KINGDOM OF THE LOST: THE ADVENTURES
OF PETER THE BRAZEN, VOLUME 8

KINGDOM OF THE LOST

THE ADVENTURES OF PETER THE BRAZEN, VOLUME 8

LORING BRENT

ILLUSTRATED BY
SAMUEL CAHAN

COVER BY
PAUL STAHR

POPULAR PUBLICATIONS · 2025

TABLE OF CONTENTS

KINGDOM OF THE LOST

*The most dangerous woman in China
had Peter the Brazen's sweetheart and
his friend's diamonds—and Peter was
going into the Jaws of Hell to get them*

1

ORDERED TO LEAVE

SOUTH AND EAST of Hainan it lies—that mystic reach of the South China Sea known to the mariners of all nations as the Jaws of Hell. The actual location of the Jaws of Hell has always been a matter of conjecture—and heated controversy. But it is agreed that the Jaws of Hell are somewhere south and east of Hainan, somewhere north of the most dangerous reef in the world—the Paracels—and offshore from that vague and mysterious borderland where China ends and French Indo-China begins.

The Paracels Reef runs northerly and southerly, and it resembles the broken backbone of an incredible monster of the sea. Stout ships, both in canvas and in steam, have broken their own backs on these barnacled vertebræ which lurk beneath the surface for hundreds of miles.

Even today, with all modern aids to navigation, ships avoid these fogbound, reef-studded waters when they can, and those that must venture into them do so with great caution.

With the passage of centuries, a terrifying legend grew and took hold of the imagination of sailing men; for neither the submerged black rocks, nor the heavy fogs prevalent so many months of the year, nor the swift and treacherous currents set up by tides and winds—none of these natural

"*Room can always be found for a sultan.*"

hazards could quite account for the mysterious disappearance, with all hands, of so many ships.

According to this legend, there is a hole in the ocean somewhere north of the Paracels—a monstrous, silent and irresistible whirlpool. And it is this hole in the ocean that is called the Jaws of Hell. Any ship straying into the outer eddying of this wicked whirl is drawn into the center and sucked down, and the ship and its men are scattered about in the gray ooze of unsounded depths.

The legend was scouted by hard-headed shipmasters. They declared that, despite the sweep of the currents in the South China Sea, such a whirlpool at such a spot would be contrary to natural laws. Yet the most hard-headed of shipmasters could not explain why, over the centuries, so many ships entered that treacherous area and vanished without trace.

It remained for an American adventurer to solve a mystery which had plagued the mariners of all nations for upwards of five centuries.

"I am afraid we have no accommodations fit for a sultan."

THE TALL YOUNG man in Room 712 of the Colonial Hotel, in Hong Kong, was making last-minute preparations for departure. His two Gladstone bags were packed and ready to be closed and buckled.

The time was four minutes of two in the morning. He had a little more than two hours in which to check out of the hotel and board the little coastwise steamer which would take him—if all went well—to Soerabaya, Java. He did not believe that all would go well, for he knew that the adventure on which he was embarking was extremely hazardous. He was preparing with meticulous care to meet trouble halfway, if trouble intruded itself.

With bags packed, he was now examining the .38 caliber Smith & Wesson revolver which had proved an able and trustworthy friend. The gun was loaded, but even that certainty did not satisfy him. Breaking it, he removed one of the shells. With a pocket knife he pried away shell brass from lead, and extracted the bullet. He decanted the powder upon a folded, thick envelope. To the little dark pile he touched a lighted match. The powder puffed into a bright gold bud of flame which hissed and instantly expired.

But the young man was not yet satisfied. He removed the other cartridges from the revolver and inserted the despoiled shell. He snapped the cylinder into place, and pulled the trigger until a brisk pop convinced him that the cap was good. Reassured now that nothing had been tampered with, he returned the other cartridges to the cylinder and dropped the revolver into his hip pocket.

He went to the dresser and picked up from it a small black metal box. In shape and appearance it resembled a small folding camera—the size that slips easily into a coat pocket. It was a compact pocket radio receiver—a device on which he had been working in his spare time for months. Actually, it represented years of research.

Until quite recently a research engineer on the staff of the General Electric Company, this young man, with a passion for radio, had dreamed of an efficient, portable radio receiver, and in this device he had transmuted his dreams into reality. It contained several interesting features: tiny amplifying tubes of great ruggedness; a unique battery of great power, light weight and exceedingly long life; and a speaker, of the power type, which was as precise as a Swiss watch and remarkable not only in its clearness and range but in its volume.

This tiny pocket receiver would, if you wished, produce sounds of a magnitude sufficient to shatter an eardrum. It required no aërial or ground connection.

He touched the dials. The high, sweet piping of ships at sea filled the bedroom. He twisted the wavelength dial. At first faintly, then with greater volume, the strains of a dance orchestra, clear, full and resonant, surged from the tiny mouth of the receiver. Chicago—eleven thousand miles away! There was a thrill for you!

His bedside telephone rang sharply. He switched off his radio and considered that other useful electrical instrument with a faint frown. He picked up the receiver, put it to his ear and listened.

A man's low voice panted, "Pete?"

"Yes."

"Come up. Chop-chop! Trouble!"

The young man replaced the telephone receiver. As he did so, knuckles rapped sharply at his door.

HE PICKED UP the radio receiver, placed it in his coat pocket, and opened the door. Three men of varying heights and ages stood in a row in the hall, all looking at him with hard, unfriendly eyes. He recognized two of them.

The tallest and oldest of the trio said, in a harsh voice, "You're Peter Moore, aren't you?"

"Yes."

"We're from the American consulate," the tall man said. "We hear you're leaving China."

Wondering just what they had heard, Moore answered, "That's right. My ship sails at noon."

"For San Francisco?"

Moore nodded. "Do you want to see my ticket?"

The shorter, younger man gave a grunt. "We know all about your ticket. You had two tickets. You were going to marry a girl, and she gave you the run-around. Her name is Susan O'Gilvie. Where is she?"

"I don't know."

The three men stared at him suspiciously, and the short one said, "Where's her ticket?"

"Right here. She isn't going to use it."

The tall, thin man was squinting at him now. "Are you sure about that?"

Peter Moore smiled briefly. "I'm taking her word for it."

"And you're sailing alone?"

"Do you doubt my word?"

"That's about the size of it," the short, stocky man answered bluntly. "There's a lot of ships clearing from Hong Kong between now and noon. We just wanted to make sure you're taking the one that goes to Frisco."

"There's been too much going on in this town tonight," the third man said, speaking for the first time. He had rusty brown hair and small green eyes. "There was a lot of trouble up on the Peak. There was a house busted into by a gang of American tars. What do you know about it?"

"Nothing."

"What do you know about an American girl named Marcia Pool who got kidnaped tonight?"

"Nothing."

"What do you know about a Eurasian woman by the name of Lotus Burma? They call her the Octopus."

Peter Moore gently shook his head. His three visitors stared at him without friendliness.

"This guy," said the short man peevishly, "never knows anything about anything. Where is the Octopus now?"

Peter Moore shrugged with an air of regret.

The tall man, glaring coldly at him, said, "Every time you hit this town, we're busy for the next month, trying to patch things up. We've got a message for you from the Consul General. It's this: take that ship to Frisco at noon—and don't take any other ship. And don't bother about coming back."

Peter Moore lighted a cigarette calmly. "Give my respects to the Consul General," he said softly, "and tell him that I will always treat his slightest whim as a command. Good night, gentlemen."

He closed the door upon them, but his feelings were not so light-hearted as his voice had sounded. Always, it seemed, at a crucial moment, when plans were ripe, some officious official interfered. This meant he would be watched. It meant that his quiet departure for Java might be hindered.

WHEN HE WAS sure that his callers were gone, he closed his bags, picked them up, opened the door, and ran to the stairs, wondering if Dan de Sylva had had previous information of the American Consul General's interest in his activities.

It was not unlikely. Dan de Sylva's espionage system was as intricate, as far-reaching, as that of a nation at war. He was a gem dealer—the brains, in fact, of the powerful and somewhat mysterious De Sylva Corporation. He and his agents in the Far East collected rare gems and jewels, and sold them to European and American clients at outrageous profits. In a world of thieves and murderers, Daniel de Sylva lived a dangerous and exotic life.

He opened the door to Moore's knock—a tall, dark, thin man of forty; a red-haired man with the sharp, angu-

lar features, the V-shaped smile, the cynical dark eyes of
Satan. His hair was of a dusky shade of red—it resembled
the play of fire in smoke.

He pulled Peter Moore into the room and swiftly,
silently shut the door. His dark, thin face was flushed and
his eyes had an excited glitter.

"Did you know," he said breathlessly, "that Susan O'Gilvie will be on that ship?"

Moore placed his bags on the floor against the wall.
"What of it?"

"What of it!" his satanic friend cried. "She'll ruin everything! She always ruins everything!"

"She won't ruin this," Moore said firmly. "Forget her."

"What's more," the gem dealer went on, "they're wise."

Moore nodded. "I just had a visit."

"What happened?"

"Three of them dropped around. They told me to be on
board the *King of Asia* when she sails at noon—or else."

De Sylva stared at him. "Who said this?"

"The Consul General sent the message. It took three of
them to deliver it."

"Now?"

"They just left."

Satan wagged his head. "This is getting too complicated.
I'm not talking about the Consul General. I'm talking
about Lotus Burma. One of my agents took her aboard
the Langpo—a sampan boy—and just reported to me. She
suspects you'll be aboard that ship. She told Miss O'Gilvie
she believed you'd be aboard."

"I expected it," Moore said quietly. "Stop worrying."

"But what'll you do if she catches you?"

"She won't catch me."

But Daniel de Sylva was not reassured. He was nervous and irritable—a prey to a thousand worries.

"I don't think you realize the danger of this job. Are you bearing in mind that Lotus Burma has in her possession two million dollars' worth of diamonds belonging to my company? Are you bearing in mind that she got those diamonds by torturing to death one of my most valued men?"

Moore smiled faintly. "Yes, Dan." His blue eyes were clear and tranquil. If he was nervous, if he was apprehensive, he did not betray it.

SATAN STARED AT him and cried, "How can you be so damned calm?" Distracted, he began pacing up and down the room.

"Oh, I know how clever you are," he said. "I know how reckless you are. I know you've slid out of a thousand tight jams. I know you're the only man in China capable of handling this job. I grant all that."

"Then why are you having this nervous breakdown?"

"I'll tell you why!" De Sylva snapped. "A man can't mix romance with this kind of job!"

"It isn't romance. I am responsible for Susan O'Gilvie. My responsibility won't end until I get her out of this country—and back to America."

"Are you telling me you aren't in love with her?"

Moore's blue eyes hardened. "Yes."

"You're a liar! You're crazy about her! You'd follow her through hell! You aren't interested in getting back my diamonds—you're only going on that ship to be near her! My God! You were going to marry her this morning and sail for Frisco at noon on your honeymoon—and you say you don't love her!"

A little wearily, Peter Moore said, "Aw, stop worrying, Dan."

"That little thrill hunter!" the gem dealer muttered, as if he had not heard. "She's almost cost you your life a dozen times already. She isn't happy if she isn't in a jam. But you'll never get her out of this. No woman alive can beat the combination of that purple drug—and Lotus Burma. Lotus Burma will never let go of her. And you'll lose my diamonds, and you'll lose your life if you mix that girl into this! You're trying to ride two horses!"

"I have to go," Moore said quietly.

"Wait a minute! You apparently don't know what this means to me. Nobody knows. Those diamonds were not insured. If I don't recover them—I'm lost. The De Sylva Corporation is lost! I'll be ruined and I'll be disgraced!"

"I'll get the diamonds. But I'll need a decoy—a bait. I want some of the finest diamonds, sapphires, emeralds and rubies you have."

Satan stared at him a moment longer—a harassed and distracted Satan. Then, unquestioningly, he went to a large square black trunk against the wall. He unlocked it and raised the lid.

He lifted out a tray and brought out a small black leather case. This he opened—and it was as if he had unlocked the source of the rainbow.

In narrow compartments of black velvet, gems blazed forth in spectacular, colorful brilliance. There was the frosty white of diamonds, the blood-red of rubies, the sea-blue of sapphires, the reptilian green of emeralds.

Peter Moore did not pause to marvel over this amazing hoard. Swiftly, he began collecting the largest stones in each compartment. He selected three diamonds the size of marbles; an emerald in the shape of a cube as clear as crème de menthe; four rubies of various sizes and cuts, and two cabochon sapphires large and blue.

Dan de Sylva gave a grunt. "You've helped yourself to a hundred and fifty thousand dollars' worth of stones—at wholesale prices," he said huskily.

"They'll do nicely," Moore said, and dropped the lot carelessly into a pants pocket.

"You've got one more item I'll need—the elephant ring you bought from the Sultan of Sakara."

The gem dealer stiffened.

"Who told you I had that ring?" he asked harshly.

"The same man who told me the sultan had been confined to an insane asylum in Singapore."

"But no one knows that!" De Sylva cried. "No one but I and one man in the British secret service knows that the Sultan of Sakara is insane!"

"Perhaps that's why I want the sultan's ring."

WITH A MYSTIFIED air, Satan produced the famous elephant ring once owned by that eccentric and amazing Oriental potentate, His Majesty Ameer Prak Chan, the Sultan of Sakara. It was in another black box, and it was a strange and astonishing jewel.

It was of purest gold, this elephant head, so large that it covered all of a man's middle finger from the hand to the knuckle. It was held in place not only by the gold band but by the trunk, which, curiously, was shaped so that it appeared to wind round and round the wearer's finger.

The eyes were emerald, the tusks were little shafts of pure diamond. And in the forehead was set a perfect sample of that venerated and talismanic stone—a star sapphire. The elephant's face, delicately carved, was whimsical. Here, one might say, was an elephant with a sense of humor. The green eyes seemed to twinkle; the mouth seemed actually to smile—a roguish smile.

Peter Moore slipped the ring onto the middle finger of his left hand, clenched his fist and brandished it about, admiring the play of light on the pure gold, the dancing of the light in the impudent emerald eyes.

"And that," De Sylva said nervously, "is worth another forty thousand. In fact, I wouldn't take forty thousand for it. The question is, am I sending good jewels after lost ones?"

The blond man looked at the elephant ring with dreamy eyes.

"They say it's a magical ring," he said. "They say it'll grant a man three wishes."

"Bunk!" De Sylva snorted. "The only magic that gems and jewels have is bad magic. There isn't a stone in that pocketful that couldn't drown a man in the blood it's spilled."

Mysteriously smiling, Peter Moore rubbed the elephant's head against the palm of his right hand.

"First wish—a successful voyage!" He shot out his hand, gripped De Sylva's, and said, "So long, Dan! I'm leaving these bags here. Don't worry about your diamonds."

He was, somewhat mysteriously, gone. Satan stared at the closed door, shook his head gloomily, and reached for a half-empty bottle of Five Star Hennessy.

2

PETER DISGUISES

REACHING THE LOBBY, Moore was aware that trouble was lurking not far away. The shorter of the three men who had recently called at his room was slumped in a chair, smoking a cigar and staring at the elevator. When he saw Moore he sprang up. And when Moore went out into the street he followed.

The trouble-maker glanced at his watch, settled his felt hat, pulled the collar of his gray trench coat up about his neck against the clammy chill of the harbor air, and climbed into the first of the line of waiting rickshas. He knew that the man from the consulate would follow. He gave his ricksha coolie an address. As the coolie started off, Moore glanced back. The short man was scrambling into a ricksha, excitedly telling his coolie to follow.

But Moore did not tell his coolie to hurry. His objective was the House with the Black Door on Wing Lok Street, a place known among the select as the Mansion of Divine Contentment; and to tourists and most white residents of Hong Kong, known not at all.

A grimy, one story stone building with corrugated steel shutters at the windows, the Mansion gave no indication that it led a charmed life.

Peter Moore paid and dismissed his coolie, advanced to the Black Door, knocked twice, then once, then twice again. The door swung open. An elderly Chinese in the servile blue of the lower class peered into his face and said, "Aie—master!" and stepped aside for Peter Moore to enter.

As he went in, the short man arrived. He leaped out and ran to the black door just as it softly closed. He banged on the black door with his fists. Moore sauntered through a labyrinth of rooms and corridors without hesitation, and came at length to a finely polished brass door, carved beautifully and ornamented with laughing lions and sneering tigers. This he opened without ceremony, entering a room with walls of golden silk and an atmosphere of the finest sandalwood incense.

A fat, living Buddha squatted on a teakwood stool in a corner. He was smoking an opium pipe—inhaling the acrid, perfumed puff from the sizzling pill at the very instant that Moore opened the door.

He stared at Moore with his tiny shoebutton eyes, and set the elaborately inlaid pipe down on the mother-of-pearl taboret beside him.

"By Buddha's hangnail!" he cried in a thin squeal of a voice. "But you are late! The man who wishes to capture a fleeing camel does not grasp a hair of its tail!"

Peter Moore was emptying his pockets and placing his recent precious acquisitions on the taboret beside the opium pipe.

The fat Chinese stared at the diamonds, the emeralds, the rubies, the sapphires with the avidity of a coarse, greedy nature.

"I grovel and abase myself in the muck of this miserable room in the presence of your magnificence. I am flattered that a being of your high purposes has crossed the threshold of my wretched abode and graced my inferior hospitality with the perfume of his noble presence. I am the slave to your bidding. Command!"

Moore was stripping off his clothing. He undressed to the last garment, tossing his clothes into a heap on the floor.

"Is the sedan chair ready, Yat Gow?"

"Ready and waiting, as is all else that you demanded, Ren-beh-tung!"

THE FAT CHINESE clapped his pudgy hands. A pair of scarlet brocaded curtains at the end of the room parted, and a tall man the color of ebony, naked to the waist, glided into the room. From the waist down he wore a blue *sarong,* for he was from the south, and on his feet he wore sapphire-blue felt sandals.

"Here, master," Yat Gow said breathlessly to Peter.

The American went to the teakwood table on which were bowls of dyes and stains. The black man dexterously applied them. He dyed Peter's hair, brows and lashes black, and he rapidly sponged a walnut stain upon his skin from head to foot. He worked swiftly and with dexterity.

While dye and stain were drying, the black slave attended to the details of Peter's face. He inserted short silver tubes in his nostrils, to change the contour of his nose and to give it a greater flare. He affixed to Peter's left earlobe a mole fashioned of soft rubber. It was complete, even with artificial hairs. And within Peter's upper lip, against the gum, he pressed a length of soft, cleverly shaped red rubber, its purpose being to increase the apparent length of his upper lip.

"By the providence of Buddha," Yat Gow piped, "his mother was a Frenchwoman and his eyes were blue—not so blue as yours, but blue. You will pass. You are of his height and of his build. You have his amazing animation. But you must acquire his strange manner of speech and his curious habits. It is a delicate and finedrawn matter, my king. Yet you are cleverer than any dozen yellow men I know, and the man who holds the eyes of a needle close enough to his own eye can see the world."

"You are full of whompee juice and black smoke," the American said, laughing. "The turban!" he cried.

Yat Gow lifted the lid of a brass-studded beefwood chest. The hidden lights of the room, a golden suffusion, played upon colors quite as vivid as those of the brilliant gems on the teakwood taboret. Here were garments fit for an Oriental nabob—the finest and richest of hand-loomed satins of cardinal red, sapphire blue, emerald green, purest white.

The turban was white. Assured that the dye and stains were dry, the American deftly wound the turban about his head in the prescribed manner—a tedious and difficult task, for in each twist, each fold of a sultan's turban is legend and history.

Next he slipped into white silk undergarments, then into baggy pantaloons of sapphire blue. A white vest embroidered with gold and worked with semi-precious stones came next. The exotic costume was topped by a long cloak of canary yellow satin with gilt braid marking all edges and a capacious pocket on either side.

The exotic nature of His Majesty Ameer Prak Chan, the Sultan of Sakara, had gone no farther than this. For footgear, good English black oxfords were correct.

Peter Moore dropped his revolver into the left pocket. The diamonds, sapphires, rubies and emeralds he scooped away from Yat Gow's gloating eyes, and poured into another pocket. To this collection he added the tiny radio receiver from his coat pocket.

He consulted himself now in the long, flawless mirror, and saw a stranger. Peter Moore, by means of clever, subtle changes, had vanished. In his place stood His Majesty the Sultan of Sakara!

Startled in spite of himself, Peter stared at his reflection. He saw a tall, slender, dark-skinned man of the most exotic description, a character, indeed, that might have stepped from the pages of an Oriental romance. His blue eyes glimmered oddly, with a touch of the sinister, in that dark countenance. He had a well-shaped nose with slightly flaring nostrils, a long upper lip.

PETER MOORE FELT himself becoming, in personality, the famous Sultan of Sakara. He smiled the sultan's wolfish grin, and the reflection in the mirror grinned back with a flash of shining white teeth.

Peter Moore whirled from the mirror, struck a pose, with chest out, hands upraised, fingers spread apart, and a strange voice issued from his chest, "Yat Gow, you oily old rascal, I will bet you fifty ticals that the fly alights on the nearer lump of sugar!"

And the fat yellow man, who comprehended no English, grinned and chortled with delight and approval, "The voice and the manners are perfect, my king!"

Peter Moore devoutly hoped so. He had met the Sultan of Sakara but once, years ago, in Saigon, and he had marked the curious polyglot accent. The Sultan of Sakara had spoken English with a strong Malayan influence and a distinct Oxford accent overlaid on that. A hard voice, indeed, to imitate.

"Do not forget," Yat Gow said, "that you carry your left shoulder a little lower than the right. And now—now let us see you walk."

Peter walked up and down the room, with a curious, exaggerated swagger, almost a strut, setting the heels down hard, turning the toes well out.

Yat Gow burst into laughter. "Perfect, your majesty! And the mole and the nose and the upper lip! Let me hear that voice just once again!"

Still in that strange voice, but now in idiomatic southern Chinese, the American adventurer said, "Yat Gow! My chair! Instantly!"

"Your echo is my answer, my king," the fat Chinese responded. "Your chair awaits! Dessoulu! The master's chest!"

"Aie!" the black man said.

He closed the lid of the beefwood chest upon his bizarre finery and lifted it to his shoulder.

"A cape against the chill of the dawn!" Yat Gow squealed.

It was of heavy brocade, a green cape, that lent the Sultan of Sakara a final pictorial touch, if one was needed. It was lined with the heaviest of white Shantung silk—a product of the proudest silkworms and the noblest artisans in the East.

Peter draped it about himself, again viewed himself in the great mirror.

"It is perfect," Yat Gow said. "And here is your money, majesty."

He gave Peter a small but heavy blue suede bag, with drawstrings of blue satin cord at the throat. Peter opened the bag, ran his hand inside and brought forth a fistful of gold—ticals, these were, the nut-shaped coinage of Siam.

He dropped the bag into one of the ample pockets. Then, with a cheery, "Blessings of Buddha upon your house!" he went to the polished brass door which the black man held open for him.

Peter Moore threaded his way back through the familiar labyrinth. On the way he detoured from his original course to enter a small booth lined with purple satin. Here, in surroundings as ancient as the Oriental worship of ancestors, was a modern toy—a wall telephone!

The Sultan of Sakara picked up the receiver and called a number—the number of the private telephone in Daniel de Sylva's hotel bedroom.

The gem dealer instantly answered. His voice was breathless.

"I am ready to go aboard," Peter said. "Have a police boat to meet me at once at Pasig Wharf."

"Good Lord—why?"

"The Sultan of Sakara must be taken to the steamer Langpo in a style befitting his station."

"It's too damned risky!" De Sylva protested.

"The harbor is crawling with pirates," Peter answered, "who would think nothing of slitting a man's throat for a glass stickpin."

"All right, all right," De Sylva said hysterically. "I'll attend to it. So long! Good luck!"

Peter abandoned his own voice and simulated the strange accents of the insane jungle monarch he was impersonating.

"Ameer Prak Chan needs no luck!" he cried, "I have rubbed the ring!"

He clicked the receiver into the hook and went to the black door. The doorman stared at him with shocked amazement, then made a low bow. He opened the door.

Peter went out, followed by the black slave carrying the beefwood chest.

A sedan chair with four bearers was in the street—a highly ornamental vehicle, in such taste as the insane sultan would no doubt have approved heartily. Crimson satin and gold braid had been used lavishly, and the poles themselves were inset with mother-of-pearl.

The four bearers sprang to attention. Dessoulu loaded the beefwood chest upon a small platform which extended outward from the rear of the chair proper.

Across the street a short man stood smoking a short fat cigar. Peter gave him a princely smile and entered the sedan chair. The short man did not return the smile. His stare was indifferent. Costumes as elegant, as colorful as the one Peter was wearing are not sensational in the streets of Hong Kong. The short man was not interested in an opium-smoking sultan. He had eyes only for a tall, blond, blue-eyed American whom he had been told to watch until the moment the *King of Asia* weighed anchor and steamed away to America.

Patiently, as the ornate chair was lifted and carried away toward the water front, the short man resumed his vigil.

3

GOING ABOARD

A LONG, RAKISH, mahogany speedboat was waiting when the sedan chair reached the Pasig Wharf, at the foot of Cleverly Street. Officers of the harbor police in white uniforms—a dozen of them—were lined along the wharf at attention when the spurious Sultan of Sakara alighted. A police captain saluted him with a crisp "Good morning, your majesty!"

Peter acknowledged this with a smile and a gesture of the left hand, that quick, jerking gesture, as of a man about to slap a mosquito—a gesture characteristic of Ameer Prak Chan.

The police captain, a grizzled veteran, betrayed no excitement and only a logical curiosity. He was accustomed to the eccentric hours and habits of southern potentates. And when he had been told that the Sultan of Sakara wished a police escort to a steamer sailing for the south at 4 a.m. he was neither excited nor inquisitive.

His logical curiosity was, however, another matter. Why, he wished to know, was his majesty traveling to Singapore on such a small and shabby ship as the Langpo, when stately liners were clearing for that port in the morning—a Messagerie Maritimes ship, a P. & O., and a Dollar liner—

all of which would land his highness in Singapore days before the Langpo, a lumbering little tub, could possibly get there?

"It is my whim," said the Sultan of Sakara.

That settled it. All rulers are whimsical. All Oriental rulers are very whimsical. And the Sultan of Sakara was notoriously one of the most whimsical rulers who ever breathed.

The black man deposited the beefwood chest in the stern of the police launch and vanished into the shades of night. The courteous white-uniformed officers waited for the sultan to arrange himself in the stern, then swarmed aboard. The lines were cast off, and the mahogany "devil-chaser" darted out across the star-studded waters toward an obscure and distant riding light.

The fog of the earlier night had cleared, and the majestic panorama of Hong Kong's harbor was spread for the delight of Peter Moore's eyes. He loved this harbor. It had become home to him. Gliding across it to the smooth rhythm of the police boat's engines, he wondered if he would ever see it again. He was filled with a sense of foreboding. He knew that he was embarking on an errand on which he might readily lose his life.

He did not underestimate the cunning and savagery of Lotus Burma—that mysterious and beautiful creature who was known, not without adequate reason, as the Octopus—and the equally mysterious and sinister powers which, he knew, she must represent.

Two hopes burned in him—that he might return Dan de Sylva's fortune in diamonds to him, and that he might dissuade Susan O'Gilvie from this worst of all her follies.

The police boat was skimming past a great liner now—one of the newest and largest ships in the transpacific run—the *King of Asia.* Back in the Mansion of Divine Contentment, in a pocket of his coat, were the tickets he had planned to use—tickets entitling him and his bride to the *King of Asia's* costliest suite—a richly merited extravagance—so he had thought when purchasing them.

With thoughtful eyes he watched the rows of lighted, brass-bound portholes stream past. A bitter smile played at his lips. He would get over it. Susan O'Gilvie would become, with time, a romantic memory. He had got what he had deserved. Susan O'Gilvie was for no man. She was no more fitted for marriage than an eagle is fitted for a cage. Nor was he. But it had been a hard lesson to learn.

The short, squat hulk of the coastwise steamer Langpo loomed close aboard now. He studied her scattered lights, her shapeless outlines, with a dreamy detachment. Susan was aboard that ship. Susan and the Octopus of Hong Kong!

The dark steamer became possessed of a mystery closely related to the unknown, the untried. He tried to shake off the illogical feeling that she was a ship of mystery; that her very air, as she crouched there, had something of the sinister in it. It struck him sharply. He could not define it. She wasn't *right.* Something was indefinably wrong.

WITH SHARPENED FACULTIES, he ran his eyes along the stolid bulk of the Langpo, telling himself that he was the victim of imagination. But the sensation was not to be dismissed so easily. It lingered in the air without definition, like an aura of evil. And it grew on him queerly that this was somehow no ordinary ship; that she was a haunted thing, a ship of trouble.

They were close alongside the accommodation ladder now. The voice of the police captain rang out sharply, "Langpo, ahoy!"

That they were being watched from the bridge was immediately evident, for a voice, cool and remote, replied, "Ahoy!"

"A passenger for Singapore!" the police captain called. "The Sultan of Sakara!"

There was hesitation. The dim figure on the wing of the bridge seemed to be pondering the announcement.

Impatiently the police captain inquired, "You are clearing for Soerabaya with a stop at Singapore, are you not?"

"Yes."

"Then let us have a little light here, please. When are you sailing?"

"At once."

The dim figure was coming down from the bridge wing. The police captain murmured to the tall, exotically garbed young man beside him, "I don't like this at all, your majesty. Are you quite sure—" His voice faded off into a mumble, became clearer with the words, "—these little coastwise packets—"

"I'm quite sure," Peter said with finality.

A greasy decklight blinked on above. In the rays of it a tall, thin man stood, peering down at the police launch.

The police captain said, "Where's your captain?"

"I am Captain Barberry," the other answered. His voice was strained. It had the tight sound of a man alarmed or afraid. It was, in addition to this, a peculiar voice. Its inflections were strange.

Peter tried to place the accent. It was neither Dutch, French, Spanish, Chinese nor Japanese, that accent. It was, in fact, like no accent Peter had ever heard. It quickened his sense of uneasiness, his doubts of the Langpo's honesty.

The police captain doubtless shared this sensation. He seemed most reluctant to permit the Sultan of Sakara to go aboard.

Captain Barberry was leaning on the handrail. Peter could not see his face. He had an impression of cropped, bristling black hair, like that of a convict, of dull, dead eyes.

"I am afraid we have no accommodations fit for a sultan," he said.

"I am not particular," the Sultan of Sakara said cheerfully.

"But we have no room whatever for another passenger."

"Room can always be found for a Sultan," the Sultan of Sakara said with a ring of command in his voice.

"Your majesty," the police captain began, "I advise—"

"My mind is made up."

Captain Barberry was peering down into his uplifted face. "But, your majesty, I believe there are other ships, finer and faster than this miserable tub, sailing for Singapore later this morning. We have the most wretched of accommodations."

The police captain, when the sultan had made no reply, said, "Captain, his majesty has the whimsical notion that he wishes to travel to Singapore by this ship."

"It is not whimsical," Peter said sharply, in the voice of a monarch whose will is being crossed. "There are certain people traveling on those other ships whom I wish to avoid. Besides, this filthy little tub appeals to my sense of the comic."

"One moment—please!" Captain Barberry begged. "I must consult the steward."

4

THE OCTOPUS

LOUNGING ON A pile of purple cushions, the most dangerous woman in China smoked a perfumed cigarette in an
amethyst holder and listened serenely to the excited expos-
tulations of the captain of the Langpo.

His strange gray face had a frightened look. A man
evidently trained to repress his impulses, Captain Barberry
was, with great difficulty, modulating his voice and restrain-
ing his alarm.

"The Sultan of Sakara insists on a passage to Singapore!"

And the woman known as the Octopus softly drawled,
"Then let him have a passage to Singapore."

"But, madam, the presence of this sultan will spoil everything!"

"On the contrary," the beautiful woman answered, "the
presence of this sultan will afford me both pleasure and
profit."

"But it is dangerous, madam. He is too important. And
it is, if you ask me, suspicious."

"Why?"

"Why should a sultan wish to travel on a ship like this
when three fine liners are sailing for Singapore a few hours
from now?"

"The Sultan of Sakara is the most whimsical monarch on earth. Let him indulge his whim. Bring him here and get under way at once."

"Yes, madam. He came in a police boat. I do not like that at all. Our papers are by no means open to close scrutiny."

"Did the police officers ask for your papers?"

"No, madam, but they were aware that we are clearing for Soerabaya via Singapore."

"Ah," Lotus Burma said contemptuously, "your blood has turned to ice water. Bring the sultan here and let us leave this wretched place immediately."

Captain Barberry departed. On deck, he instructed men to carry his majesty's trunk aboard and to stow it in Stateroom Six. The Sultan of Sakara climbed the ladder to the deck and got a better view of the captain's face.

It was a strange, gray face, somehow sinister, somehow evil. In it was a strange blending of many races—the sensuous lips of the Latins, the peaked brows of the Near East, and the almond eyes of the Far East, yet they were slate gray and dead. A stirringly odd face. It made the American wonder.

"If you please, your majesty—this way." Again, that strange impression of utterly unfamiliar accents, or a blending of many accents, and with it a ghostly feeling. A fantastic thought occurred to Peter: it was as if this voice were being projected out of Captain Barberry's mouth from a lost age. It was curious and it was preposterous. Yet he could not rid himself of the conviction that there was creeping mystery, creeping horror, aboard this slattern of the seas.

He followed Captain Barberry to a door midway around

the after turn of the deck. This door bore no numeral or letter.

Captain Barberry pushed open the door, and for a moment Peter's presence of mind, his assurance, deserted him.

"Come, come, this is not my stateroom," he protested.

"No, your majesty," the strange voice whispered.

Peter had caught a glimpse of royal purple hangings, of a slender woman reclining on a tumbled mass of purple cushions. A tendril of incense smoke reached out to encircle his head like a ghostly arm. The fumes were sweet and spicy in his nostrils.

"The Sultan of Sakara, madam," Captain Barberry said, and withdrew. The door clicked shut behind Peter Moore, and he was face to face again with Lotus Burma, the most mysterious woman he had ever known, and the most barbarically beautiful.

But the instant the door closed he was himself again. He did what the Sultan of Sakara would certainly have done under the circumstances, for that insane young monarch had been a connoisseur of beautiful women. In them, indeed, Peter suspected, Ameer Prak Chan had found his doom.

HE WALKED ACROSS the room with a strut and a swagger, stopped, kissed the tips of his fingers, and sent the caress, as if it had bulk and body, snapping from the tips of his fingers. His eyes whimsically followed its imagined course. The kiss bounced against the ceiling, and his dancing eyes followed it to the dangerous and beautiful creature reclining on the cushions.

She studied him with a lazy and mysterious smile. She

was queenly in a gown of royal purple. Her features were as symmetrical as a porcelain Buddha's. Her eyes were large and lustrous, like wet grapes. Her skin was like cream—not white, not yellow, but a soft and amazing shade in between. She had the slim perfection of a goddess. She was ageless. She might have been twenty or forty.

A slim, graceful arm moved in languid gesture as she placed a stiletto on an amethyst holder to her red lips, puffed and breathed out the smoke in an enchanted vapor.

There was something hypnotic about this woman—a dangerous, secret charm. In her was perfectly expressed the exotic lure of all Eastern lands. Peter could understand how Susan might have been fascinated by this amazing woman. In spite of his danger, he was stirred, as he had been in his previous encounter with her. For the beauty of Lotus Burma was of the kind that challenges the masculinity of any man.

In a sweet, husky contralto she said, drawling, "I am flattered, your majesty. And I am charmed."

"This," said the spurious sultan enthusiastically, "should be a voyage of—shall we say infinitely delightful possibilities?"

She laughed softly. Her eyes glowed with a tantalizing mystery. "Shall we? Who knows? I understand you are a great gambler?"

The Sultan of Sakara uttered the quick, barking laughter which was characteristic of the Sultan of Sakara. "I'll gamble now, my princess! I'll wager this ring against that rope of pearls that I'll be madly in love with you before we touch Singapore!"

Lotus Burma laughed again and fingered the rope of

pearls. They were priceless—blue pearls. And ropes of black pearls were twined about her slim wrists.

He was extending his hand, and Lotus Burma bent forward a little to inspect the ring. Her eyes became bright. "Ah! The elephant ring! How charming! How whimsical!"

And Peter knew that Lotus Burma firmly intended to possess that ring before this remarkable voyage was over. Would she possess the ring—or would he possess two million dollars' worth of diamonds belonging rightfully to the great but threatened De Sylva Corporation?

She was still staring at the ring, smiling. Only in her mouth was the legend of her cruelty confirmed. It was a lovely mouth, a sensuous mouth, a mouth capable of infinite passion and infinite barbarity. She had tortured to death the De Sylva agent who had had the diamonds—by stabbing him repeatedly with a long silver pin! Perhaps her cruelty explained her lips. They were as vividly red as the lips of a mythological vampire.

The astounding black veil of her lashes lifted. Her eyes glowed at him. She lowered the amethyst holder and looked into his eyes with a faint, mysterious smile.

"It is the most beautiful ring in the world!"

In spite of himself, Peter was fascinated. Her languor, her sensuousness, made her as dangerous as a lazily awakening python.

"IS IT TRUE," she said lightly, "that you play a game of marbles with precious stones?"

He laughed again. He got down on his knees and plunged a hand into one of the capacious pockets of his satin coat. He brought out a small fistful of stones. He tossed a diamond and a sapphire into the air and caught them in his other hand. He opened both hands and sent the stones tumbling across the carpet.

Lotus Burma swiftly leaned forward. One of the stones, a sapphire, had rolled within reach. She studied it, turning it quickly about in her long, slender fingers, letting the light strike blue fire from its facets.

"A pretty thing," she said. "Chantaboun."

But she was watching him as he crawled about, gathering up the scattered stones, and laughing, with derision. Her laughter was, to Peter, a betrayal. It implied so much. It was indulgent.

It conveyed to him that she had heard the stories of Ameer Prak Chan's childishness over precious stones. It conveyed that she considered him the softest kind of victim.

"Let us make a bet," she said, as if with inspiration. "Do you hear that rumbling and grinding, your majesty?"

The Sultan of Sakara cocked his turbaned head. "I do!"

"It means our anchor is coming out of the mud. Presently our engines will turn. But—look! We are pointed, not toward the sea but toward the City of Hong Kong. We must turn about sharply. In turning, we will veer to one side or the other. Which will it be—port or starboard?"

"Starboard!" the sultan cried.

"We will fill a glass to the very brim with water," Lotus Burma said gayly. She sprang up and went to a washstand in a corner of the large room. She took a drinking glass from a wall socket and filled it.

Peter watched her with shimmering eyes. He knew that his proving, for her benefit, the legend that the Sultan of Sakara played marbles with precious stones had filled her with instant contempt. And he wondered what her game would be. But he felt that just so long as she did not penetrate his disguise he was safe. Just so long as she believed him to be the sultan, she would not dare murder him for the elephant ring or his precious stones, because the Hong Kong police knew that he was a passenger on this ship for Singapore.

She was returning with the glass, walking with great care, watching the brimming glass with large and shining eyes. The purple robe clung to her and revealed the slim, delicate perfection of her body. It was hard to believe that a woman so beautifully made could be so vicious.

He was still kneeling, looking up at her. She was within a dozen inches of him, holding the glass so steadily that not a drop had been spilled. Amazing control! Perfume from her slim body reached him, seemed to wrap about him in a sweet, alluring wave. It was the most seductive perfume he had ever smelled. It seemed to breathe from her body with a promise of mysterious and unimaginable delights. In him it prompted a sudden, upthrusting wave of heat.

She lowered the glass to the carpet beside him. It was still full.

"The ship will tilt slightly when she turns about. If she tilts to starboard, water will be spilled out on this side, and if she tilts to port, water will spill from this side."

She seemed to have entered gayly into the caprice.

"What shall we bet, your majesty?"

HIS VOICE AUTOMATICALLY said, "Precious stones, my princess!" for he had planned on saying that; but his heart stood still and his brain went cold.

In frosted letters upon the side of the glass was the name

of a ship. The name was not that, however, of this ship. It was Aronga. And as he stared at the name a chill wave of apprehension swept along his spine, and the sense of creeping mystery returned with an impact that would have left his face a bleached white had it not been for the walnut stain.

For the Aronga was one of that host of mystery ships—a ship lost without trace ten or twelve years ago in the Jaws of Hell! She had left Hong Kong for Saigon on a night in December. And she had never been reported again. She had vanished as if, indeed, the sea had suddenly opened up and engulfed her. What was that glass doing here?

"You see?" Lotus Burma gayly cried. "Not a drop was spilled!"

"Not a drop!" the sultan breathed.

"But why are you so shocked?"

"I have never seen such steadiness in a woman. It is amazing!"

She laughed softly. "The engines are starting! We are about to turn! You say starboard! I say port! Hai-yah! We shall bet!"

She reached under one of the cushions. Her hand returned with a black box about ten inches wide by four in width, by three in depth. It was tied shut with black satin ribbon. She removed the ribbon.

She lifted the lid—and Peter Moore's eyes were shocked by the frosty white stabbing glitter of more diamonds than he had ever seen in one mass in his life.

The box was as brimful of diamonds as was the Aronga's drinking glass with water. Diamonds of all shapes and sizes. All blue white. All doubtless perfect. Without question the De Sylva diamonds—the treasure trove for which he had come aboard this ship prepared to risk his life!

He had a reckless impulse to snatch the box from her hand, to run to the rail, to leap overboard and swim for his life. It would have been the easiest way. And it would have been a practical way. He was a strong swimmer. He had recently mastered the art of staying under water for minutes at a time. He could surely escape.

But he would not snatch the diamonds. He was, as Dan de Sylva had declared, riding two horses. He could not leave this mysterious ship until he had exerted all his powers to deliver Susan O'Gilvie from this woman. De Sylva had said, "You can't mix romance with this kind of job." And De Sylva was right.

"They dazzle you!" Lotus Burma cried. She scooped a dozen of them into the palm of her hand. She spilled these onto the carpet beside the drinking glass. "I will bet these against that sapphire, that diamond and that ruby!"

"You are a woman after my own heart," Peter exclaimed, matching her gusto. "I will take that bet, my princess!"

She closed the box, wrapped the ribbon about it, and tossed it back carelessly among the purple cushions. It might have been as worthless as, say, a box of candy. Two million dollars' worth of diamonds! Her very casualness was disconcerting—it plainly indicated her indifference to danger. Quite possibly she had nothing whatever to fear.

SHE WAS KNEELING opposite him—on the other side of the glass of water. She was staring into it with her hands raised above it. She was like a sorceress gazing into a crystal, compelling from it the secrets of the past, the present, the future. Uneasiness stole over the Sultan of Sakara.

As if in a dream, he saw water forming in a rising, round mound against the left hand lip of the glass. The mound broke over gently, and water flowed down over the frosted name of the lost ship.

"Port!" Lotus Burma cried. "I win the bet!"

She snatched up the diamond, the ruby and the sapphire which he had placed beside the glass. She snatched up the diamonds she had placed on the other side.

The Sultan of Sakara rose with a flashing grin. He went to the door and he said, "Beautiful women are always too lucky. We will have other bets. I love to bet."

"I, too, love to bet, your majesty." There was a betraying gleam in her eyes as they lingered a moment on the fabulous elephant ring. It was stark, quickly shuttered greed.

He knew that it was her simple plan to possess the ring and the rest of his precious stones before the Langpo reached Singapore. One by one, she would somehow contrive to secure them, and in such a way that he could make no complaint to the authorities had he wished.

He had, of course, no interest in the authorities. When Singapore was reached, Peter intended to walk ashore not only with the diamonds De Sylva had lent him but the contents of that box of hers, too. Her wits against his! He would have been amazed to know the fantastic designs of the fate in store for him.

He had left Lotus Burma's quarters more hurriedly than appearances would indicate. The air of that place had grown too thick for him. Not the perfume of that exotic, beautiful, cruel woman, or the incense from the braziers. Two shocks had come too quickly for him—first the drinking glass bearing the name of that ghost ship, the Aronga; then the sudden, sensational display of the fortune in diamonds.

He needed to breathe, to slip out of his role for a moment, to think. And he wanted to look over this mysterious ship.

On deck, with the door of her room closed behind him, he set his thoughts in order. The lure of that sinister woman was still upon him. He was conscious of an actual wish, a sharp desire, to return to her now. It was a terrific power she had over men, like a false beacon luring a ship to destruction.

Common sense washed that impulse away, was replaced by a sensation no less troublesome and infinitely more grotesque. It was the old feeling that the Langpo was a ship creeping with mystery. The strangeness of Captain Barberry returned to perplex him afresh.

5

MYSTERY SHIP

HE STROLLED FORWARD. The Langpo was sliding out of the strait and into the open sea, softly wheezing along. Peter found his stateroom, Number Six, halfway down the deck on the port side. A light was burning over the washstand. His beefwood trunk had been placed beside the bunk.

Peter placed his pocket radio receiver in the trunk and looked about the room. It was typical of all the staterooms he had seen on ships of the Langpo's class. A double decker bunk against one wall; a wardrobe built across one corner—always too short to hang an overcoat or a pair of pants full length; a washstand beside the narrow seat which ran beneath the window; a faded green carpet on the floor; a smell of staleness.

A bulb of low wattage pulsed above the washstand mirror. The old familiarity of his surroundings restored to Peter a sense of ease and security. He heard the grinding and rumbling of a winch as a hatch was covered; he felt the steady shuddering of woodwork. All of this was rational and homelike.

Then his roving glance changed to alight on the towel rack. Three white hand towels—typical ship's towels—were hung on the rack. On each the name of a ship was sewn in red thread. But the name he read was not that of the Langpo. It was Pelgrasse.

The Pelgrasse was another mystery of the China coast! She had been a Greek ship, bound from Hong Kong to Athens. On a spring morning, six or seven years ago, the Pelgrasse had left Singapore—and never been seen again! She, too, had fitted into that old blood-chilling legend. She, too, had been engulfed in the Jaws of Hell!

The drinking glass in Lotus Burma's room might have been a coincidence. But the two together could not be dismissed so easily.

What, Peter wanted to know, were the towels and the drinking glass of two ghost ships, reputed victims of the Jaws of Hell, doing on this ship?

Shivering a little, he opened the door and looked across the deck. Three men, deckhands or stewards, walked forward along the deck through the shaft of light from his doorway.

As they passed, all three glanced at him, and he was so startled that he gasped. Not only did each member of this trio have the strange, dull gray eyes of Captain Barberry, but they strikingly resembled him in other particulars!

They had the same slack mouths, the same colorless, flat hair, the same narrow foreheads. Even the contours of their faces were identical. And in each of them Peter got the impression of a heavy-boned body—and of an order of intelligence hardly higher than that of an idiot. They seemed to drool. They were like three robots, as they mechanically planted their feet and picked them up again—three men with that idiotic vacancy of eye, that

impression that they were machines of flesh and blood.
Dull-eyed men! Gray men! What race was this? It was
baffling.

It was as if ghosts were staring at him. There was no
flicker of interest, no brightening in the eyes of these men.
If a man's very soul had perished, his eyes might resemble
these.

The men passed on, and Peter Moore stepped quickly on
deck, his heart thumping, his spine cold, sweat prickling
on his brows and chin.

Gray shadows, they retreated, setting their feet down
with slow and dull precision. In passing, their feet had
made no sound. They vanished.

Until recently it had not occurred to Peter that the ship
on which Lotus Burma had booked passage to Java might
prove to be an unusual ship. He realized now that it was
the most extraordinary ship on which he had ever traveled.

ACROSS FROM THE doorway of his stateroom was a lifeboat under a tarpaulin. An ordinary lifeboat, dried out by
tropical suns—the kind of a lifeboat you would expect
to find on a ship like the Langpo. A lap-straked double-
ender. At one end, high on the cutwater, was an eyebolt,
placed there for towing purposes. Something dark and dry
drooped from the eye-bolt.

Curiously Peter went to it, examined it. Seaweed. Dry
enough to crumple up and blow away. It was a wisp of
seaweed, not yellow weed, but grayish blue—the kind of
seaweed found only at great depths!

True, this type of weed often detached itself from rocks
and floated to the surface. But its presence in this eyebolt
was discomforting. It quickened the sense of mystery

which seemed to touch everywhere about this ship—
mystery and unreality.

Peter had the eerie sensation that he was aboard a
haunted ship manned by ghosts. Certainly, in all his travels,
he had never encountered humans so strange as these, or on
any ship on which he had ever sailed had he seen seamen
look or act so queerly as these. Why did they look alike?

His mind played with fantastic theories. Was this ship
actually commanded by Lotus Burma—a woman notorious for black practices, infamous for the way she controlled
the destinies of men?

Was she actually a sorceress? He could not rid himself
of the mystic feeling he had had when she peered into the
drinking glass brimful of water, or of the feeling that in her
darkly Oriental soul were queerly occult powers.

This was dangerous territory, yet something was wrong
with the very heartbeat of the Langpo, an uneasiness to
her rhythm, a stealth to the very way she crept through
the black water.

Definitely and decisively, something was wrong with
this ship; but he could not guess what it might be.

He walked to a fidley hatch to investigate, and found
that all engine-room hatches were covered with frosted
glass, and were screwed or nailed down tight. Why? There
was a deck grating near by, and he found that by backing
away from it he could see into the engine room through a
small aperture between steam pipes.

He saw a portion of the engine room, a familiar enough
glimpse of steam gauges and throttle handles. A man was
standing on the steel deck looking up at the gauges.

His face was clearly lighted by a pulsing bulb overhead.

Peter stared down at it with fascination. It was the face of a corpse—a corpse magically animated with the grimaces of life, but with the dull eyes of death. It might have been Captain Barberry—or either of those three. Who were these men?

Peter shivered a little. Again he was swept by the chilling suspicion that this ship of mystery was manned by ghosts—living ghosts of flesh and blood—dead men with the breath of life blown into them by the black magic of Lotus Burma.

THEN THIS FANTASTIC suspicion was driven away by an odor as from another world. Perfume! A familiar, haunting fragrance. It came on the wind, and with it came a woman, who set her little high heels down sharply.

She went past him in the darkness, walking rapidly. He did not see her face, but he would have known that quick step, that alert, gallant little head, the slender, diminutive figure, anywhere.

She wore a gray fur coat—and he recognized the coat. It was chinchilla, most expensive fur in existence. That coat had cost its wearer no less than fifty thousand dollars.

She walked rapidly, her high heels tapping sharply on the deck. For a moment Peter could not move. He had reassured himself that when he met Susan O'Gilvie again he would be calm and collected; that he would deal with the situation coolly. He had even made himself believe that he would not be upset when he saw her; that he had hardened himself so successfully against her that she would fail to move him.

His present symptoms were, however, not those of a man immune. Quite as if she exerted an irresistible magnetism, he followed her aft. The thrill hunter had gone to the taff-rail. With her gloved hands upon it, she looked somehow forlorn. He went to the rail some eight feet away from her and watched her.

Dimly, in the lights of the receding city, he could see her profile—a crisp and beautiful profile.

Her fragrance reached him again—and made him thrill again. He saw her shoulders twitch and twitch again. And he wondered what she was thinking about. An impulse grew strong in him to walk over to her, to crush her into his arms; to demand of her that she give up this latest pursuit of thrills.

Perhaps she was crying. Perhaps she was sorry for him. She turned away from the lights of the city. She stared up at him a moment, but her eyes were not wet. They were beautiful eyes, the color of fresh violets. And they were bright with excitement. She stared at him a moment, then turned and walked away, and the staccato of her heels on the deck was like the rippling tattoo of castanets.

In that glimpse of her, Susan O'Gilvie had looked very warm, very vital. But the glimpse had told nothing of her voice and very little of her reckless personality. At a glance, Susan O'Gilvie was a normal girl—and an exceptionally beautiful girl. But glimpses and glances were very deceiving.

Reputed to be the richest young woman in America, if not in the world, Susan O'Gilvie was an insatiable thrill hunter—a girl with a craving, a hunter for adventurous excitement that nothing could appease. Time after time, since she had been in Asia, she had plunged herself into dangerous predicaments, and had frantically called upon

Peter Moore to help. Since the eventful night of their meeting on the transpacific crossing, she had—always with the most innocent of intentions—drawn him into one dangerous Oriental complication after another. It was as if she had deliberately spun a web of enchantment about the young man, a web with threads of gold.

For almost two years this had been going on. And for these two years, Peter had refused to consider marriage because of Susan's great wealth. He had weakened very recently. Their marriage was to have taken place this morning. And until a few hours ago, he had considered himself the happiest and luckiest man on earth.

His thrill hunter had, in a few swift hours, changed all that. Unable to resist the lure of adventure, she had fallen under the influence of Lotus Burma. Doubtless, the Octopus had promised Susan thrills, adventure, excitement. And she had, at the same time, acquainted her with the most insidious, most amazing drug of which Peter had ever heard—a scented purple stuff which gave to its victims a ruthless sense of exaltation and power.

He knew that he had lost Susan forever, but he considered her a definite responsibility. It was his intention to take her ashore in Singapore and to take her aboard a ship bound for the United States.

That was Peter Moore's plan, and somehow he intended to carry it through.

WHEN SUSAN O'GILVIE entered Lotus Burma's room her cheeks were flushed and her eyes were starry with excitement. Lotus Burma lazily regarded her from under half-lowered lids, the amethyst cigarette holder dropping from a corner of her beautiful, cruel, red mouth.

Breathlessly Susan burst out, "Who is it—in the turban and the satin cape?"

And the Octopus, lazily studying her, drawled, "The Sultan of Sakara, my dear."

With this girl she used a voice that was a caress, soft and purring—her most hypnotic inflection. To bend this spirited American girl to her plans, to cause her to expel Peter Moore from her heart, had been a difficult task; because the girl had been so madly in love with that reckless adventurer. But the promise of Oriental adventure more exciting than Peter could ever offer, of a glimpse into the inner life of Asia's most exotic peoples, had won her.

Looking at Susan O'Gilvie now, Lotus Burma was satisfied. She had not erred in selecting Susan. Susan fulfilled all of the requirements of the order which the Octopus was obeying. The American girl was beautiful and she was healthy. She was the most beautiful white girl Lotus Burma had ever seen, with a slim, beautiful body over which any man might reasonably lose his reason.

Susan was smiling expectantly, and her violet eyes were radiant.

"And who is the Sultan of Sakara?"

"You've never heard of him?"

"Never!"

"He is the most amusing young despot in the Far East. His sultanate is in the northern end of Malaya, not far from the Siamese border. He is tremendously rich, very eccentric and very charming. His mother was a Frenchwoman. He was educated at Oxford. He is mad about horse racing, gambling, precious stones—and women. He is considered a connoisseur of women. His reputation is dangerous. He is half Malay—a very dangerous mixture."

"I'll be on my guard," Susan said lightly.

On the deck, on the starboard side, Peter Moore, at a partly opened window, had heard most of this. He complimented himself on having made a correct impression on Lotus Burma. But his interest was centered in the American girl and in the symptoms she was betraying—symptoms with which he had reason to be painfully familiar. For here, to Susan, was another thrill. A half-mad, half-breed sultan! At present he was more afraid of Susan, however, than of Lotus Burma. Susan knew him so well, his mannerisms, his tricks of voice and gesture. If she penetrated his disguise, she would, he was certain, betray him to Lotus Burma.

There was an unexpected and shocking development. The door of the room opened and Captain Barberry came in. His strange gray face was working. Only his eyes, with their hunted, dead look, betrayed no emotion.

"Madam," he gasped, "he is aboard this ship!"

Lotus Burma narrowed her eyes.

"Peter Moore?" she snapped.

"Yes, madam! I am certain!"

She darted a glance at Susan.

"Tsi-Lo-Lan, you are to have nothing to do with this fellow!"

Tsi-Lo-Lan—Chinese for violet—was the woman's name for Susan, because of the color of her eyes.

Susan said firmly, "I have no intention of seeing that man!"

PETER MOORE BACKED away from the window with a

sudden tightening of muscles in his solar plexus, as if he expected a fist to be driven there. His first reaction to that announcement was one of anger. Obviously, some one who knew him well—and some one no doubt in the crew had seen him and recognized him, despite his elaborate and, as he had thought, perfect disguise.

In the course of many adventures in Oriental lands, he had assumed many disguises, but he had been certain that none he had ever worn could be compared to this. When he had played the part of the Sultan of Sakara just a little longer, had perfected the sultan's curious accent and more fully mastered his habitual gestures, he was certain that he could deceive even Susan, who knew him better, perhaps, than any one on earth.

Yet some one had suspected or guessed—had somehow penetrated to the truth.

It meant that his entire elaborate plan was ruined. He could not secure the De Sylva diamonds, and he could make no progress with his plan to spirit Susan ashore and out of Lotus Burma's power, in Singapore.

More than that, his very life was threatened. For he—Peter Moore—was Lotus Burma's sworn enemy, and she would not hesitate to put him to death. In so far as help from any source was concerned, he was lost. This mystery ship was unquestionably under Lotus Burma's command, and its queer dead-faced men were so many slaves.

In his anger and anxiety, he was striding along the deck, his satin cape floating out behind, crackling in the wind. He could overcome the wireless operator, and flash a message to Hong Kong for help. He might signal a ship in the American battle fleet. His request for help might or might not be denied. For he was on a sort of blacklist with all the authorities.

This plan, however, appealed to him. The Langpo and her mystery were richly deserving of official investigation. And in the confusion of a high seas search he might be able to forward his other plans. He did not know what type of wireless equipment was installed on the Langpo, but he was well versed in wireless telegraphy, and quite familiar with the various types of installations in shipboard use, for he had been a wireless operator for several years in the China run from America, and in the China coastwise trade.

He found the wireless room forward of the funnel, and saw, with relief, that the plate over the door was that of the Radio Corporation of America.

As he reached for the knob of the door, the door swung open. He stepped quickly back to avoid being bowled over by it. A man was silhouetted in the dazzling lights which hung over the instruments.

Staring at him, Peter Moore forgot his dramatic plan. He had intended to rush in, to overpower the operator—to knock him senseless, if necessary—and to transmit messages to Hong Kong and the Asiatic fleet. But he did not even move. He was so shocked that he could not move. The brooding mystery of the Langpo in that instant seemed to pounce upon him and overwhelm him with its chilling terror.

For the man in the wifeless room doorway, in his gray trench coat, his gray felt hat, was *himself!* With the hair at the nape of his neck stirring, Peter Moore stared into the shockingly familiar face of Peter Moore!

6

MYSTERY SHIP

THE PETER MOORE in the wireless room doorway had a half-smoked cigarette in his lips, held at a certain angle. How well did the Peter Moore on deck, the Peter Moore garbed as the Sultan of Sakara, know that particular angle!

A chill wind seemed to be blowing through the brain of the spurious Sultan of Sakara. In all his adventures in China, in all his encounters with Oriental magic, he had never received a shock so stupefying as this.

The man who was himself, the man who blocked the wireless room doorway, was regarding him with a faint, pleasant grin.

The Sultan of Sakara fiercely asked, "Who are you?" He wanted to hear this man speak—wanted to hear the sound of his own voices issuing from another's lips.

"My name is Moore—Peter Moore," the other said.

The man who was impersonating a sultan did not know. He could not be sure. He knew that he would not recognize his own voice as his own. Yet he did not need that assurance. He was convinced now that he was under the sway of malignant occult powers. He could not even believe now in the reality of this ship, with its animated dead men for a crew. He could not even believe that he had actually seen

Susan O'Gilvie a few minutes ago, or that he had been face to face with a flesh-and-blood Lotus Burma.

He felt certain that he had somehow been made the victim of occult powers, of a species of Yogism. It was as if he were actually, not Peter Moore, but the childishly insane Sultan of Sakara. He knew that certain sorcerers and, presumably, sorceresses, of tribes in the remote fastnesses of the Indo-Chinese jungle practiced these tactics—that by a kind of hypnosis they could exchange the spirit of one man for the spirit of another.

He had always been skeptical of these legends, but he could not be skeptical now. And if he had been actually transformed—had actually become the Sultan of Sakara, then the man in the doorway was actually Peter Moore, and he had lost his soul.

It was a grotesque and fantastic assumption, yet the impersonator of the Malayan nabob had seen too much tonight to believe that this ship of mystery was explainable by the rules of common sense and logic. She was a ship of creeping terror and mystery beyond reasonable explanation.

Pleasantly, the man in the doorway said, "A nice night, isn't it?"

"Delightful!" agreed the Sultan of Sakara.

The man in the gray trenchcoat passed him and strolled down the deck, with cigarette smoke floating off his wide shoulders. The man in the white turban stared after him as the spirit of a dead man might stare at the body he had recently inhabited.

The shocking apparition of Peter Moore proceeded forward and vanished into a doorway. The Sultan of Sakara

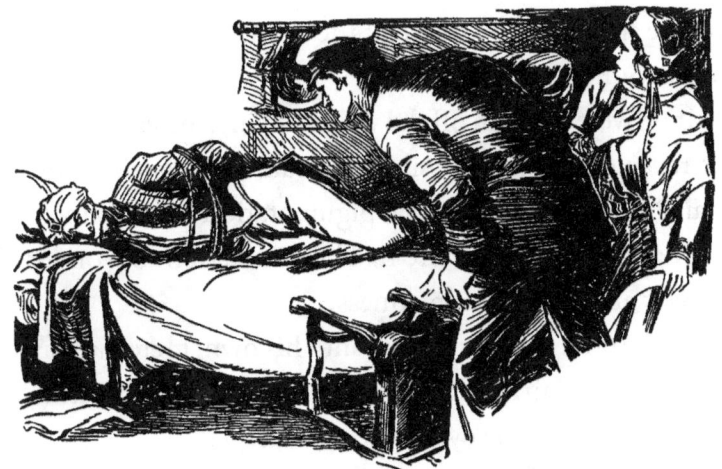

"What happened to you? Who did this?"

followed. It was Stateroom 8—two doors removed from his own. The man in the trenchcoat came out with a fresh pack of cigarettes in his hand. He walked on, vanishing around the turn of the deck.

The Sultan of Sakara passed the doorway of Stateroom 8. He hesitated, turned back with rapidly pumping heart. The light was still on.

FAMILIAR OBJECTS WERE strewn about the room, and about the washstand. Luggage which was his own—or identical with it. One of the bags was open on the bunk. He looked into it—and saw shirts, neckties, underwear, socks—either his own, or identical with his own.

He examined the razor, the toothbrush, the shaving cream and the toothpaste on the washstand. Again—his own, or identical with his own!

A thumping at the back of his head made him feel giddy. He stared at his face in the mirror. Shaken to the roots of his being, half-sick with fear, uncertain as to what his course should be, he stared at the brown face and blue eyes of the Sultan of Sakara.

If he were to clean off the walnut stain, whose face would be revealed? Was it possible to clean off the stain? Was it stain? Or was it the natural pigmentation of his skin?

Never before in his life had he had reason to wonder if he was at the brink of madness.

He left the room and went into his own. Here, he stared again into a mirror. He saw a brown face with a straight nose, firm lips, blue eyes. His own face?

"Good God," he growled, "who am I?"

If he were under the influence of Lotus Burma's sorcery, it was logical that she had placed him in this state for a purpose. Was her purpose simply to secure the elephant ring and the decoy stones—or had she some more devious reason for bending him to her will? Was this her revenge on his presumptiveness?

He reasoned: "This is absolutely fantastic, preposterous, and silly. I have not changed. I am still thinking with my own brain, and not one of my purposes has been changed. I am the man who talked with Dan de Sylva a few hours ago. I am the man who went to Yat Gow's and got this costume. I came aboard this ship to secure those diamonds. I'm going to get them."

A tenderness of his upper gums gave him a better grip on sanity. It was the clever red rubber strip which Yat Gow's black slave had placed there, to give his upper lip a longer appearance. His nostrils were sensitive, too. The silver tubes! He began to smile. He touched the clever rubber mole on his left earlobe. It was dead to the touch.

He wasn't, thank God, the Sultan of Sakara, after all!

He was Peter Moore. And the other man—? Another Peter Moore? An identical twin? Or a trick of that beautiful sorceress?

He went on deck again, anxious for another glimpse of this man who was identical with—or actually was—Peter Moore. But he saw nothing of him.

In the stern, he stopped, placed his elbows on the worn rail and stared out into the uncompromising blackness of the night. Far off, he saw a lighthouse beaconing. The Langpo was well at sea now. There was not even a glow to the north to indicate where Hong Kong lay. Off to starboard somewhere was Macao, but he could see nothing of that great opium center of South China.

The blackness was beginning to give way to gray. A ghostly light was threatening the night. Dawn would be here presently. There was a dampness in the air, a promise of fog. He could see no stars, no moonglow.

He had the premonition that dreadful things would happen when this ship reached that stretch of the South China Sea known as the Jaws of Hell.

HE TURNED AWAY from the rail. At his elbow was the partly-opened window at which he had stood listening to the conversation between Susan and Lotus Burma.

Lights still burned in that enchanted room, but it was empty now. Lotus Burma had retired. He presumed that she slept in an adjoining room.

His eyes darted about the room, and were suddenly attracted by a gleam in the midst of the purple cushions. It was the box containing the de Sylva diamonds! With careless indifference, she left it lying there, unwatched, unguarded, a fortune in diamonds!

It proved merely what he had sensed before. She was without fear. Her feeling for thieves, for enemies, was one of contempt and scorn. He could walk into that room now and walk out with the de Sylva diamonds. Yet, what would be the use? She had absolute control over this ship.

A wave of weariness swept over the Sultan of Sakara. He had had no sleep tonight, and none the previous night. His eyeballs itched. His lungs and heart ached, but he dared not sleep—dared not, literally, be caught napping.

He took a turn about the deck, but saw no one. The light still burned in Room 8, but the man who was Peter Moore—or so startlingly resembled him—was not there.

The dampness became more noticeable. A dead gray light filtered through the blackness. Dawn was coming. In its spectral light, the Sultan of Sakara saw, looming ahead perhaps two miles away, a great wall of fog. It stretched to east and west as far as he could see, and the face of it rose up until it vanished into the gloom of clouds.

A boy of sixteen or seventeen passed him, dressed in steward's whites, softly stroking a triangle of bronze wire with a leather-covered stick. The triangle sang softly, in a minor key.

Breakfast! In spite of his apprehension, his nerve fag, the Sultan of Sakara was hungry. He followed the steward below.

Captain Barberry and the man in the gray trenchcoat were already at table in the small, grimy dining saloon. Peter Moore—or his double—no longer wore the trenchcoat, but he was familiar in a suit of double-breasted blue serge, a blue tie, a tan shirt.

He was sitting halfway down the table from the captain,

devouring ham and eggs, the flaccid ham and the anæmic eggs of China. The Sultan of Sakara seated himself in a chair opposite, and gave him two quick glances.

Relief surged over the Sultan of Sakara. Two swift glances had reassured him. He had stared into his own face, in the process of shaving, too many years to be fooled. Without a hat, and with fairly good light from a chandelier flooding his hair and face, the difference, while slight, was, to the real Peter Moore, sufficient.

It was in the hairline and the sideburns. The impostor's hair grew down to a slightly sharper point on his forehead than did Peter Moore's, and his sideburns, cut short, as were Peter's, were fractionally wider.

Not one person of Peter's wide collection of acquaintances would have noticed these subtle differences. And Peter wondered if Susan would notice them. He also wondered what this careful imitator's game was. Something, no doubt, to do with Lotus Burma. The diamonds? Possibly.

But he was not worried about the impostor's game. That he had a very passable duplicate aboard this mystery ship suited his own plans perfectly. It would distract suspicion from himself. But he realized that if Susan O'Gilvie saw this man in adequate light—studied his face for more than a few seconds—she would recognize him—and no doubt betray him.

BUT HIS GESTURES, his mannerisms, were perfect. He was trying to make Captain Barberry talk. And the master of the Langpo appeared to be most reluctant.

"What's your nationality, captain?"

The gray eyes glanced at him vacantly. "I am Eurasian."

"But what's your country?"

"China."

"North or South?"

"North."

In good Mandarin Chinese, the impostor asked his next question: "Does an honest man reach up to straighten his hat under a ripe peach tree?"

A grimace, a distorted smile, momentarily twisted Captain Barberry's lips, but he did not answer the question.

The impostor asked him other questions. How long had he been at sea? What countries had he visited? Captain Barberry grew surly, then silent. He gave grunts for answers. His slack mouth trembled. Grotesque muscle knots ridged along his heavy jaw bones. The impression he gave was one of stupidity tinged with a growing fear. His vacant eyes swam. He reached up from time to time to pluck at a cowlick of his drab, flat hair which hung down on his idiotic forehead.

He seemed frightened, but he did not seem resentful. And it was hard indeed to imagine a spark of resentment or any similar emotion lighting those dead eyes. He gave the effect of a man completely cowed. And he gave the effect of wincing when the stranger's questions were too sharp or too insistent.

The stranger tried a variety of tongues—Cantonese, Japanese, Indo-Chinese. But he was met by the cloudy wall of those haunted, hunted eyes—and grunts.

These eyes became more and more distracted. They slid about uneasily at first, then frantically, in their sockets.

The ruthless questioning was interrupted by a deep and awful sobbing in the very bowels of the ship. This sound translated itself into a hissing surge of steam, then a melancholy bellowing. The Langpo's whistle was announcing the fog.

Captain Barberry's eyes slid across Peter's walnut-stained face. He clicked his coffee cup into its saucer and sprang up. Like an uneasy ghost, he took himself out of the saloon.

The impostor was through with his ham and eggs. He lit a cigarette and smiled across the table at the Sultan of Sakara, with his left eyebrow slightly raised—a smile that was, or should have been, familiar enough to the dark man in the turban.

"You're the Sultan of Sakara, aren't you?"

The Sultan of Sakara answered with the Sultan of Sakara's particular grin—a somewhat wolfish grimace, with eyes squeezed almost shut. He nodded.

"I recognized you from photographs—and that ring. My name's Peter Moore."

The impersonator held his cigarette well down in the crotch formed by the forefinger and middle finger of his right hand.

The Sultan of Sakara, who had lit a cigarette, held his in the tips of his fingers.

The spurious Peter Moore let smoke trickle from his nostrils.

The Sultan of Sakara squirted smoke through his teeth.

"I am charmed to meet you at last, Mr. Moore. I've heard about you, of course."

THE TWO MEN shook hands. The stranger dropped his elbows to the cloth and bent forward. His eyes sparkled with interest. They narrowed. He darted glances about the dingy little room and said, low-voiced: "If you'll pardon me, your majesty, I'm curious to know why you are traveling on a ship like this. There are three large, fast, luxurious ships sailing from Hong Kong this morning."

"It was a whim," his majesty replied.

"Has it struck you there's anything strange—mystifying—about this ship?"

"Strange? Mystifying?" the sultan repeated with that Malayan-Oxford accent.

"That captain—the crew! They're like ghosts. I've been in every part of the Far East—and their nationality baffles me."

"I'm afraid I'm at a loss, Mr. Moore."

He was sparring, and he knew that the other man, a clever student of his methods, of his very processes of thought, was doing likewise—trying to fit him into a baffling picture.

The stranger said quietly, "I dropped into the wireless room last night to send a message. The operator said the wireless equipment was out of order. I offered to fix it. I used to be a wireless operator."

"Really?"

"For years! He declined my offer. Why, your majesty? Because the wireless apparatus isn't real! It's made of papier-mâché!"

The sultan's eyes gleamed. "How fantastic!"

"The entire ship is fantastic, your majesty. You booked passage for Singapore, did you not?"

"I did, Mr. Moore."

The man across from him shrugged. "So did I. I hope we get there. But I'm dubious. If there was any way to send a message from this ship, I'd send it. I'd send an S.O.S. Wouldn't you?"

The Sultan of Sakara pursed his lips with the air of a man in troubled thought.

He wondered just what the stranger was driving at.

"We have an expression in America," the synthetic Peter Moore said, "that covers this ship very neatly. Phony."

"Yes, I've heard of it. A very pungent and useful word, Mr. Moore."

"It applies to this ship. She is phony. So is everybody on board." He hesitated, gave that familiar, lifted-eyebrow smile. "Except you and me, of course, your majesty."

"But what would be the purpose of it?"

The stranger shrugged again. The sultan recognized that shrug. It was perfect. "This is the China coast. *Maskee!* And some time tomorrow, we'll be entering the Jaws of Hell. I'll see you later."

He got up and picked up his hat and trenchcoat.

"I'll be seeing you," the Sultan of Sakara said with dry good humor, "in Davy Jones's locker!"

The stranger gave him a quick, surprised grin—and went out. The sultan finished his breakfast in solitary grandeur, then went on deck and proceeded to the wireless room. There was no answer to his knock. He tried the knob. The door opened upon familiar instruments. There was no one in the room.

He quickly examined the switchboard, the switches and some of the instruments. He did not have to look far to verify what his impersonator had said. The instruments were of pressed wood or carved wood, cleverly fashioned and cleverly lacquered or painted.

Not one of them was real.

With this latest item to add to the long list of baffling mysteries, he went on deck. The Langpo was in dense fog now, and the whistle was blowing at short intervals. Thick gray vapor went streaming aft, obscuring any object more than fifty feet away. The Langpo was proceeding through the fog at her usual speed, which, in itself, was mysterious.

7

CAUGHT!

THE SULTAN OF Sakara sauntered around to Room 8, and knocked. His impersonator was not at home, but the door was unlocked. Without hesitation, the sultan went in. He wanted to find out just what the man's business was aboard this ship.

He went through the unknown's luggage with the meticulous care of a Japanese spy. He looked for secret hiding places in the luggage. And when he found nothing of interest there, he explored the washstand and the bunk.

Under the bunk, in the life preserver rack, very cunningly concealed, was an unlabeled bottle with an ornamental glass stopper. He took out the stopper and sniffed the pale blue liquid. It smelled like fine hair tonic. But it wasn't hair tonic. Precious stuff, this. It was the most expensive hair bleach that money could buy. And it would appear that the impersonator was not as blond as he looked.

If the spurious Sultan of Sakara had wished to spoil the spurious Peter Moore's game, he might have done so by pouring the contents of that bottle down the drain. But he did not wish to. He wanted to wait for developments. In all his life, he had never been so curious about a man.

There was a rattling at the door handle. He was, presumably, trapped. But he did not attempt to hide the bottle.

The door opened. The blond man in the gray hat and the gray trenchcoat started into the room, then stopped.

He said, with an apologetic grin, "I beg your pardon, sultan, but I thought this was my room."

"It is your room. Come right in."

The apologetic grin vanished. The man in the trenchcoat glanced swiftly about the room, but his eyes returned to the bottle of pale-blue stuff in Peter's hand, and the skin about his blue eyes tightened a little.

He came into the small room, closing the door firmly behind him. He placed his back against the door, took out a cigarette and lighted it. He exhaled the smoke through his nostrils.

"A cat," he said, "was killed one time because it got curious."

"You must pardon my intrusion," the sultan said. "I was naturally curious. When you failed to recognize me, I knew you were not my old friend Peter Moore. I suspected you at once. But I was amazed by the resemblance. You are not Peter Moore."

"No?" the other drawled. "That puts us in a hell of a mess, doesn't it? I'm not Peter Moore—and you're not the Sultan of Sakara! The Sultan of Sakara is an old friend of mine. In Paris. When you failed to recognize me, I knew you were not my old friend the Sultan of Sakara. But I was amazed by the resemblance. You *are* Peter Moore!"

The stranger was no longer grinning. There was a nasty twist to his mouth. His eyes were half-closed and somewhat menacing.

"Get this, Moore. Keep out of my business or I'll spoil yours! You're a trouble-maker—but don't let me catch you making trouble for me!"

"There's a possibility," Peter quietly suggested, "that we could be useful to each other."

The unknown gave a short, barking laugh. "On the principle that a rat knows the way of rats?" he jeered. "Not a chance! I don't want your help. We don't know each other. I don't want to know you. Now, get the hell out of here." This was said in English. He added to it an insult in Chinese—the filthiest, most blasphemous insult in the language.

PETER HESITATED A moment, tempted to smack him on the jaw. A glimpse of a figure in gray approaching along the deck made him think better of the impulse. He stepped out on deck as Lotus Burma emerged, like a wraith, from the fog.

The Octopus was so preoccupied that she did not see him until she was almost past. Yards of soft gray crêpe de Chine were wrapped about her, Burmese fashion. Her golden skin and ink-black hair were startling above the gray silk.

She saw the Sultan of Sakara and gave him a quick, somewhat contemptuous smile. Then she saw the man in the doorway. Her step faltered. The smile did not go away, but it subtly changed and the eyes went narrow and greenly shimmering. Here was hatred in terms of utter contempt. Behind this was gloating—triumph? She went on quickly.

And Peter gleaned that this was the first meeting between her and his impersonator since the latter had come aboard. Certainly, she had not recognized him as an impostor. Peter glanced at the man in the doorway. The unknown was not smiling. His mouth and eyes were hard with determination.

And Peter, taking himself away, wondered again what the fellow's game was.

He returned to his own stateroom, undressed and turned in. He ached with sleeplessness, but before he dozed off, he made a decision. He would secure the diamonds tonight. He did not know why the man in Room 8 was aboard, but he would take no chances with those diamonds!

He was asleep almost the instant his head touched the pillow. The booming of the fog whistle did not even penetrate his dreams. They were not happy dreams. In them, Susan was in some difficulty, a prisoner in a great gray castle, and he was helpless. He tried vainly to rescue her.

Late in the afternoon, a knocking at his door awakened him. A steward was at the door with a note. When Peter saw the handwriting on the envelope, his heart suddenly began beating rapidly. He read the note.

> H.R.H. the SULTAN OF SAKARA.
>
> YOUR HIGHNESS:
>
> I'd be delighted if you'd have tea—or cocktails—with me— and pardon the informality of this. Will you?
>
> Sincerely,
>
> SUSAN O'GILVIE.

Peter told the steward to wait. Sooner or later, he would have to face Susan—would have to undergo the scrutiny of her clever violet eyes. It might be wise to meet that test now—have it over with.

He examined himself in the washstand mirror. To

himself, with that strangely flaring nose, that slightly protuberant upper lip, that walnut skin, he looked utterly strange. He was convinced that the man who was posing as himself had not penetrated his disguise, but had either guessed his identity or been informed of it.

He dressed carefully, selecting a fresh white turban, a sapphire-blue jacket and canary-yellow trousers.

When he was ready, the steward conducted him to Miss O'Gilvie's suite. It was next door to but not connected with Lotus Burma's suite, and it comprised a small sitting room and a bedroom.

SUSAN OPENED THE door to his knock—a slim, beautiful, eager-eyed girl in a blue tea gown. It was their first actual meeting since she had told him, the night before, that she would never marry him—that she never wanted to see him again.

It surprised him that she looked no different. To be sure, she was not angry now. But she was excited. Her eyes were brilliant and her cheeks were feverishly flushed. Excitement always did this to Susan—her whole being seemed to quicken, to glow. He had never seen her more beautiful than she was this afternoon.

Standing there, looking up at him with those large, amazing eyes, he forgot his apprehension, his fear of discovery. She was so lovely, so slim, so softly appealing that he wanted to cry out, to crush her in his arms. Instead, he gave her the Sultan of Sakara's famous wolfish smile, and he accompanied it with a gesture of his left hand, that quick, jerking gesture, as of a man about to slap a mosquito—a gesture for which Ameer Prak Chan was equally famous.

The girl with violet eyes was looking sharply into his face and something in her eyes seemed to quicken. His heart began to hammer again. Did she recognize him? Was she going to pretend that she didn't?

Then she cried: "I am delighted and flattered, your highness!"

With a deep bow, he retorted, "Oh, I assure you, my dear lady, it is I who am honored!"

She seemed pleased. She seemed thrilled. But even if she had guessed his identity, she might have seemed both pleased and thrilled. For Susan was unpredictable. If she had guessed his identity, she might be delighted at his boldness. She might, on the other hand, be acting. He was certain he had lost Susan forever—that she was determined to wash him and all memory of him from her life and from her mind.

She was charming—her old blithe, gay self. She had heard a little of the Sultan of Sakara. She wanted to hear more. She had an insatiable thirst for adventurous thrills. She wanted to hear stories which were adventurous and thrilling. Very obviously, she had not regretted her decision to wash Peter Moore out of her life. She had dedicated her life to the pursuit of adventure.

He talked and she drew him out. Well-versed in the life and activities of Ameer Prak Chan, he told her hair-raising and blood-chilling stories of the Malayan jungles—of tiger and boar hunts, of ghosts, of fabulous mines. She was fascinated.

He was presently convinced that Susan O'Gilvie had not guessed who he was. He talked and gestured with the greatest care, and he took care that she saw nothing of his profile.

His curiosity carried him presently into dangerous waters. As she was pouring tea, he said, with an air of apology, "Miss O'Gilvie, didn't I read in yesterday's Hong Kong papers that you were to be married today?"

She gave him a quick smile. "You did. But it's off."

"Wasn't the young man named Peter Moore?"

Her smile became a little fixed. "Yes, your highness."

"Isn't that the young man I've seen aboard this ship?"

The smile vanished and the lovely red mouth became stern. "It is," she answered. "He is a fool to follow me."

"Love is a cruel mistress."

Susan smiled again, a little bitterly. "That's why I stopped being in love. I don't want love. I don't want marriage."

He could have said, "You wanted it badly enough for almost two years—until you met this devil woman!" But what he said was, "Ah, you American girls! Freedom! It's all you want."

"It isn't all I want," Susan declared. "I want adventure—excitement." Her eyes were hard and glittering. She meant it, very definitely. She had gone over wholly to adventure, to the romance of dangerous thrills.

TWO YEARS AGO, when he first met Susan, Peter had sensed the two sides to her nature. With one of them, very shortly after that first meeting, she loved him. She had told him frankly she adored him. And she had followed him over the face of China. But during this time, the other nature had developed until now it appeared that *Dr. Jekyll* had become completely *Mr. Hyde*.

He had never loved her adventurous side, and he had

hated to see it gradually dominate her. Susan in search of a thrill, of new and untried excitements had been a trial, a growing problem.

She did not want to talk about Peter Moore. She babbled about the adventures she had had and of adventures in strange lands which she hoped to experience. He was forced to conclude that Susan was on this ship of her own free will—and he wondered what her fate would be— wondered where this strange ship, with its ghostly crew, was taking all of them.

She had heard about the Jaws of Hell—was perfectly fascinated by the weird tales she had heard. He did not tell her of his discovery of the Aronga's drinking glass or the Pelgrasse's towels, or of the wireless room with its papier-mâché equipment. All of these mysteries would explain themselves in due course. But he asked her what she thought of the crew.

Susan had paid no attention to the crew. She said: "I think Captain Barberry is perfectly fascinating. He has such weird eyes!"

He left her parlor presently with the feeling that he was safe from discovery by Susan as long as he never let her look too long at his profile.

At dinner that night, as at breakfast, no one appeared in the dingy little dining saloon but Captain Barberry and the two impostors. The fraudulent Peter Moore ignored the spurious Sultan of Sakara and addressed all of his remarks to the captain. He again tried to draw out the captain, to make him talk, but that gray-faced, strange man gave him no satisfaction. He never once lifted those cloudy, mystifying eyes from his plate, and his answers were in the form of grunts and monosyllables.

After dinner Peter took a turn about the deck.

The Langpo was still ploughing through dense fog at full speed, sounding her whistle at thirty-second intervals. She wallowed and creaked in a long cross-swell.

He wondered again what her destination might be. And he knew that both he and the insolent stranger were completely at Lotus Burma's mercy. He retired to his room and removed his pocket radio receiver from the beefwood chest—and wished now that he had devoted all of his time to developing a portable wireless transmitter instead of a receiver.

He turned on the dials, and adjusted the volume control so that the speaker produced the softest of sounds. The air was full of a shrill piping. He could hardly tune it out. He recognized call letters and signatures. The Langpo was very close to the Asiatic squadron of the American fleet! But there was no way of signaling for help.

Restless, he put the receiver away and went back on deck. The Langpo's disregard of the fog made him uneasy. Why should she be driven at such speed through this fog?

8

TORTURE

HE WALKED AFT. As he passed the windows of Lotus Burma's parlor, he saw her talking to a steward. She was evidently giving him some instructions, for the steward kept bobbing his head like an idiot trying vainly to understand. But he apparently understood. She went to the door of her bedroom and vanished. The steward waited at the door. After a moment, she handed him the purple satin gown she had been wearing. The steward, bobbing his head in that idiotic way, took the gown and went out by way of the door at the after end of the room.

The Sultan of Sakara waited. He could not see much of the bedroom, but through the crack he caught glimpses first, of a naked arm, then of a naked foot. And presently the light in the bedroom went out.

He would, he decided, give her a half hour in which to fall asleep. He walked forward and searched about among the donkey engines in the peak until he found what he wanted. It was a length of iron wire smaller in diameter than a fine pencil lead, and was wrapped around the broken insulation on a steam pipe. He unwrapped the wire and coiled it up. There was approximately twelve feet of it. The coil he stowed away in a pocket.

He returned aft and looked in Lotus Burma's parlor. He could see one end of the black jewel box protruding from the purple cushions, and his heart began to pound more rapidly.

Then he went to the door. It was not locked. He opened it and went in, with his heart hammering. He knew what he was about to do would precipitate trouble. He wanted to precipitate trouble. He wanted to bring a hazy picture into focus.

With quick strides, he went to the great tumbled pile of cushions. He picked up the box. As he did so, he saw, from the tail of his eye, a figure flit past the windows on the port side.

The diamond thief leaped to one of the purple brocade wall hangings—slipped behind it as the door latch rattled. He flattened himself against the wall, with his head back. He heard the door open. A man's voice called, "Miss Burma! Miss Burma!"

A triangle of light fell on Peter's forehead just above his left eye. By going up on his tiptoes, his eye reached the rent in the cloth. He saw Captain Barberry standing in the middle of the room, his lips working, his eyes staring wide.

The bedroom door squeaked. Peter could not see Lotus Burma. But he heard the swish of satin as she entered the room.

"Madam, she is weeping. She is hysterical," Captain Barberry said.

"Bring her here," the woman snapped.

The captain went out. Over the hammering of his heart, Peter heard her moving about. Then she moved into his range of vision. Over jade-green pajamas she was wearing a negligee of scarlet satin. She was fitting a cigarette into the amethyst holder. She held the cigarette into an incense brazier, puffed, straightened up. In the palm of her left hand, the man behind the curtain glimpsed a small white object. It might have been a flake of polished ivory—or alabaster.

Dust in the heavy curtain made him want to cough. It tickled his throat until his very restraint caused tears to gush into his eyes. The sharp eyes of Lotus Burma were darting about the room. She stared at the pile of pillows, then at the curtain behind which Peter was hiding. He could have sworn she started impulsively toward him, as if, by some clairvoyant power, she actually detected his presence.

THEN THE DOOR rattled and opened and Susan came into the room, followed by the captain. Susan was dressed as she had been when he saw her that afternoon. But she was no longer the radiant, adventurous girl of teatime. Her eyes and cheeks were red and swollen. Her hair was rumpled. Her clothing was disarranged. She had evidently thrown herself on her bed and given way to hysterics. She was still sobbing, still blind with tears.

"I don't want to see you!" Susan cried.

"You were having hysterics," Lotus Burma said severely. "Is it because that man is on this ship?"

"No. I'm afraid."

"What are you afraid of?"

"I don't know," the girl wailed. "Everything's so strange. This ship's so strange. These—these men are so queer. Who are they? Where is this ship going?"

"You will find out in due time."

"But you told me we were going to Java. You were lying to me. Who are these horrible men?" Her voice was rising. She was screaming now. "I don't want to go on with this. I'm afraid."

Quietly, the Octopus woman said, "Hold her, captain."

"No!" Susan screamed. "Keep away from me, you horrible creature!"

But the captain had seized her by the elbows from behind. She struggled. She screamed. She kicked at him. But Captain Barberry did not release her. She began laughing and sobbing at once.

Lotus Burma approached her. The meaning of the white glint Peter had seen in the palm of her hand now became clear to him. It was a small alabaster phial with a kingfisher jade stopper.

He held himself grimly. He wanted to spring out, dash the phial from her hand. But he controlled himself.

The Octopus woman seized Susan by the throat, pushed her head back. And when Susan wriggled away, Lotus Burma grasped a handful of the girl's hair, close to the scalp, and twisted it. Susan screamed and became limp. She might have fainted.

Lotus Burma unstoppered the phial and pressed the mouth of it between Susan's lips. A drop or two of the incredible purple drug escaped, trickling down the girl's chin.

The woman released her and stepped back. Peter, staring with fascination, saw a subtle change, then a more striking change come over Susan. She no longer wept. Her head came up. Magically, she took on an aspect of haughty dignity. She became regal.

Her eyes began to glow, a curious smile appeared at her bruised lips. She was a different girl.

"You can release her now," Lotus Burma said.

Captain Barberry let her go. Her eyes seemed to flash.

"Do you feel better now, Tsi-Lo-Lan?" the woman asked.

"Yes, Miss Burma. I feel—I feel quite myself."

"You have no desire to leave this ship now?"

The girl gave her an imperious little smile. "Why, no," she said in a puzzled voice. Her sweet, timid personality was gone. She was as haughty, as self-possessed as any queen.

"You long for the greatest adventure that life can hold?"

"Of course I do!"

"Perhaps you wish to retire now, Tsi-Lo-Lan."

"I do."

She left the room. Captain Barberry hesitated.

"Have her watched every moment," Lotus Burma directed. "If we lose her—you lose your head."

"Yes, madam," the man said. His eyes were more vacant than ever. His sagging lower lip was shining wet with saliva.

He went to the door and out on deck. Lotus Burma stood in the center of the room, with her back to the hanging behind which Peter stood, then she turned and walked from view.

He again heard the squeaking of the bedroom door. Above the throbbing of the woodwork, he heard her moving about in her bedroom. He permitted a full half hour to pass before he moved. Then he slipped from behind the curtain, and, with the box of diamonds under his arm, swiftly crossed the room and let himself out on deck.

RETURNING QUICKLY TO his room, he encountered no

one. He went rapidly to work. He untied the black ribbon from the box and opened it. For a moment, he let his eyes feast on that glittering, icy mass of diamonds—two million dollars' worth of the finest stones in the Orient! Then he added to the treasure the rest of the stones—the diamonds, sapphires, rubies and emeralds—which he had borrowed from Daniel de Sylva. Last to go into the box was the fabulous elephant ring.

Whimsically, he rubbed the elephant head down his cheek and said, "Bring me luck!" Closing the box, he swiftly wired the lid down. He went on deck again, and now he proceeded with utmost caution. But he met no one.

Fog swirled about him. Moisture, collecting on the rigging, dripped on deck. The fog whistle blew at monotonous intervals, and it had a hoarse, dreary sound. Far off, he heard a ship's answer—a deep bellow of an answer, and he presumed that the ship, invisible, was a large one, a liner.

When he had hidden the box of diamonds, he did not immediately return to his stateroom. From one of the forward lifeboats, he removed about thirty feet of weathered rope. This he carried into his room. He scattered the contents of the beefwood chest about the room. He turned out the light and got into bed—with the rope.

He began the slow and laborious job of lashing himself into the bunk, working upwards from his feet. Lashing his wrists together was the most difficult, but he succeeded finally, and when the final slipknot had been laboriously worked into place, he was lashed there, helpless.

In more ways than one, he was taking long chances. By stealing the diamonds, he had, in effect, planted a bomb. The bomb would blow up when Lotus Burma discovered her diamonds were missing. The Langpo would, he hoped, cease being a ship of baffling mystery and become a ship popping with trouble. The rope tied so tightly about him was uncomfortable and prevented sleep. Hours passed. The Sultan of Sakara was suddenly aware of a tension within himself—an awareness of something missing.

The fog whistle had stopped blowing! Dawn came shortly—a cold and wretched light—and gave him another surprise. Through the window he could see that the fog was not gone—it was as thick as ever! He could see it drifting in a great gray cloud past the window—dense fog. Why had the whistle stopped sounding its warning?

Listening, he believed he heard, faintly, the voices of other ships in the fog—once, the shrill warning of a destroyer, then, the bass, jovial booming of a large steamer.

The light increased. And he was suddenly aware of agitation on deck. Men were running to and fro. Voices, muffled by fog, were shouting. Men raced past his window.

He did not believe that the ship was in trouble, or the engines would have stopped.

Silence was presently restored. He heard nothing for perhaps a half hour but the steady vibration of the woodwork, the creaking and groaning of the hull as it responded to the throb of the engines and the lifting and falling of long ground swells.

Then, far away, a man's voice arose in a thin wail of pain. The wailing continued for several minutes, and it was of a character that started the hairs on Peter's neck to bristling. **PRESENTLY, FOOTSTEPS SOUNDED** on the deck outside his room. A hand seized the knob and jerked the door open.

"Your majesty!" a woman's voice shrilled. Then: "Oh, good God!"

It was Lotus Burma, but a Lotus Burma changed almost beyond recognition. Her hair was in disorder. Her face was pale. Her lips were raw.

Behind her, vacant of eye, slack of jaw, loomed Captain Barberry.

She stumbled into the room and stared at him. Wildly she cried, "What happened to you? Who did this?"

She stripped the gag from his mouth. He wet his paralyzed lips. "I—don't—know, madam."

"You've been robbed!"

"Yes."

"The ring—where's the ring?"

"Gone! Everything's gone!"

She shrieked: "My diamonds, too! Captain, take off these ropes!" She was wringing her hands. She was distracted, frantic.

The man on the bed reflected: "Whatever happens, this is worth all the trouble." Her haughty disdain, her coolness, her contempt were of the past.

"Didn't you see the robber?" she panted.

"No, madam. In the dark, some one pounced on me. I heard this person ransacking my trunk. I felt the ring being snatched off my finger. I saw no one."

Lotus Burma gave a despairing wail. Then, with better control: "We will find the robber. Never fear! I think we have already found him."

She stormed out of the little stateroom and vanished, followed by the vacant-eyed, wet-mouthed captain. And the howls of pain Peter had heard were continued.

He went on deck. The sounds as of a man in agony were coming from somewhere aft. They were, indeed, issuing from Lotas Burma's parlor—from the lips of the insolent stranger who had come aboard in Hong Kong cleverly disguised as Peter Moore. He was screaming with pain.

Through a window, the Sultan of Sakara saw him. He was being subjected to an old, a medieval method of torture—one called the *strappado*. He was seated in a chair, with his legs and body strapped to it. His arms, drawn out back of him—back of the chair—were bound at the wrist with rope. A stout rope led from this binding up and over an iron hook in the ceiling, and down to the hands of two sailors standing near the open doorway.

They had pulled enough of the rope up and over the hook, so that the luckless adventurer was clear of the floor—and the chair was clear of the floor. The weight of himself and the heavy chair was being supported by those delicate sockets where arms met shoulders. The weight was threatening to dislocate them—to pull the bones out of the sockets, and the pain must have been agonizing.

This spurious Peter Moore was pale and glistening with sweat. His mouth was working. Shrieks were being wrenched from him. And mingled with the shrieks of the tortured man were those of the furious woman.

She shrieked: "Where did you hide them?"

And the suffering man answered, "I didn't! I didn't steal them!"

He fainted then. "Lower him," Lotus Burma said. "When he recovers consciousness—up he goes again!"

The Sultan of Sakara sauntered aft. Lotus Burma had just gone forward. Peter heard her screaming at members of the crew. Men were swarming all about the decks. Hatch covers had been removed. Men were climbing in and out of holds like hungry rats—these ghostly, vacant-eyed men who looked like brothers. Every square inch of the slatternly old tub would be gone over. But they would not, Peter believed, find the diamonds.

He said to the two sailors, the torturers, "Get busy, you dogs! Hunt for that black box! I will attend to this rascal!" And he delivered this in such a ferocious tone that the two sailors leaped to obey him.

Thus he was alone with the stranger when he recovered his senses. The fellow stared at him with bloodshot, pain-racked eyes. His chest rose and fell with short gasps, sobs. But when he saw the man in the turban standing over him, he controlled his sobs. His face hardened, and the ghost of a smile flitted across his lips.

"Yeah," he whispered. "I was a damned fool to come busting into your game. But I thought you were sailing on the *King of Asia*. Don't worry, I won't squeal. What's going to happen to us?"

"We'll probably be dumped overboard," Peter said cheerfully, "minus our heads—if she finds those diamonds."

"Did you hide them safely?"

"She'll never find them. But she won't do any more of this."

"Keep your turban on. I can take it. You know damned well the Sultan of Sakara loves torture. If you stop this they'll have that mole off your left ear-lobe before you can bat an eye. Where's this old hooker going?"

"I don't know."

"Listen! In case anything happens to me—if you get out of this mess safely—I'm—"

"Some one's coming!"

9

A MYSTERY IS SOLVED

SOME ONE WAS running down the deck. It was Susan O'Gilvie. Close behind her came Lotus Burma and Captain Barberry.

The girl ran into the room, glanced at the Sultan of Sakara, then at the man lashed to the chair, and cried: "Oh, Peter! What are they doing to you?"

She had evidently been awakened by the tortured man's screams. She wore a frilly blue negligee over her night-gown. Her eyes were still dark with sleep.

Lotus Burma said hysterically: "I told you this man would make trouble! I should have had his throat cut! I should have had him lashed in irons and thrown overboard! I was a fool to indulge your silly whim!"

"My whim?" Susan cried. "You were afraid of him! You've always been afraid of him. Why are you doing this? What has he done?"

"He stole my diamonds—the boxful! He has hidden them somewhere on this ship. And the sultan's—he stole all of his stones and the elephant ring. Hoist him, captain!"

Captain Barberry seized the rope. Susan shrieked: "Don't you dare!" She ran around to the front of the chair, and for the first time since he had come aboard, Susan had a full glimpse of his face. She began, tremulously, "Peter—" Then she checked herself. Her eyes grew wide. She uttered a small, hysterical laugh. "This man," she announced, "is not Peter Moore!"

Lotus Burma's face seemed to stiffen. "You're lying!"

"Look for yourself," Susan cried. "He hasn't Peter's eyes. And look at his hair. In a hundred ways, he's different."

The octopus woman seemed uncertain. She looked steadily into Susan's eyes, then into the impostor's face.

"Who are you?" she snapped.

"My name is Jim Saunders," the man answered. "I am the United States Vice Consul at Foochow. The Consul General in Hong Kong put this job up to me. And he knows, of course, that I'm on this ship. If anything happens to me—if I don't return—what's going to happen to you?"

Lotus Burma stared at him with the ferocity of a tiger about to pounce upon a victim.

"What are you doing on this ship?"

Jim Saunders gave her his twisted grin. "Nothing much, Miss Burma. Just checking up on you. There was a little kidnaping job pulled off in Hong Kong eight or ten hours before you sailed. A girl called Marcia Pool would have been fed to an octopus if the man I'm impersonating hadn't stepped in and stopped you."

The octopus woman cried: "It's a lie!"

"Oh, sure, it's all a lie. The truth is, I'm Mahatma Ghandi, looking for a new place to go on a fast."

"What are you doing on this ship?" Lotus Burma repeated wrathfully.

"Just what I said. Checking you up. We've got kind of curious about your mysterious disappearances. We wondered where you holed up when you weren't pulling off a little job somewhere."

"You will never leave this ship alive!"

"No?" Saunders jeered. "It's up to you, baby. If I don't show up in Hong Kong inside of sixty days, you'd better stay holed up the rest of your life."

In a breathless voice, Susan said, "Of all the utterly amazing—" She turned, with a quick eager smile, to the Sultan of Sakara. And it caught that Oriental nabob completely off guard. He was presenting his profile, and his face must have worn some characteristic expression. For Susan cried: "Peter! It's you!"

LOTUS BURMA STARED at him only for a moment. Then she shrieked orders. Men came swarming, but Peter did not try to escape. He had anticipated this development. Sooner or later, it was inevitable. He was roughly searched, then his arms were roped.

The octopus woman wore a look of triumph. Color flowed back into her beautiful face. Her dark-green eyes sparkled and flashed.

With arms folded on chest, she looked up into his dark face.

"Perhaps," she said, "you wish to tell me where my diamonds are."

Susan whimpered, "Peter, tell her! Don't let her torture you."

"They're overboard," he said calmly.

Lotus Burma lost some of her composure. "You're lying! Where are my diamonds?"

"Overboard!"

"That's right," Jim Saunders said cheerfully. "I saw him throw 'em over myself."

"Take this man away," the octopus woman ordered. "Lock him up!"

And when Jim Saunders had been taken away, she reiterated her question. "Where are those diamonds?"

And when Peter repeated his answer, she said, "Take him forward. We will let him swing awhile by the thumbs. Perhaps he will remember."

Susan began to scream. Lotus Burma clapped a hand over the girl's convulsing mouth. Captain Barberry seized Susan's hands from behind, held her rigidly while the woman poured a dose of the fantastic purple drug into Susan's mouth.

Her struggling ceased. Once again, that magical, almost frightening transformation took place in her. She became calm. Her chin came up. Her eyes glowed mysteriously.

Peter said, "Can't you fight that stuff off, Susan?"

And she stared at him regally. "You shall be punished for following me!"

He was taken forward, and on his way he made a new discovery—new fuel for mystery! The decks, the deck cabins, the holds were swarming with men as a Chinese beggar swarms with vermin. Dozens of them! Countless times as many men as were required, by the law of any known country, in the crew of a ship of this size! They scrambled out in the fog, these fantastic gray men, with their idiots' eyes—as alike as rats in a cellar!

A simple but effective torture machine was made ready for Peter Moore. One of the cargo booms was unshipped and lifted, so that the great buff arm was at an angle of forty-five degrees. From the upper and outer end of this, a rope was run through a block. The lashing about Peter's wrists was removed. Sailors lashed marlin about the upper ends of his thumbs, and the ends of these small ropes were spliced to the end of the rope dangling from the boom.

Four men laid hold of the other end of the rope. It was tightened until his arms were lifted over his head, until he was standing on tiptoe.

A white-faced she-devil of vengeance, Lotus Burma said, "Where are those diamonds?"

"Overboard!"

"Hoist him up!"

The four men heaved on the rope. They hauled until Peter's feet were dangling three feet off the steel deck.

The octopus woman cried, "When you are ready to talk, I will be ready to listen. In a half hour, my friend, I think you will become quite talkative."

But Peter, for reasons of his own, thought otherwise. From a friend, one Dekka, a Tibetan who had been schooled in the ways of Yogism, he had learned priceless tricks. He had learned the mastery of pain. He had learned that process of mental concentration whereby he could, when he wished, deaden pain in any part of his body. He could, if he wished, render himself totally unconscious for hours at a time. He might, it was true, suffer some after-effects from this form of torture, but Lotus Burma could not—if he willed otherwise—wring from him the answer she wanted.

She did not stay long. She left to supervise the thorough search of the ship. The four men made the rope fast to a cleat and departed, too. Left alone, he wondered if he had hidden the diamonds successfully. Such a minute search made him believe that, in time, the black metal box must be found.

THE LANGPO ROLLED heavily in the swell. Fog poured down upon her, as if from an inexhaustible vat. It was so thick that, as he twisted at the end of the rope, he could never see farther than fifty feet in any direction. The bridge was only twenty or twenty-five feet away from him. At times, the three figures on the bridge were completely obscured. And since early this morning—at dawn—the fog whistle had stopped.

Why? He could not believe that it had been out of order for such a length of time.

The steady rolling of the ship caused him to swing. He swung from side to side, in greater and greater arcs, like a pendulum. The pain in his thumbs was becoming intense. He brought his mind to bear on it. And as the pain crept down his arms and flowed, like a fiery liquid, into his shoulders, he sent numbness into those areas, too. He endured no actual pain, only a slight discomfort, and, with this, a certain cloudiness of mind which always accompanied his use of Yogism.

But his brain was sufficiently clear so that he was aware of a new and puzzling mystery; the Langpo was proceeding through the fog at unabated speed. She was—or should have been—close to that stretch of the South China Sea known for centuries to mariners as the Jaws of Hell—that feared and hated spot where stout ships vanished with their crews and left not the slightest trace.

Peter recalled the fantastic legends he had heard of the great whirlpool—the silent maelstrom which drew the most powerful ship into its center and sucked it down to the ooze of unsounded depths.

He had never taken stock in that superstition. Yet he wondered why this ship was maneuvering so erratically. These were certainly dangerous waters. Not far from here, to the south, was the Paracels Reef—most dangerous reef in the world. He had been in these waters many times, and he had never known ship officers to take the chances these men were taking.

He presently became aware of a new development. Distantly, through the fog, he heard the muffled warning voices of other ships. One, a deep, triple-throated voice, undoubtedly that of a large ship, was, to Peter, uncomfortably close on the port bow. There were two other ships off to starboard.

One of these ships, with a thin, husky whistle, grew closer while the other two were gradually left astern. Then he saw that more men were gathered on the bridge. Now, there were at least ten men on the bridge. A group of them clustered on each wing, staring into the fog toward the ship with the thin, hoarse whistle. Of minor interest was the fact that all of these men were wearing dark glasses—glasses of a curious amber-violet tint, and he wondered if these strangely colored lenses enabled the men to see better in the fog.

Peter now observed that the dozens of men were being herded along the decks. Other men, presumably officers, were giving them some kind of instructions. And presently all these men began to disappear. Some went into cabins. Others went into holds.

It was baffling and somehow sinister. And the growing

nearness of the thin, husky whistle made Peter growingly uneasy. Why did this ship not sound her whistle?

SIX MEN CAME along the deck toward him, dragging along a strange looking machine. It consisted of powerful springs and long steel levers. There were two steel arms mounted upon a metal plate in a parallel position and about eight feet apart. To each of these arms was attached with thin wire the two ends of a great mass of iron chain.

He studied it for some time until he reasoned that it was a crude but rather clever form of catapult—a double catapult for hurling a great length of chain. But he could not guess its purpose.

A suspicion stole into his mind, but he rejected it as fanciful, grotesque. Yet the thin, hoarse whistle of that steamer off the port bow was closer each time it sounded. And he was now aware that the Langpo had checked her speed.

There would be, he was certain, a collision. It seemed unavoidable. At any instant, he would see the vague bulk of the unknown steamer loom up out of the fog. And he would be at the focal point of the wreck!

When the unseen ship was so close that his very flesh quivered and danced to the vibration of her whistle, the Langpo's whistle uttered a sharp, short blast.

It was instantly answered by a series of panic toots—the danger signal of the sea. The Langpo should have reversed her engines instantly. But she did not reverse. She crept steadily, stealthily on—toward that frantically tooting whistle.

He could picture the surprise, the consternation of her crew—having heard no answering whistle all this time, now to hear that single, mysterious blast. It would throw them into a panic. And Peter allowed that insistent suspicion to swarm in upon him now. He believed he was at the verge of solving that old, old mystery of the sea—being shown the truth about the dreaded, legendary Jaws of Hell.

He had hardly formed this thought in his head when things began to happen. Before he could shout a warning, the Langpo's whistle began to blow steadily. And at that instant, out of the fog, the strange ship loomed—almost bow on!

Peter caught a glimpse of the name on those squat, strong bows—the *City of Amoy*. He knew this ship. She was one of the obscure little tramps in the China trade of which the world would never hear unless, perhaps, she vanished and became another mystery of the seas—a nine-day wonder. Ships like the *City of Amoy* quietly went about their work, carrying rich cargoes from east to west and west to east.

As the squat, wide bows of the tramp went past, Peter saw men frantically waving from the bridge. Other men were running about. That lone blast from the Langpo's brazen throat had, as he had suspected, reduced her personnel to confusion and panic.

But there was no confusion aboard the Langpo. Her tremendous crew acted swiftly, efficiently—with the skill and sureness of long practice.

PETER WATCHED THE six men below him with that strange, crude catapult. He watched them aim it. One of them touched a trigger. And the purpose of that ingenious machine was promptly explained. With a smashing sound of released springs, the chain went sailing up and off the deck, writhing through the fog like a long and amazing snake.

Its target was the wireless antenna. And it found that target with swift and incredible accuracy. As if it were a giant's hand, it snatched the wires from the masts, and the broken wires became entangled with rigging and funnel guys, effectively short-circuiting the wireless machine and rendering it useless.

Meanwhile the two ships had come close alongside. The whistle of the Langpo continued to fill the fogbound world with an unceasing blast of sound.

What followed was nightmare. The sides of the two ships ground softly together. Smoke shot with sparks rose in clouds from friction. Grappling hooks were thrown from the Langpo, fore and aft. And simultaneously, the tremendous crew of the Langpo went into action. They swarmed from hatches and doorways, yelling and shrieking. In a dark wave, they went over the rail and aboard the doomed *City of Amoy*. Each of them carried a knife—a long knife like a cutlass, but shorter, with more of a curve to it—the wickedest knife Peter had ever seen. More wicked than any dirk. More wicked than any Malay *parang*.

But in the vanguard went men with carbines, firing as they went. Now—not till now—the Langpo stopped whistling. And in place of that strenuous blast came the yells and cries of terrified men.

Taken in a state of cleverly induced panic, taken completely by surprise, the crew of the *City of Amoy* offered little resistance. Peter saw the gray horde sweep upon those luckless men. And not only men, but women. Two young women, presumably passengers, came running out of a doorway. Howling idiots seized them—seized them by the hair and slashed their throats.

A man was climbing into the rigging. A swarm of the gray men pursued him up the shrouds. They overtook him. He was dragged down and his throat was cut.

Aft, some of the engineroom crew were resisting. Men ran into cabins and came out with pistols. One of them had a rifle. They stood their ground, firing into the invaders, but they did not resist long. They vanished beneath a surging tide of the murderers.

Twisting grotesquely at the end of the rope, Peter felt weak and sick. Fury swept him in hot waves. Yet beneath these surges of wrath was a feeling of stunned amazement He had been a privileged witness to the answer to a riddle of the ages. With his own eyes he was seeing what happened to the ships—and had been happening to them for centuries—the ships which were so mysteriously lost with all hands in the Jaws of Hell! Or so he believed.

Everything—or almost everything—was explained now. Everything, in fact, but the greatest riddle of all. Who were these gray-faced, idiot-eyed assassins? Of what race?

His speculations were forgotten as he watched the systematic way the gray men went about the rest of their work. While some of them bound heavy pieces of iron to their victims and threw them overboard, others went about gutting the ship. Gangplanks were laid between the two ships. Winches hissed, rattled and sang. Cargo hoists went into play. And the cargo of the stricken ship was swiftly transferred to the holds of the Langpo.

When the last of her cargo and stores had been transferred, her lifeboats and liferafts—and all similar objects

"You will be killed if you start trouble!"

which might leave a clue upon the water—were chopped up, reduced to kindling. All this débris, in splinters, was dumped into the gutted holds.

Crude bombs were now lowered into all holds. The *City of Amoy* was beginning perceptibly to settle. Her seacocks, Peter suspected, had been opened.

The grappling hooks were thrown off, and the piratical crew came swarming back aboard the Langpo. Smoke in black clouds belched from the hatches of the doomed ship.

The Langpo backed away, but Peter saw the end of it before the *City of Amoy* was lost in the fog—lost forever. Great explosions sent fragments of wood and metal spraying upward through the hatches, and the tramp began to settle rapidly by the stern.

As he watched, she rolled to starboard—rolled until water flowed into the hatches. She settled more swiftly then.

Another vast explosion told that one or more of her boilers had blown up.

The *City of Amoy* plunged, stern first, with a great slobbering and gurgling and rushing of air—a ship's death rattle. And then the enveloping fog closed in.

For perhaps forty minutes, the Langpo lingered in that neighborhood, with engines stopped. Then she got under way.

To Peter Moore, it had been one of the most incredible performances he had ever witnessed. Events had taken place so swiftly that it was hard to believe they had actually taken place. From start to finish, that surprise attack, with its swift, ruthless slaughtering of those innocent men and women, the looting of the cargo holds, the firing and sinking of the prey, had consumed something less than two hours. He had never seen men work with such speed, such sureness, such precision. They had acted with the mechanical certainty of robots.

10

A WOMAN'S ANGER

SHORTLY AFTER THE Langpo was again under way, Lotus Burma came forward. There was confidence in her air, a faint smile at her red lips. But when she saw Peter's face, the confidence went out of her. Her smile went, leaving her lips with a bleeding look. And her eyes were pools of desolation.

It had been a contest of wills—a clash that had been inevitable. In the test, his had stood and remained strong—and hers had cracked. She had been whipped by this man who hung by his thumbs. She knew she was whipped—that her will had succumbed before his. And in knowing it, it was as if all hope, all fire, had run out of her, leaving nothing in its place but dismay, a mounting terror.

She ran her fingers through her disarrayed hair and screamed at him, "Where are those diamonds?"

Twisting slowly—swinging at the end of that rope—Peter looked down at her. "You'll never find them."

"I'll kill you!"

"Will that help you find them?" He knew now, definitely, that so long as she did not find the diamonds, his life was safe.

"I'll bleed you to death."

"I'm not afraid of death."

She knew that, too. Susan came into view, with the look of a sleepwalker. Her eyes were dazed. She put her feet down uncertainly. And he wondered if this was how she looked when the effects of that strange purple drug wore off—or if she were in a state of shock, almost of collapse, from what she had seen—the wholesale slaughter aboard the freighter.

She stared up at Peter, then she ran to the cleat where the rope was made fast. She threw off the turns and let him down to the deck so rapidly that his knees buckled.

Lotus Burma clutched his elbows and dragged him to his feet. She shook him fiercely. "For God's sake," she panted, "tell me where those diamonds are!" She was hysterical. Her voice ran thin and cracked. Tears welled into her eyes. She shook him as if he were a child. She whimpered, "Where are they?"

"You'll never find them," he said quietly. And he knew why she was so terrified. "Unless," he said, "you care to drive a bargain."

"What is it?"

"Have this ship put into the nearest port—Kwang-chow or Hue. Put Miss O'Gilivie, Jim Saunders and me ashore. When you have done that, I'll tell you where those diamonds are."

"Then they are still aboard!"

"You'll never find them. You'd have to tear this ship apart splinter by splinter to find them."

Lotus Burma stared at him a moment in uncertainty. Then she shook her head.

"I will put you and Saunders ashore—but not her."

"Then you'll never find the diamonds."

"If I do not find the diamonds, neither you nor Saunders will be seen again!"

Susan cried, "Peter! Don't be silly. Let her put you and Saunders ashore. I'll stay."

"No—the three of us, or none of us."

Lotus Burma's beautiful, cruel face had hardened again.

"Very well," she said. "You will stay aboard. But you will be dreadfully sorry."

MEMBERS OF THAT strange crew took Peter below decks—locked him into a small room which had once been a paint locker. It still reeked of turpentine and linseed oil, and it contained Jim Saunders.

The American vice consul was at the porthole when the door opened and Peter was pushed into the room. Screwed into one eyesocket, like a monocle, was a triangular fragment of amber-violet glass with rounded edges. He removed it and said shakily, "What the hell's been going on?"

Peter realized that Saunders could have seen nothing of that recent, blood-chilling attack on the helpless freighter, as it had all occurred on the other side of the ship.

He told Saunders briefly what had taken place and said, concluding: "The way they worked is proof that this gang is at the bottom of all the mysteries which have been chalked up to that mythological whirlpool—the Jaws of Hell. You never saw such teamwork. You never saw efficiency like it! They murdered that crew, transferred the cargo and scuttled that ship—did every detail of it with the precision of a machine. Before we're through with this, I think we'll be at the bottom of one of the most amazing mysteries the world ever knew."

"Who in the devil are these men?"

"We'll soon learn. I'm absolutely convinced that Lotus Burma is taking orders."

"But who's the big shot?"

Peter shrugged.

Saunders said, "What did she do to you?"

"Strung me up by the thumbs."

"Did you spill the beans?"

"I did not. I tried to drive a bargain—offered to tell her where I'd hidden them if she'd put the three of us ashore at Kwang-chow or Hue. She would agree to put you and me ashore—but not Miss O'Gilvie. I refused."

Jim Saunders grinned. "Well, that's okay with me. My orders were to follow her through hell and high water—bring back a complete report. The way things look, I'll go through plenty of hell and high water, but I won't turn in the report. Anyhow, I'm glad you're aboard. I've heard a lot about you. You're a great guy. I feel a hell of a sight better with you in the same boat."

Peter said, "The consul general knew what a dangerous assignment this was. Why were you the goat?"

"China—and you. I was a victim of the well-known, pernicious chit system. When I came out here, five years ago, I thought the chit system was wonderful. Just sign a little piece of paper for anything you wanted—and it became money! I'm so deep in debt that it would take me forty years to get out from under."

The vice consul's smile was cynical. "The big boss called me to Hong Kong—had me on the carpet. Said I was a disgrace to the service. Then he discovered that I looked enough like you to be a twin brother. He thought he might put that to some good use. For better than eight months I've been studying up on you—studying your photographs, learning all your little mannerisms and tricks of speech—even how you smile and smoke a cigarette. When I was letter-perfect, the chance came—to track down Lotus Burma to her lair. If I made good on this assignment, the big chief was to take up all my chits—and give me a promotion."

"That," Peter guessed, "was why those three men from the consulate called on me—to make sure I was not taking this ship."

"Yes. We had you watched. We were sure you were taking the *King of Asia* to Frisco. But it wouldn't have made any difference. It didn't make any difference—your being aboard, I mean. I'm damned glad you are."

PETER SAID NOTHING. He was sorry for Jim Saunders. He went to the porthole and looked out. Gray fog swirled past. He could just see the water. The Langpo was forging ahead at full speed.

Behind him, Saunders said, "By golly, here's something absolutely uncanny. Look through it."

It was the fragment of amber-violet glass he had had in his eyesocket when Peter came in. It had evidently been broken from a lens, for the outer edges of the triangle were rounded, for fitting into a spectacle frame. Peter recalled the dark glasses he had seen the men on the bridge wearing.

He held the fragment of dark glass to his eye and, closing the other, looked out the porthole into the fog. As if by magic, he saw, three or four hundred yards away, a fishing junk—a brown, shapeless mass.

He closed that eye, opened the other and peered into solid fog!

He muttered, "Saunders, this is impossible!" He tried the glass again, and again he saw the fishing junk, this time farther abeam. Beyond the junk, through a thin opalescence, he made out the black form of an island.

Peter Moore was suddenly, peculiarly excited, as he had never been in his life. The possibilities of this glass exploded upon him, made his heart thump. To him, scientifically, this little triangle of glass was as exciting, as important as if he had been able to see, with it, at close range, the inhabitants of Mars.

Much more important! He had the thrill of a scientific discoverer—the thrill that Leeuwenhoek must have experienced when he saw, through the first microscope, specimens of life wriggling about, too tiny for the unaided eye to see; the thrill Galileo must have enjoyed when, with the first telescope the world had ever known, he magnified the diameter of stars and the moon.

The practical value—the value to humanity, to mariners, to aviators—of this magical fragment of glass electrified him. A lens—a glass of magic formula—with which the human eye could see through fog!

In his scientific studies, he had known that the infrared ray would penetrate through fog; that photographs could actually be taken on a plate sensitive only to those invisible red waves through the densest fog. But that was a scientific principle he could readily understand. He had seen photographs taken with aërial cameras of mountains more than two hundred miles distant—mountains which, because of the haze, were invisible to the naked eye. But he could understand that phenomenon. He could not, however, grasp or understand the principle by which this amazing lens worked.

Without understanding it, he could understand much of what had taken place to mystify him on this most mystifying of ships. He could understand why her officers drove her at full tilt through dense fog. Long, long before the *City of Amoy* had loomed out of the mist for Peter to see, the men on the Langpo's bridge wings had seen her clearly— every detail of her. Doubtless, they had selected her from a dozen—a score—of fogbound ships!

HE SAID, EXCITEDLY, "This is the greatest contribution to science since the invention of wireless telegraphy!"

And Saunders drawled, "Yeah? Is it a contribution? How are you going to contribute it? How are you going to hand it over to the world? Is she worth it?"

"What do you mean?"

"Is that O'Gilvie girl worth more to the world than this little piece of glass? Give your word to that Burma woman—and trade our lives for those diamonds. She'll put you and me ashore, and we can either make a fortune— millions—with this little piece of glass—have it analyzed— and patent the formula—or we can present the world with the greatest gift, as you say, since wireless telegraphy. Think of the ships and the planes that have been smashed—the loss of lives—because the human eye can't penetrate fog! But perhaps it couldn't be analyzed."

"It could be analyzed," Peter said.

"Is any girl worth it? She gave you the air, didn't she?

And what makes you think you can save her by sticking around?"

"There isn't much chance," Peter admitted. "No, I've got to stick. But I'll do this. I'll let her put you ashore—and she can have the diamonds."

"Nothing doing!" Saunders grinned. "It's my job, you know—sticking to the bitter end, too."

They fell to speculating about their destination, but speculation was useless. Never in his life had Peter seen men who resembled these strange, gray-faced, empty-eyed creatures; they were hardly human. It occurred to him that the men of distant planets might resemble these strange, bloodless men. It also occurred to him—a thought quite as fantastic—that these men were not moderns at all, but that they sprang from ancient times. And they were a human paradox—the lifeless living! But only in this latter guess was he at all close to the horrible truth.

SOUNDS ON DECK puzzled the two young men—ripping, tearing sounds. They speculated about these noises. It was as if the Lango were being wrenched to pieces.

They took turns looking out the porthole, using the triangle of magical amber-violet glass—the lens with which this strange race of men had held sway over the Jaws of Hell—for how long?

Neither Peter nor Jim Saunders could guess their direction. As the day advanced, they entered a zone of strange islands. Peter guessed that they were westing—that the destination of the Langpo was somewhere west of the island of Hainan; that they were proceeding into the Gulf of Tonkin.

All about them were islands—strange islands—so

strange that the two young men wondered—and shivered a little. It was as if they were steaming through the islands of the dead. Few men, they knew, had seen these islands for the northern bight of the Gulf of Tonkin is an area of almost perpetual fog. Here, cold currents swirl and sweep in from the South China Sea, and meet the hot, fetid breath of the Cambodian jungles, and the moisture of the air, suddenly chilled, turns to fog.

They were black and lifeless islands, and some were not islands at all, but black pinnacles of rock which rose up from the floor of the sea and were thrust above the water like the points of great ebony daggers.

With unchecked speed, the mystery ship ploughed through these hazardous waters.

The light was beginning to fade when the paint locker door was opened.

Three members of the crew, each armed with one of the long, curved daggers which Peter had seen in their hands when they swarmed upon the helpless *City of Amoy,* came in.

Three pairs of cold, vacant gray eyes stared in at the two young men. A thin voice said, "You may go on deck. But you are still her prisoners. You are warned you will be killed if you start trouble."

The two prisoners accompanied them on deck.

Here, an amazing sight greeted them. The teakwood deck had been pried up, torn loose from the steel flooring. The teakwood rail was in splinters, lying all about. The contents of cabins were strewn about the deck. And scores of the gray-faced men were at work, destroying the cabins themselves.

And it dawned on Peter that Lotus Burma was taking him at his word—she was tearing this ship into splinters to find the hiding place of those diamonds!

She glanced at him wildly when he and the vice consul approached. It was a blurred glance. Her eyes looked feverish. There were hectic spots on her cheeks. She was nervously lacing and unlacing her fingers. She was like a woman on the verge of madness. And the ship was a scene of utter madness.

WHEN HE PASSED her, she called: "I humble myself before you. I throw myself on your mercy. Where are those diamonds?"

"Why," he said coldly, "should I show you mercy? Are you showing that girl mercy?"

"My brother will kill me!"

"Look here," Jim Saunders said impatiently. "If those diamonds meant so much to you, why did you leave them lying around? Why didn't you hide them—lock them up?"

"I did not dream any one would dare take them! Mr. Moore, if you will tell me where they are, I will intercede for you."

"With whom?"

"My brother! I will save your life!"

"Where is your brother?"

"What does it matter?" she cried. "Will you?"

"No."

She began to scream. She shrieked curses. She made blood-curdling threats. She would have him drawn and quartered! She would have him stripped naked, smeared with honey and staked out for the ants to devour! It was as if she had completely lost her reason; but Peter divined that this was the grip of an intolerable fear. Fear, no doubt, of her brother. She was beside herself.

When cursing and reviling and threatening had no effect, she resorted to pleas. Once again, she all but groveled at his feet. It was an incredible performance—and it was an amazing glimpse of a woman in the shadow of an incalculable horror. He had once believed that nothing could shake this woman from her queenly poise. And he wondered what threat hung over her that could terrify her so.

When he started away, she cried: "I warn you—you are doomed to a living death!"

Indifferently, he walked on. He went to Room Six. His cabin was gutted. The bunk had been taken out and torn to shreds. The woodwork had been wrenched out, and it lay in Splinters on the deck. The carpet had been taken up and the floor pried up. What remained of his belongings he found in the litter on deck—in a tangle of teakwood planking. He found shreds of the beefwood trunk, and he found tatters of the costly satin jackets and capes and turbans which had once comprised his wardrobe.

And in the midst of this amazing wreckage he found what he was anxiously looking for—the priceless, tiny radio receiver. It was scratched. The case was dented, and back unhinged. But it had miraculously escaped destruction at the hands of these ruthless vandals.

He snapped the lid down and dusted it off. He touched the dials. A shrill signalling—the faraway voice of a Japanese warship surged from the metallic throat. He switched it off. It was uninjured! He dropped it into a hip pocket.

He accompanied Saunders to his room which, likewise,

had been completely gutted. His clothing had been torn to shreds.

The two men picked their way through wreckage into the bows. Evidently, they were free to roam about the ship.

He wondered for the hundredth time what his fate was to be—and Jim Saunders'—and Susan's. Susan, he supposed, had locked herself in her suite—was having hysterics. Often, in the past, he had helped her out of her predicaments. But the feeling was strong in him that this was a predicament from which no one could help her. And equally strong was the conviction that she no longer wished his help. Definitely he had lost Susan—forever.

11

LOST KINGDOM

THE LANGPO WAS drawing close to land. On either side
of them now the dagger-like pinnacle rocks rose out of
the water, gleaming wet from the fog, cruelly sharp. No
mariner without the magical aid of these leases would have
dared enter these waters.

Dead ahead was a smooth black wall. It ran sheerly
upward to incredible heights. Its upper surfaces caught
the reflected gleam of sunlight. The wall was like black
glass—almost as smooth. It must have extended upward
to a height of five thousand feet—perhaps more. A sheer
black cliff a mile high!

The bows of the Langpo were aimed straight at the base
of this stupendous cliff. And once again, a chill of apprehension trickled along Peter's spine, He wondered where
this strange crew was taking the Langpo. The black cliff
marked the end of a fiord—a narrow arm of the sea, with
high embankments on each side, with the black spearheads
protruding from the sea all but shutting off what must have
been a perilous channel.

He could see no river flowing into this fiord, no inlet
of any kind at the end of it, and no sign of wharfs or piers

anywhere. The Langpo, if not soon checked, would batter in her bows on that monstrous, glassy black cliff.

The experience was bleakly similar to that of a nightmare—the kind of nightmare in which one visits the land of the dead, with stark, black hills all about—a land of chilling blackness and mists, a dreadful land in which not a blade of grass can be seen. He had the illusion that the ship was floating swiftly through the air, her keel just clearing these ugly black poniards.

Simultaneously, the two men saw the cave dead ahead—a great archway in the foot of the black cliff. This natural arch must have been at least two hundred feet in height by a thousand feet in width. The Langpo was making straight for this mammoth entrance.

The arch looked higher and higher as the ship neared it. Within was blackness—the blackness of charcoal, the blackness of eternity. As the ship approached, bats flew out of the great cave with a whirring rush—black clouds of them.

A DAMP, COLD breath was exhaled from the cave—more chilling than the fog. A shadow fell over the ship. The two young men stared. Dying daylight, diffused by the fog, penetrated only a short distance into this enormous, abysmal chamber of perpetual night. The ship's lights blinked on. Random rays sparkled on great black stalagmites and stalactites, some as large as temple spires, some reaching down from the lofty black roof to join others reaching up from the water—a formation, doubtless, of prehistoric time, before the ocean flowed into this cavern.

In the half-light, these great tapering spears of blackness lost all resemblance to spires and took on a likeness to monstrous fangs. It was as if the ship were steaming straight into the gaping maws of a monster of impossible dimensions—into the jaws of what doom?

Still at unchecked speed, the Langpo went clanking on, her lights reflected on black water, on glittering black spears. And Peter had the feeling that the world of reason was lost—that beyond these monstrous black sculpturings lay an experience too preposterous even to be imagined.

And the likeness of this strange entrance from the sea to a monster's maws made him wonder if that imaginative phrase, the Jaws of Hell, had been originally derived from this ghostly place.

Dead ahead now he saw another wall—doubtless the back wall of the cave. Here, decidedly, was a dead end. The Langpo was slowing. He looked about to see the man at the wheel spinning the spokes. The bows veered to starboard. Close behind Peter a man stood with a great sledgehammer—a man who might have been an imp in the farther reaches of hell.

The bows swung in close to a black wall. Dimly, in the poor light, Peter saw a round, dully-gleaming patch set into the black wall. The man behind him struck this circular area with the sledgehammer. Brazenly ringing metal answered the blow. Jim Saunders said; in a strangled voice, "Good Lord!"

Peter turned about. The black wall dead ahead was opening! And Peter saw that what he had taken to be a solid wall—the end of the passage—was in reality a pair of massive doors, of bronze, discolored by time to the blackness of the rock itself.

These doors, or gates, two feet thick, were fully a hundred

and fifty feet in height, and each leaf must have been forty feet wide. Evidently, the single sledgehammer blow had worked a system of levers, by which the doors were operated.

Slowly, in utter silence, the great bronze gates swung ajar. Beyond was apparently the end of this remarkable cavernous passage. It was a basin, roughly round, perhaps six hundred feet in diameter. And for the first time since this strange, mystic journey into the northern bight of the Gulf of Tonkin had begun, Peter Moore saw evidences of human occupation.

To the left of the basin, on a great shelf of rock, was the paraphernalia and litter of a small shipyard, with ways of sufficient size to accommodate a ship of the Langpo's tonnage. On the opposite side of this great basin was another shelf, perhaps a dozen feet above the water, and here was an assortment of cargo-handling gear. Dead ahead, at the very end of this inner passage, was another door in the black rock wall. But this door was relatively small—not more than fifteen feet in height by twenty in width. Beyond that door lay what?

PETER LOOKED OVERHEAD as the Langpo steamed cautiously into the basin. He saw that crude but mighty arms, or levers, operated the great bronze doors. The ship proceeded to the right hand side of the basin, to the wharf-like ledge. The man with the sledgehammer sprang ashore, and trotted to a bronze plate, or stud, set flush in the nearest wall. This he struck a mighty blow with the sledgehammer—and the mighty bronze sea gates slowly and silently swung shut behind the steamer.

The basin at once began to hum and to ring with activity.

The large crew of the Langpo swarmed about. The hatch covers had been taken off, the cargo booms unshipped, as the ship entered this inner cave. Now began the bustle of unloading cargo.

In the midst of this excitement, Captain Barberry appeared and told the two young men to follow him. A gangplank had been placed between the deck and the rock shelf. As the three men started toward it, Lotus Burma and Susan appeared. And it was hard for Peter to see, in the former, the imperious creature with whom he had clashed both in Hong Kong and aboard this ship of mystery. No longer was she the flashing-eyed, regal beauty. She looked old and haggard, with gaunt cheeks and sunken, lacklustre eyes.

Susan was remote, imperious, utterly aloof. Evidently under the influence of the strange purple drug, she hardly condescended to notice Peter and the vice consul. Peter suffered a shock when he saw what she was wearing. A purple chiffon gown—nothing more. Nothing under it, nothing over it. It was as revealing as only sheer chiffon can be, and it left few doubts of the beauty of her slender, virginal figure. It made him angry, but he said nothing. Yet he wondered if that star-struck girl realized in any measure what all of this portended.

In silence, the little group advanced on the small bronze door. As they approached it, this door, somewhat magically, opened. Some secret control had been touched, of course, but the working of this machinery was baffling to the two Americans.

The door was a solid slab of the tough metal, hinged at the top. It swung upward. Peter found himself staring down a long tunnel. It sloped slightly downward, and it must have been a full quarter mile in length. At the far end he saw an oblong of palest green—too pale for grass, too dark for water. Tile, perhaps. And between him and that distant rectangle of light were more of the bronze doors, equally spaced, at least a dozen of them, all lifted.

The entrance to whatever city or pirate's rendezvous this place would prove to be was, at least from this end, well-nigh impenetrable.

As they walked down the slope, and as the rectangle of pale-green light grew larger, Peter's heart began to thump. He had long ago suspected that this place was utterly strange to him. He had explored the regions of southern China and northern Cambodia, yet he knew there were mighty mountain ranges and areas of dense jungle impenetrable to any man.

Yet, apprehensive and excited as he was, he was totally unprepared for the shock that awaited him at the mouth of the tunnel, A valley extending as far as eye could reach—a great valley enclosed by sheer, crystalline black walls a mile high or higher—a place of bizarre, startling architecture—a civilization which he definitely knew was utterly unknown to the great civilization outside. Of all this he was assured in a swift glance.

Thus did Peter Moore find the Kingdom of the Lost.

12

THE END OF LOTUS

THE VALLEY ENDED sharply here at the great precipice through which the tunnel ran. From this end of the valley to a distance of about a mile, the valley was narrow—actually a cañon, or gorge—less than a half mile wide. Farther away, it was wider. At a distance of perhaps ten miles it must have been three or more miles in width.

The tunnel which they had traversed gave upon a great open space, a sort of plaza or square, measuring perhaps a quarter mile along a side, and paved with pale-green tile.

To the left of this square was a gray building which resembled a prison—a large building without windows or apertures of any sort. To the right of the square was a fairyland palace—a Turkish palace! In the intricacy of its architecture, in the brilliance of its flashing colors, it might have served as a model for Maxfield Parrish. Weblike bridges sprang out of the great Central mass of white marble to minarets and dome-topped towers. Roofs were of gold leaf, of lapis lazuli, of rose quartz. It was barbarically, incredibly beautiful.

But even more exciting than this elaborate structure was one which, in entering the plaza from the tunnel, he faced. It was a fantastic lighthouse, yet it was like no

lighthouse he had ever seen. It was of some brilliant blue
stone. Perhaps two hundred feet in diameter at the base,
it sprang from the ground like a gigantic blue candle. A
spiral staircase wound around the outside of it. A few feet
from the top of it were the only windows it contained.
They encircled this remarkable tower at that point. And
between these windows and the very apex of the tower was
a shimmering area, which Peter was to learn was a mass of
precious stones, set there to blaze by sunlight and moonlight and starlight—fat diamonds and rubies and sapphires
and emeralds.

The spiraling staircase eventually ended in a flat roof or
platform of softly glowing yellow metal. And this, Peter
would learn, was a floor of gold.

His eyes leaped up to the shimmering stones, to the
yellow glow of golden planks, then dropped down again
to the base of the tower. Here—all about the base of the
tower, was a thicket of what might have been bamboo
shoots, growing in a thick and well tended formation. But
they were not bamboo shoots—they were iron spears with
cruel barbs. He glanced again to the top of this fantastic,
gigantic candle, then his eyes dropped to that small forest
of barbed spears.

Peter heard the outer gate of the tunnel clang shut, and
he presumed that the other eleven gates had similarly
closed. A moment later he saw a figure—a tall man—
descending the spiral staircase.

Beyond the tower was a wall of gray stone which
extended in a severe line straight across the valley, shutting off the palace, the tower and the great gray prisonlike
structure on the left from whatever might be beyond.

This wall was a massive, impressive affair perhaps fifty feet in height, and its purpose, he guessed, was to wall off a chosen few from a rabble, for he had seen such walls before. Beyond that wall the valley extended indefinitely, its sheer black walls rising up to incredible heights, at least a mile. And as far as Peter could see on either side, these mountainsides were not only unscalable, but there was no crack or fissure of any kind to be seen.

Sentries, with rifles at shoulder, paced up and down along the great wall.

PETER SAW THAT construction of some kind was taking place at one point along the wall—a fantastic structure of colored stones—marble, perhaps, or glass—and that workmen were swarming over it like industrious ants. From this distance, the structure had an appearance of such delicacy, such fragility that it would not have surprised him if it had collapsed at a breath of wind, or the rude slamming of a door.

The man who was descending the spiral staircase of the blue tower reached the bottom. He threaded his way through the maze of spears and strode off toward the palace.

The last light of day was going. There was no fog in this astounding valley, and already the evening star was visible. Matching it, lights began to come on, to twinkle in the fairyland palace to his right.

Jim Saunders was muttering exclamations under his breath.

"I've been the length and breadth of this damned country," he said, "and I never saw this place. What's more, I never heard of this place. It beats hell!"

Lotus Burma, overhearing him, said stonily, "You will find it *is* hell, my friend. He who enters here—" She left the unpleasant sentence unfinished.

Saunders said to Peter, "What do you make of this valley, Pete?"

And Peter answered, "It may be part of the great Rift Valley—you've heard of it."

"Not me."

"Its supposed to exist in several parts of the world, and its supposed to vary in width and depth. They've found part of it in Africa. I think the Mediterranean is supposed to be part of it. Other parts of it are supposed to be in the Pacific."

"What caused it?"

"Scientists have fought about that," Peter answered "The most generally accepted theory is that, millions of years ago, when the earth was still a molten mass, the moon or some planet exerted a pull away from the sun. The earth, caught between the two forces, pulled apart a little. They say this caused the Rift Valley. Most of it healed up with lava and erosion matter, but parts of it remain sharply— as this one, perhaps. This crack may have once extended hundreds of miles into the earth, but it's been filled over millions of centuries."

"What's your guess about this outfit?"

"Just as good as my guess as to what's going to happen to us."

Captain Barberry said in his colorless-voice, "I warn you men that you are under close observation. I warn you to start no trouble."

He was conducting them toward the palace—that fanciful confection of marble and gold and lapis lazuli and rarest colored quartzes and alabaster.

At the base of it were gardens, then came a series of terraces. Over the lowest of these a canopy of golden silk was stretched, and under this canopy a group had gathered.

Jim Saunders said excitedly: "Pete, why the hell hasn't this place ever been spotted by flyers?"

"They don't dare travel this route, because of the fogs. It's the most dangerous flying country in the world—high peaks, impenetrable jungles, no emergency landing spots—and fogs the year round."

Peter glanced at Susan, walking some distance away from him, in that outrageous purple chiffon garment. But she was paying no heed to him.

AS THEY APPROACHED the terrace, Peter made out the faces of that silent group gathered there. And he knew that the central figure was the ruler of this incredible place.

He sat on a throne of some dark wood, nara-wood, no doubt, a great bulk of a man, obscured by shadows until Peter was within twenty feet of him and then, in the blue gloom, saw him clearly—saw him and was shocked.

Instantly he realized that here was no petty monarch—no effete Oriental princeling, but a man of strength and ruthless power and monstrous contempt.

He wore a beard—a fierce and barbaric beard as red as the embers of a fire. A red, thick mouth was grim. The nose was large with flaring nostrils. And the eyes were as savage as those of a tiger. He wore a robe of royal purple.

Peter guessed his age at thirty-five—and sent quick glances at this amazing monarch's attendants. A score of men, some armed, some not, and a sprinkling of women.

He was astonished that only a few of them, none of the women, were of the strange, clammy breed which had populated the Langpo.

Three, at least, of the women were lovely, and one of them was surpassingly beautiful. She was, doubtless, a princess; a slender thing with eyes like cornflowers, a tender bud of a mouth, and hair, long rippling hair, of the most entrancing shade of red Peter Moore had ever glimpsed.

She stood not far from the monarch, her blue eyes softly shining, her mouth soft and lovely with compassion. She, too, wore purple—a soft and flowing garment, embroidered with gold and precious stones, which enhanced the slim perfection of her small body. Peter heard Jim Saunders' gasp of wonderment.

It was a shocking contrast—that slender, fragile girl, standing so close to that red-bearded monster on the dark wood dais.

He was bending forward, with one elbow on outthrust knee, his bearded chin planted on a mighty fist. A Visigoth, this man might have been.

He was staring at Susan O'Gilvie. His tigerish, yellow-green eyes ran swiftly from her face along the revealing garment to her feet, with their tiny purple slippers.

The fierce, yellow-green eyes dismissed the two Americans, then sprang to the white, agonized face of Lotus Burma.

In a leaden voice she intoned: "I have honor in presenting to his imperial majesty King Hassan Barbarossa these strangers from another land. All three are American subjects, my majesty."

The red-bearded monarch spoke. "Ah," he said softly. It

was like a purr—the purr of a ruthless cat animal. "This is the bride you have fetched me."

"Yes, my majesty."

The eyes of Hassan Barbarossa, like swarming bees, again ran down that gossamer garment which so poorly concealed the slim, lovely figure of the American heiress.

He said sharply, "These men? What are they doing here?"

And Lotus Burma falteringly answered, "Both came aboard the ship in Hong Kong, my brother, and—and I could not put them off."

"Why not?"

"I did not know what to do." Her voice was whimpering. She was wringing her hands. "One—the light one, is an American vice consul. The American consul general in Hong Kong knows he came aboard the Langpo. The other is an American adventurer. His name is Peter Moore. Throughout China, he is known as Peter the Brazen."

KING HASSAN BARBAROSSA drew in his breath through clenched teeth, exhaled it in the same gusty fashion. His eyes grew red-rimmed. Here, indeed, was a man of dangerous temper.

Wrathfully, he said, "You have made your last mistake, Lotus Barbarossa! For years you have been making mistakes—playing with danger. Long ago, your hatred of the white race made you useless. You could not be my servant, my emissary into that other world. No! You must taste power! You must indulge in political intrigue—you must make mistakes!

"You should not have permitted this vice consul aboard that ship. You should not have permitted this other man to enter my kingdom at all. Why was he brought here alive? Why was he not killed? Answer me!"

Lotus Burma—Lotus Barbarossa—dropped to her knees. She extended shaking hands imploringly.

"My brother, I have done my best. I have failed. But I have done my best. Do not condemn me," she sobbed. "During the voyage, this man, this Peter Moore, robbed me." She halted, choking.

"Of what?" King Hassan roared.

"Diamonds! Two million dollars' worth of diamonds. I thought they were safe. I thought no one would dare touch them. This man stole them and hid them."

"Where?"

"Somewhere on the ship! I don't know where. I had the ship searched and all but torn apart. I had this man hung by his thumbs for hours—but he would not tell."

"This man?" Hassan Barbarossa jabbed a thumb at Peter.

"Yes, my majesty."

"He stole my diamonds and would not tell you where he had concealed them?"

"Yes, my brother."

King Barbarossa bent forward and stared at Peter. His tigerish eyes peered into the walnut-stained face, the defiant blue eyes.

"Perhaps you care to tell me where you hid those diamonds, my friend."

And when Peter, with arms folded on chest, stood and smiled mysteriously and said nothing, the king of this amazing land nodded slowly, with an ironical gleam in his savage, malevolent eyes.

Quietly, menacingly, he said, "I will show you, my adventurous, thieving friend, that it does not pay to balk the will of Hassan Barbarossa. Lotus—" he paused with a mysterious significance.

She wailed, with arms still outstretched, "My brother—my blood brother—"

"I sentence you—"

The frantic woman crawled to him on her knees. Her dark hair was spilled down, almost obscuring her convulsing face.

She reached the dais, and clambered upon it. She clasped the knees of Hassan Barbarossa, whimpering, sobbing.

"Let me be banished!" she shrieked.

He struck her with the flat of his hand. Lotus Barbarossa fell backwards, with a hand clasped to the red welt forming on her white cheek.

"—to the death of whirling ecstasy!" he concluded.

The woman screamed: "My brother! My king!"

Coldly, he said: "Go. Now!"

DREARILY, GRAY-FACED, HAGGARD of eye, Lotus Barbarossa picked herself up from the black tile. She looked behind her. Breathlessly, Peter followed her wild stare. She staggered away. Then, as if by imperial edict of his majesty, the red-bearded one—the first rays of the moon fell into the valley—and silvered the thousand-foot shaft with its spiral staircase.

The wretched woman took her departure without further protest. Silently, the group watched her go—watched her cross the plaza—watched her start that spiral climb.

Peter's heart was beating with a dull and heavy ache. He was not sorry for Lotus Barbarossa. In all his experience in Far Eastern lands, he had never met a woman so cruel, so brutal, so completely without civilized instincts. The pain in his heart was for Susan, so young, so helpless, so virginal. Death would be far preferable to her fate at the hands of this red-bearded giant.

Hours seemed to pass as the condemned woman dragged herself to the golden floor at the top of the blue column.

He saw Lotus Barbarossa stagger out upon the golden floor far above—a small, slim figure in the ghostly moonlight. And he saw her slowly start to whirl. Faster and faster she whirled, until the purple robe she wore belled out in the small cyclone of her own creation, until she was a blur almost imperceptible to the naked eye.

He had seen whirling dervishes, he had seen the devil dances of Java, but he had never before seen a dancer spin with such rapidity as this. It was as if, through aching eyes, he saw her spinning at the very core of the universe; and in this spinning he knew that the unfortunate woman was expected to reach a divine exhilaration—a state of spirit in which she became one with all the ecstasies.

SUDDENLY, SHE TOPPLED into space. She had whirled herself into the dubious ecstasy of certain, hideous death. The whirling speck tumbled swiftly toward earth. And with its falling came a scream so shrill, so terrible, that Peter shuddered.

He did not see that slender, beautiful body impaled on the horrible, barbed spears at the base of the tower. But a thin, forlorn scream from Susan assured him that she had reached the end of her fall.

Susan did not faint. She cried angrily, "Horrible! Barbaric! Hideous!"

Strong white teeth gleamed in the red beard of the monarch.

"My little bride," he whispered, "will learn not to be so tender hearted with traitors."

Susan shivered. She was, Peter well knew, at the verge of collapse—frightened, horrified as she had never been in her life.

She cried: "You loathsome monster!"

He laughed. "You will come to love me. You will come to me on my own terms."

Shifting those fierce, yellow-green eyes to Peter, he drawled contemptuously, "And you, my adventure loving friend. I will think about you. I assure you I will give you at least two minutes, between tonight and tomorrow morning, of my undivided thought. I think I have heard of you. I think I have heard of your deeds and your daring. And I think you will find you have come to a land where deeds of daring are most, most difficult of accomplishment."

He was smiling cruelly in that amazing red beard. "I think I have heard that you are an electrical genius—an inventor. I am interested in such things. Greatly. We will have a little talk at dinner, for you are to be my honored guests tonight."

Peter was chilled by the very tones of that voice, for it was, like its owner, a thing of ruthless strength and cruelty beyond imagining.

"Ailena!" said Hassan Barbarossa.

The lovely red-haired girl spoke breathlessly: "Yes, my brother?"

"You, my most charming sister, will, I am sure, be delighted to act as hostess. Take these gentlemen to the bronze room—for bronze is the metal of men, and take my bride to the silver room, for silver is the metal of the moon and of virginal women. See that they are furnished with appropriate clothing." He rubbed his large hands together and smacked his lips. "We have guests tonight, Ailena! Guests! Tonight we banquet in the hall of gold."

"Yes, my brother." She dropped a curtsey to him and turned with a faint, melancholy smile to Susan O'Gilvie and the two men. "If you will please follow me."

Hassan Barbarossa grasped his beard close to the chin with one hand and with his tigerish eyes watched Susan until she had gone from sight.

Peter missed none of this, and he admired Susan for her courage. She was eaten by a malignant terror, yet her step did not falter. Her courage lasted until they were away from the terrace, had entered an arched corridor of purple tile which seemed to lead into the interior of the palace.

13

NO HOPE

ONCE BEYOND THE range of those greedy, yellow-green eyes, Susan all but collapsed. She seized Peter's nearest hand and began to tremble. She made small whimpering sounds. Then she burst into unconstrained sobbing and threw her arms fiercely about his neck. She pressed her hot, wet face tight against his.

"You've got to save me," she sobbed. "You must get me out of this horrible place!"

The proud princess had broken at last. She was, clinging to him, a frightened girl, sobbing, trembling.

The red-haired girl and Jim Saunders, who had been walking ahead, stopped and looked back.

"There must be some way to get out of this place," Susan clamored. "You must find the way, Peter!"

Princess Ailena was watching them with large, tragic eyes.

"There is no way out of this place," she said. "Except the way you came. And he would not let you go."

"There must be a way!" Susan wailed. "Farther up the valley!"

"There is no way at any part of the valley," the red-haired girl said sadly. "Thousands have tried."

"Peter," Susan panted, "we could fight our way out!"

"Against a dozen thick bronze doors?" the princess cried. "Against men who are armed?"

"I don't believe you!" Susan gasped.

The red-haired girl sighed. "I am so sorry for you poor people. I would love to help you. But I am telling the truth. There is no escape from this place. In almost four hundred years, thousands have tried—and none has succeeded. It is like a bottle with the cork driven in tight."

Susan shuddered. Her arms were wrapped so tightly about Peter's neck that she was almost choking him.

"Peter! You've got to do something! You must save me from that horrible beast! You can! You're so clever—so strong! Get me out of here! I'll go back to America with you! I will! I'll never make trouble again. I'll promise!"

The red-haired girl met Peter's eyes and sadly shook her shining head. His heart ached for Susan. How many times—at the threat of great danger had she said just these things? And each time, when she was clear of the danger, had she changed her mind? Great perils were like a drug. Once she was clear of actual danger, she was thrilled by what she had been through, and promptly thirsted for new thrills.

She babbled on, clinging to him as if she would never let him go. She declared that she loved him—that, not for one moment, had she stopped loving him.

"Darling, you know how I adore you. I'm cured of wanting thrills. Really, I'm cured. Look at me! Look at my eyes!"

She held him off. He looked into the wet, amethyst blurs of her eyes. She did not know what she was saying. In her terror of Hassan Barbarossa, she was half out of her mind. She saw, in her proposed marriage to that loathsome man, terrors exceeding any with which she had ever been threatened.

But on one point she was rational enough. She fully admitted her blame for trapping the three of them in this predicament. Once again, she had jeopardized not only her own life, but Peter's. And, once again, she was sorry— so sorry. And once again, she insisted that his cleverness, his resourcefulness, his courage, would deliver her safely from this hell!

Peter comforted her as best he could. He was sorry for Susan—Susan, the incurable thrill-hunter. But this time he saw no hope.

JIM SAUNDERS WAS watching Susan with a strange expression—with saddened eyes and a cynical smile. He knew Susan's reputation. Every consul and vice consul in the Far East knew her for a dangerous young woman— dangerous to herself and every one with whom she came in contact. He sympathized with her present hysterical terror, but he took no stock in her frantic promises. For he knew that Susan, beautiful, spoiled Susan, was incurable.

The red-haired girl, who did not know Susan's reputation as a seeker of dangerous adventure, saw only the American girl's grief and terror. Her own eyes were moist with pity, and her lovely pink mouth was sad. From time to time, she shook her head a little, as if in realization of the hopelessness of any kind of attempt to escape from the Kingdom of the Lost.

Hysterically, Susan was saying, "Don't you suppose he'd let me buy my way out? Wouldn't he let me ransom myself,

Peter? I'd give him millions! I'd give him every dollar I possess!"

Princess Ailena said, "Money means nothing to Hassan Barbarossa. He is one of the richest men in the world—if not the richest. He has seen you and he wants you. I have seen him look at other girls. But never as he looked at you. You will become his favorite wife."

Susan burst into fresh sobbing and clung more fiercely to Peter. Peter heard the red-haired girl say softly, "Oh, I am so sorry for you poor, poor people!"

"How many wives has he?" Jim Saunders asked.

"Eleven. She will be the twelfth."

"I'd rather die!"

The vice consul looked up and down the corridor. He said, "Princess, who is this Hassan Barbarossa?"

"He is the fifteenth direct descendent of Hassan Barbarossa who came here from Turkey in the year 1567."

Peter gasped: "Redbeard, the Turkish pirate?"

The girl shook her head. "No, my friend. Redbeard was Arouj, or Orux Barbarossa. Hassan was his eldest son, but likewise a pirate. In the year 1567 he vanished—he came here with his band. He was driven out of the Mediterranean. Hassan the First came to the Far East in his caravel and somehow found this place. We are taught that he had a prophetic vision, and that he followed the vision and found his way through the great cave and into this valley."

"What is this valley called?" Peter asked.

"It is called the Valley of the Barbarossas, the Black Valley, and the Kingdom of the Lost. Truly it is a kingdom of the lost. For any one who enters this place is surely lost. Hassan the First built those great bronze sea doors through which the ship passed that brought you here. And he built the dozen bronze doors through which you passed when you came here from the ship."

"How are those dozen doors controlled?" Peter interrupted.

"Did you notice the windows in the top of the tower of the whirling death? It is the guard tower. It was built by Hassan the Second. The eldest member of one family—the Jenghas—has always been the keeper of that tower—the keeper of the key. It goes from father to son. The present Jengha was standing to the left of my brother when you were presented—the tall, very tall man. He came down from the tower as you crossed the square. The tower is his sacred trust. He alone has the key to the room where the great lever is that opens those dozen bronze doors. The mechanism runs down through the tower and underground—under the great blue plaza and under the hill itself."

"If we could get possession of that key and get into that tower," the vice consul said dreamily, "we could open those doors and get out!"

PRINCESS AILENA LOOKED up into Jim Saunders's handsome dark face and her eyes glowed with pity.

"It is utterly impossible. Many have tried—all have failed. In the highest dome of the palace are a dozen high power repeating rifles, all pointing at the doorway of the tower—all set rigidly in cement. By the time any one who wanted to reach the control room in the tower had climbed as far as the doorway, some servant, under the king's orders, would have reached the dome—or turret—where these guns are. All of us—women as well as men—are trained to do that. A lever is simply pulled. Instantly, the guns begin firing—shooting their bullets with deadly accuracy at that doorway.

"A few years ago, a party of eight British and Belgian captives tried it. They drew lots. The one who was to sacrifice himself dashed up the stairway. The others waited near the tunnel entrance, ready to escape. When he reached the doorway, he was simply riddled with bullets.

"Seventy years ago, two American seamen and an Australian sea captain overpowered Jengha's grandfather, then the keeper of the tower. But he swallowed the key. They promptly cut him open—got the key out of his stomach. But the man who ran up the spiral was killed by bullets before he reached the doorway."

Jim Saunders said, "If we could get the key, then have some one prevent any one from going up to that turret, where the rifles are—"

The red-haired girl was shaking her head. "It is necessary to pass a dozen armed guards to reach the turret."

"How about a night attack?"

"At night, oil flares are set all along the spiral staircase."

"Some night the fog might be thick enough—"

"Never! The fog seldom comes over the valley. Although the surrounding country is always thick with fog, rising air currents keep the air clear above the valley. But when fog does occasionally form over us, it never drops lower into the valley than the top of the tower. It was the fog that determined the height of the tower when it was built."

"Why is the control room in that tower?"

"Because it commands the entire valley."

The vice consul said wearily, "Well, that scheme is out.

But how about dynamite? Could we blast our way through those twelve bronze doors?"

"There is no dynamite nor anything like it in the valley," the princess said. "The Barbarossas have always been afraid of heavy explosives in any form. None has ever been brought into the valley. They have been afraid of accidental explosions in the tunnel—afraid of anything which might bottle us up."

JIM SAUNDERS ASKED her what was the purpose of the prisonlike gray building on their left when they had emerged from the tunnel into the great square.

"It is where the crew and the warriors and workers for the ship are trained. They are selected from the valley people in early childhood and placed in that building under trainers. Submission—obedience to command—is beaten into them from childhood."

"Who is Captain Barberry?" Peter inquired.

"He is one of them. He, too, is nothing but a slave."

"Who are these valley people?" Saunders asked.

"They are the descendants of the original thirty men and women whom Hassan the First brought here as slaves in the Sixteenth Century."

"How many are there now?"

"It is impossible to say—but at least a hundred thousand."

"Do you mean," Peter said incredulously, "that these thousands are all descendants of that original thirty?"

"Yes."

"There's been no outside blood brought in?"

"Only in the past few years."

"But that's impossible," the vice consul protested. "You say that original thirty landed here in 1567?"

"Yes. Eighteen women, twelve men."

"And their descendants now number over a hundred thousand?"

"Yes."

Jim Saunders shook his head. "Impossible."

"No," Peter disagreed. "It's possible. A dollar doubled twenty times amounts to more than a million. Thirty people would have doubled at least four times every century."

"Five," Princess Ailena corrected him. "And perhaps six. Because these unfortunate women begin having children long before they're twenty. Some are as young as fourteen. And most of these women have more than two children—some as many as ten or twelve."

Susan said, "Oh, how horrible!"

Peter had been doing some rapid mental calculation. He said: "If your population doubled with each generation, thirty people in three and a half centuries—or, roughly, seventeen generations—would have multiplied to almost four million. The childbirth death rate must be terrific, both for mothers and children."

"There have been horrible epidemics," the red-haired girl said.

And this, to Peter, was one more mystery cleared up. Thus was explained why the crew of the Langpo were so alike—creatures of ratty hair and vacant eyes. It was the pernicious and horrible result of in-breeding. Thus was explained their appearance of idiocy, for it is the inevitable result of such close intermarriage that the worst traits be emphasized generation after generation.

"But how about the Barbarossas?" he asked.

"That is different," the red-haired girl answered. "Hassan the First brought with him three elderly wives and seven children. When he died, his eldest son—Hassan the Second—became king. He was dissatisfied with the women of the valley, so he sent his ship out time after time until a girl was brought in who pleased him."

"What happened to the girls who didn't please him?" Susan asked.

"They were sacrificed."

"Killed?"

"Yes. He was very brutal. All of the Hassans with red beards have been brutal men. Only once in three or four generations is a red Barbarossa born. He is always called Hassan, and he becomes the king, even if he is a younger brother. Hassan the Second married a Chinese girl who was captured in a fight with a great war jusk early in the Seventeenth Century. When he tired of her, he had other girls seized and brought to him from scuttled ships. That has since been the custom of the rulers."

"What perfectly loathsome men!" Susan breathed. She had recovered a little from her original terror—was really fascinated by what Princess Ailena was telling them.

She said now: "Would you help us if you could?"

And the red-haired girl, with her gentle smile, answered, "I would love to. But I am helpless, as much a prisoner as you."

"HAVEN'T YOU EVER been out of this place?"

"I have never been beyond the twelfth bronze door."

"Would you like to escape?"

"Oh, my dear, all my life I've dreamed of escape. Sometimes I cry. Sometimes I cannot eat or sleep for days and nights. But there is no hope. My brother says I am not clever enough to be sent out as an emissary—as an outworld contact—as my sister Lotus was. He says I am too innocent."

"Was Lotus really your sister?" Susan asked.

"A half-sister, as Hassan is a half-brother. His father had twenty wives, with children by six of them. Lotus's mother was a Chinese princess."

"Among us," Susan said, "we might work out a plan of escape."

"If we only could! But we cannot. I am helpless. My heart breaks and bleeds for you. But what can I do? Shall we go on? My brother will expect us at the banquet. He does not care to be kept waiting."

Susan clung to Peter's arm. She hugged that arm against her side. She was afraid—so afraid. And so contrite!

The purple corridor ended in a large white hall. A flight of stairs led to upper regions. The three Americans followed Princess Ailena up these stairs and through a labyrinth of halls. At length they came to a room with a new bronze door, elaborately carved and inlaid with fanciful steel and copper flowers.

"This is our room?" the vice consul asked.

"Yes," said the red-haired girl.

"When I make my report to the consul general," Saunders said dryly, "don't let me forget to mention these copper flowers, Pete. He'll be relieved to know we had flowers on our door."

Susan gulped, "Oh, how can you be so callous?"

The vice consul looked at her, "That's so. We're only

going to die. How're we going to die, princess? Do we get boiled in oil, or are we tossed to the lions?"

The red-haired girl gave him a shining glance.

"You are brave men to laugh at death," she said.

14

MONARCH SUPREME

PETER OPENED THE bronze door. It gave upon a spacious bedroom which might have served an emperor. It was luxuries, with rich Moorish tapestries on the walls, glossy Turkish rugs on the floor. In the center of the room was a huge bronze bed with an ornate bronze canopy depending by massive chains from the lofty ceiling. All the furniture in the room was of bronze—bronze stools and chairs—hand-wrought and beautiful.

At one end of the room was a window in the shape of a Moorish arch, covered with an ornate, hand-wrought bronze grille. It looked out over the great stone wall and the valley.

Jim Saunders was asking questions of the red-haired girl. How long was the valley? How high was it at the lowest point? What did the valley people do? What were their industries? Why, until recently, had no captive, men or women, been sent among them for the purpose of putting fresh blood in the race? What race were the thirty originally?

Princess Ailena answered his questions willingly, in her sweet, musical voice. The valley, she said, was about two hundred miles in length and the cliff at either side was always sheer and never less than a mile in height. There were no fissures or cracks by which escape was possible.

"The rock is of a peculiar character. It is so hard that it will dull the edge of any tool in a few blows. Yet it will chip off easily. It is impossible—if that is what you're thinking of, to chip, or cut or carve out any kind of steps or toeholds up to the top of it. It has been tried. Hassn the Fifth wanted to make another exit from the valley, because he was afraid that the one might some day be bottled up. He had thousands of workmen attempt, at different places, to carve steps. But it was impossible."

Peter said: "If the sea gates were blocked, this entire valley would be bottled up."

The red-haired girl nodded. "There is still another way to bottle it. Between the sixth and seventh gates, the roof, you may have noticed, is of bronze. It is a slab of bronze two feet thick. Above it is a great vertical slab of bronze which can be dropped down, filling the tunnel. It slides down in sockets, or slides of bronze, which are built far into the wall on either side. If that great bronze slab were dropped, it would bottle up the entire valley forever—and it would be the same if the sea doors were shut and somehow jammed. It was placed there by Hassan the First and Second in case the royal family ever wished to escape. There is a ring set in the wall which we—the royal family—learn about as children. If there is a rebellion, or anything of that sort, among the valley people, we can escape and bottle up the valley forever. Each successive king has been worried about the sea gates. The greatest care is taken with them, and the mechanism is always being inspected and repaired."

Princess Ailena answered other questions. The people

of the valley had very little to do. The soil of the valley was not very fertile. They grew rice and some other crops, but there was not enough food.

"IT IS HASSAN'S wish that the valley people be poorly nourished. They are like ravenous wolves, yet their gnawing hunger makes them obedient to his slightest command. They will slave and fight and toil and die for Hassan."

Peter asked her if there had been rebellions.

"There have been a few, but they are quickly put down. The ruler deals with ail rebellions in the same way. He finds out who the ringleaders are—then gives these ringleaders the glorious chance to whirl themselves off the tower. In this way, for almost four hundred years, all the men and women among the valley people who might have qualities of leadership are weeded out and destroyed. It had been the purpose of the Barbarossa to mold these poor people into the lowest possible form."

"Why?" Saunders asked.

"Slavelike obedience!"

"Isn't there danger of over-population?"

"Hassan—all the Barbarossas—have wanted a tremendous population of these half-starved, willing slaves. Hassan would prefer many millions of them."

Susan shuddered. "Why are they so gray?"

"Partly because of their very low intelligence—inbreeding—and partly because they are clay eaters."

"Clay eaters!"

"Yes. There are great banks of this clay in the upper end of the valley. Eating this clay dulls their hunger and it contains some drug which also dulls the mind. All of this

Susan cried faintly, "I detest you!"

fits in with the Barbarossa plans some day to overwhelm the world."

Jim Saunders said dryly, "A great general once said that an army travels best on a full stomach."

"The Barbarossas do not think so," Princess Ailena replied. "The Barbarossas believe in an army of hungry, wolflike men and women—accustomed to starvation—who are obedient to any command and who are not afraid of death. This has been driven into them as a religion. It goes back, I think, to Mohammedanism—the belief that the after life is glorious."

"Aren't there many suicides?" Saunders interrupted.

"No. Very few, in fact. The valley people believe that they can enter the kingdom of heaven only through the intervention of the Barbarossas. A suicide goes to hell."

"Isn't the whirling death a form of suicide?" Peter asked.

"Not in the eyes of the valley people. Any more than dying in battle would be suicide. If it is Hassan's wish that they whirl to death from the tower, or die in battle, then they are certain of paradise."

Peter asked her what race the original thirty were.

"Many races were represented," the girl answered. "There were many Turks, of course, and some Egyptians and Greeks and Italians. There was an Englishwoman, and there were Chinese and Javanese, and I believe there was a little Malay girl, the daughter of a raja. These people, soon after their enslavement here, began to have children. There was no marriage. There never has been. The Barbarossas forbade marriage. They wanted promiscuity, so that the race would develop rapidly—and so that all the finer instincts of the people would be destroyed. But the birth rate has been falling. A result of this hideous inbreeding which the Barbarossas did not foresee was that the race would eventually become sterile."

"So now," Peter said, "he has begun to import men and women to send in there to invigorate the race."

"Yes. Mostly girls. Any girl in his harem, any girl who is brought in here as a captive who displeases him or to whom he is indifferent, is sent into the valley. You can imagine the fate of these poor girls. A beautiful young woman among those human wolves! Is it any wonder that they go mad and that the children they bear are insane at birth?"

SUSAN SEIZED PETER by the arm. She was shaking. "If—if we can't escape from this horrible place," she panted, "and if I show your brother how I hate him, would I—" she stopped.

The princess cried, "Ah, but you won't be banished! Never! He would not let you go. And, believe me, marrying him, much as you may loathe him now, would be far preferable to banishment among those horrible valley men."

"I'll die!" Susan sobbed. "I'll kill myself first."

"Perhaps you will not feel so badly after a little time. Any fate is better than being banished to the valley."

"I would kill myself!" Susan cried hysterically.

"I should warn you that if you do, your body will be fed to his leopards."

"Who would care—why should I care what happened to my dead body?"

Ailena Barbarossa began to cry. "My dear, if only I could help you!"

Jim Saunders said brusquely, "Don't worry, Susan. We're all going to get out of here. Aren't we, Pete?"

"We're going to try."

"You've wriggled out of worse jams than this."

The red-haired girl asked them how many ships Captain Barberry had raided and sunk.

"One," Peter answered.

"There should have been more. Captain Barberry will probably be thrashed for that—and exiled to the valley for further punishment. The food shortage grows worse here every year—especially salt. We have plenty, but the valley people have only what is left. That is why so many of the valley people are lepers."

Susan groaned, "Does lack of salt cause leprosy?"

"So I have heard. A doctor from India, who was captured and brought here a number of years ago, said that the lack of salt was what caused the leprosy in India. The blood turns thin, the legs and arms become terribly swollen. I think it is called œdema. They become covered with a rash, and finally they have all the symptoms of leprosy. If our supply of salt were shut off, I believe every one in this dreadful place would be dead in a very short while—a few years.

"It is almost impossible to supply enough salt to the valley people. It is growing more dangerous every year to attack ships in the Jaws of Hell. For many ships are equipped with a machine which will transmit and receive messages to and from other ships and similar machines on shore. The wireless."

Peter recalled the papier-mâché wireless equipped aboard the Langpo. He asked the girl if she knew anything of wireless telegraphy or the radio. She had heard the names, but the machines themselves were a mystery to her. **PETER WAS PUZZLED.** "If the Barbarossas have been shut off from the world in this valley for four hundred years, how have they kept abreast of the times with ships? Where, for example, did they get the Langpo?"

"From the time of Hassan the First, that has been the Barbarossas' greatest problem. As the types of sailing ships changed, and then, when sailing ships changed to steamships, the rulers have had to obtain each new type and study it and master it. The changing types of sailing ships were not so difficult, but steamships were a tremendous problem, in spite of the fact that emissaries have always been sent out into the world, and have brought back all the latest ideas. Many of the younger sons served as sailors and officers on merchant ships, then returned here to apply their knowledge."

"Was the Langpo built to their order?"

"Oh, no. The Langpo was a British freighter, the Teneriffe. She was taken in a raid about sixteen years ago. All our ships have been taken in raids. The Langpo was taken, of course, in the Jaws of Hell, her crew was murdered, and our old ship was sunk at that spot. That is always the procedure. Since the Langpo was taken, she has been completely altered at least twice a year. Every detail of her is changed so that she cannot be recognized. Her cabins are torn down and rebuilt differently. Her funnel is made thicker or thinner, or taller or shorter. Everything about her is transformed. When she sails out of the cave next time, not even the marine architect who designed her would recognize her."

Jim Saunders asked, "What will she do? Just where will she go?"

"She will go to Hong Kong or Shanghai or perhaps a Japanese port and load with salt. Not a full load. There will be room left in her holds for a cargo of other supplies which will be taken from the ships she raids in the Jaws of Hell on her return trip here."

Peter was still puzzled. "What do her officers do about clearance papers? How do they know what ships to attack—that is, what ships will happen to have the needed cargoes?"

"The king's emissaries attend to all that. That was Lotus Barbarossa's task. She bribed petty port officials for clearance papers, and it is never difficult to learn about ships and cargoes. Our only real difficulty occurs when there is a war. Then the seas are combed by warships, clearance papers are most difficult to obtain, and there is great secrecy regarding the movements of ships.

"The World War all but ended us. Time after time, our

raider was stopped and searched by warships. But our cargoes were always innocent—mostly salt. And we were fortunate in being far from the Oriental war zone. We had to stop making trips to other countries. Our raider would go out only in the densest fog and attack only the smallest ships. Then our raiders would creep up in the fog—seeing their crew without their crew seeing our men—and fire on them and kill as many men as possible before our raider became visible to them. But it was very difficult. Many of our men were killed."

"How does it happen that your brother knows nothing about wireless telegraphy—or has never used it on the present raiding ship?" Peter asked.

"Hassan is a strange man in all ways, He is a monumental egoist. His conceit is utterly incredible. I have seen him stand before a mirror for hours admiring himself. He believes that he is not only the most handsome but the cleverest and strongest man in the world. You can tell him nothing. He scorns the radio."

"How old," Susan tremulously asked, "is—Hassan?"

"Forty-eight. He has been our ruler since he was sixteen. He is the fifteenth Hassan in direct succession."

"Has he ever been out of here?"

"Never. He hates the outworld. Since the war, his hatred has become an obsession. And from all reports he gets from his emissaries, it is not a place he cares for. He knows he is the last absolute monarch on earth, since the collapse of the absolute monarchy of Siam, and he is determined to remain so. He wants no democratic or socialistic ideas here. I believe he is more than a little mad. No man could be such a self-worshiper without being a little insane. He believes that he and his men are invulnerable."

"Doesn't he realize," the vice consul broke in, "that wireless telegraphy has been in use for thirty-five years?"

"He does not care. He hates modern inventions. His father had an electric light plant installed in this palace. My brother had it ripped out. He would really prefer to go raiding in a sailing ship as his ancestors did. He even hates steam. Some day soon he plans to capture large ships and to sail out in them and overwhelm the world with his gray idiots!"

JIM SAUNDERS LAUGHED. "He wouldn't get far. One good battlewagon would blow his fleet off the face of the earth!"

"This mass of gray idiots—lepers—turned loose in any civilized country would be horrible," Susan wailed.

"I suppose," the vice consul said to the red-haired girl, "you've never seen an airplane, a motion picture, or heard a radio."

"Never. I know what these things are, vaguely, because I read a great deal. Many books and magazines are brought from raided ships. I do nothing but read—and dream of getting out of this dreadful place. You can't imagine how I long to see the great civilized world—the cities, the wonders of this marvelous modern age. Most of all, I want to see the United States. I would give my life for a month in the outworld!"

The vice consul said, "I'd give my life, princess, for the fun of showing it to you!"

She looked at him with her gentle smile, and suddenly

blushed and lowered her eyes. "I think," she said, "we had better prepare for the banquet."

"Not yet!" Saunders protested. "There are a million more things we want to know. Who taught you to speak English?"

"My mother. She was an American woman, captured and brought here from a little British tramp freighter twenty-five years ago. She taught me to love the United States as if it were my own country. I think of it as my own country."

Jim Saunders remarked, as he had earlier to Peter, that it was incredible that this valley could exist without the outer world knowing about it. And the princess repeated what Peter had said.

"Only a man in an airplane could discover the secret of this valley. And I believe that the men who fly airplanes cannot see through fog, as we can with our amber-violet glasses. It is almost always foggy here—not in the valley, but all around it."

Peter asked her about the amber-violet lenses with which human eyes could magically see through fog, but Princess Ailena knew only that it was a secret handed down from king to successive king.

"The glasses are made in a room in the cellar of this palace by my brother. All I know is that he uses various kinds of sand and chemicals and that he smelts the sand into glass over a terrific heat."

"I still don't understand," Jim Saunders said, "why he wants to stay here."

"You cannot realize how he hates the outer world. He wants only to destroy it. He does not believe what his emissaries tell him. He cannot believe that billions of people live in the outer world. He thinks of it as a small place—that it was weakened, almost destroyed, by the World War."

"Who are the guards we saw on the stone wall?" Saunders asked.

"They are recruited from the ranks of those who are being trained for raiding."

Peter strode to the window and returned to the group in the doorway. "Look here, princess. If we could figure out some plan of escape, would you help us?"

"Oh, I would, I would!" the girl cried. "I sometimes think I'll go mad. How I'd love to see the outworld—to hear its music!"

A PLAN, QUITE vague as to outline, was forming in Peter's mind. In predicaments of this nature, his rule had always been to make one good friend in the enemy's camp, if possible. Here, in this beautiful redhead, was the friend. And, unless he was mistaken, she was, in the opinion of Jim Saunders, already something more than a friend.

Peter asked her if she had never heard music from the outside world.

"Never!" she cried.

He thought of the tiny, portable radio receiver in his hip pocket. He produced it and turned the dials. He turned the wave-length dial, adjusted the amplifier—and music gushed from the little metal throat.

It was the Colonial Hotel orchestra, in Hong Kong. And the dance it was playing was a lively foxtrot.

Princess Ailena clasped her hands and stared with incredulous eyes at the little instrument in Peter's hand. She cried, "How marvelous! Oh, how marvelous!"

"People are dancing to that in Hong Kong," Jim Saunders said. "That thing, princess, is a radio receiver."

"It is incredible? We have had strange wooden instruments, like boxes, but beautifully made and full of strange machinery. But no one knew their purpose. Don't let Hassan see this! He would destroy it!"

Her eyes were feasting on the little black box in his hand from which poured this magic of lilting musk.

She marvelled, "People are dancing to that music in Hong Kong! Ah, if I were only dancing to it!"

"You are!" Jim Saunders cried. He caught her in his arms and whirled her down the room. The red-haired girl knew no steps, but she was feather-light, amazingly graceful. She clung to him and laughed, and when the orchestra stopped, she said breathlessly, "But we are not in Hong Kong!"

"Perhaps, with your help," Peter said, "we can be—some day!"

"If we only could! We four!"

"We'll do it!" Saunders cried. "It's a date—a date to dance in Hong Kong!" He frowned. "Let me see. Ah, yes! I've got a free evening one week from tonight!"

Princess Ailena's lovely face saddened.

"But there is no way. And now we must prepare for the banquet, or King Hassan will be furious. We will go—but we will return soon."

She said that to Jim Saunders, and Saunders looked down rapturously into her lovely, flushed face, with its shining, ecstatic eyes. Unmistakably, these were the symptoms of love at first sight.

Susan did not want to go. She clung to Peter and wept inconsolably. With Jim Saunders and this strange, lovely red-haired princess, it might have been love at first sight. It was, with Susan, the re-discovery or the rebirth of the only love she had known. She told Peter so. She had been a fool to have acted against their plans to be married in Hong Kong, to sail for San Francisco on their honeymoon.

"I don't deserve you. I'm not worth it, darling. But if you'll just get us out of here, I'll promise. I'll make it up to you. I'll be so good. You'll be proud of me!"

The red-haired girl said gently, "We must go now. At once!"

JIM SAUNDERS SIGHED and said, "Oh, don't go. There are a million more questions."

She smiled and said sweetly, "I'll answer one more!"

"Has any one ever told you how beautiful you are— Ailena?"

The red-haired girl blushed and laughed.

"Or," said that bold young man, "that you have the bluest eyes in the world and the loveliest smile—"

"We must go!" she gasped. "There is no more time to waste! Servants will bring you fresh clothing at once."

Jim Saunders had a hurt look. "Is it a waste of time, Ailena, dancing with me?"

"Ah, no. I meant— Listen! If you have no more serious questions, we must go."

"How large is the royal family?"

"Never more than two hundred, including the servants."

"Are the servants valley people?"

"No. They are of the royal blood. It is a strange rule we have. Only the brothers and sisters of the reigning king and his sons and daughters are royalty. The rest all become servants. And when the population of this palace exceeds two hundred, the superfluous ones are condemned to death by the reigning king. If I were to live until Hassan's death, I would then automatically become, with my surviving brothers and sisters and their children, a servant in the palace."

Jim Saunders said suspiciously, "What do you mean, Ailena—if you were to live until your brother's death?"

"Ah," she said without emotion, "I have been condemned. There are now just two hundred of us. When my brother marries this poor girl, I will be superfluous. He has said I am the superfluous one—that I am to die by the whirling death the night of his marriage. He says I am useless to him—that I am too innocent to be an emissary, too delicate to be a servant."

She took Susan by the arm and gently led her out of the room, shutting the door on the two stunned young men.

Jim Saunders said finally, "Oh, my God. Did you hear that? He's going to make her jump off the tower the night he marries Susan! Pete, we've got to do something!"

With something of the ferocity of a caged cat animal, the vice consul strode to the grilled window and hack.

His face was pale, his eyes were dark. He looked menacing.

"By God, I'll reduce their quota!" he shouted. "I'll kill that devil with my bare hands! I'll strangle him with his own beard!"

He was panting, glaring at Peter, clenching his fists. He began to curse. He consigned Hassan Barbarossa to the darkest, hottest regions known. He was on the verge of tears—tears of helpless fury.

"Sure!" he shouted. "This had to happen to me! Did you

ever see any one like her? The one girl I've met in all my life I've fallen for—and we're all going to be killed!"

He cursed Hassan Barbarossa more thoroughly, then bitterly said, "Hell, I suppose we ought to congratulate ourselves! We've found the answer to one of the oldest mysteries in the Far East—the Jaws of Hell!" He laughed harshly. "You pay your money and you take your choice— we whirl off the tower or we join the rest of the idiots!"

As if for the first time, the vice consul appeared to realize that he was a doomed man, that happiness, life were to be snatched from him.

Peter, listening to him curse and rave, pitied him. Yet he hardly heard this human tempest. The plan in his mind was still vague, still formless, but it was at least a plan's beginning. Obviously, Hassan the Fifteenth trusted his sister Ailena because of her very innocence. That was one card in the beginning of a hand. Another was, perhaps, Hassan's very egoism. Peter only hoped he could fill the rest of that hand—and win!

15

THE BOASTER

THE DOOR OPENED. Two middle-aged men came in with clothing, which they left on the bed. One of them said, "His majesty will expect you shortly."

Jim Saunders roared: "Tell his majesty to go to hell!"

The two servants stared at him, but made no response, and withdrew, closing the door again.

Jim Saunders whirled on Peter and cried: "Shouldn't I have said that? What difference does it make? To hell with him!"

"Take it easy," Peter said. "We may get out of here—if we work on it. We may get these girls out of here. Let's try not to get killed off in a hurry."

"What do you want me to do?"

"That's all—take it easy."

"I'd like to murder him with my bare hands!"

"You wouldn't get the chance. And what good would it do? You'd be dead the next instant. Try to cool off."

"But he's going to murder that girl!"

"Maybe not. Maybe we can find a way out."

Jim Saunders grunted. "All I've got to say is, you're an incurable optimist. But I'll pipe down. I'll be as gentle as a lamb."

"Until the time comes."

"Oh, sure. Until the time comes!"

The clothing the servants had brought proved to be modern—dark suits, white shirts and accessories.

They had just finished changing to these clothes when there was a knock at the door. The two young women had returned. Each wore a purple robe, and these robes, with their heavy gold and silver embroidery, the gems with which they were fringed, must have been at least one hundred years old. Peter had seen old plates of such costumes, and they dated back to the time of Napoleon, or further.

Susan ran to Peter, threw her arms about him, and began to sob again. She was no longer, she said, sorry for herself. She was only sorry for the hopeless predicament in which her selfishness, her obstinacy had placed him and Jim Saunders.

Peter comforted her. He said, "We may find a way to get out of here. All four of us may escape. Try not to worry."

All this time, Jim Saunders had been facing Princess Ailena, murmuring to her, making fierce gestures with his hands. Quite possibly, he was telling her what he had told Peter—that he loved her and that it maddened him to realize how futile this infatuation was.

The red-haired girl was pale, with bright pink spots at her cheekbones, and her lower lip was trembling and her eyes were shining like misty stars.

Suddenly, a golden gong boomed. It rang out in slow and measured strokes, deep and vibrant and mellow. It seemed to fill the world with its rich resonance.

Princess Ailena ran to the door and cried, "Come! He will punish me if we are late!"

IN ALL HIS experience, his travels, his adventures in the Far East, Peter Moore had never seen a setting more bizarre, more remarkable than that in which the banquet was laid. Hassan Barbarossa had called it the Hall of Gold. And he seemed to have spoken quite literally. The walls of the great room were walls of gold, and the great beamed ceiling was of gold, perhaps gold foil, perhaps thin gold sheets—but gold.

The floor was of deep blue tile. These tiles, about a foot square, had each in the center a five-pointed star of gold. The effect was dazzling, as unreal as an opium dream. And it was intensified by the great banquet table itself. The cloth was cloth of gold, and the service was heavy gold.

It had places for thirty people, and at each place were gold plates and eating implements. In the precise center of the long table was a great golden bowl filled and overflowing with exotic fruit—mangosteens, mangoes, plantains, figs, passion fruit, tiny custard bananas.

People of varying ages and in various costumes were standing at all but five of the places when the two Americans, the princess and the richest girl in the world entered.

Servants instructed them in low whispers where to sit. Otherwise, no one spoke. Susan O'Gilvie was to sit to the right of his majesty, Peter to his left. On Susan's right Jim Saunders was placed. But Princess Ailena's seat was well toward the other end of the table.

Beside Peter was a tall, very fair, plump girl of about eighteen, with small, close-set eyes, a sensuous red mouth. She was staring at him with insolence and scorn.

In a flat voice, she said, "I am Princess Nairobe—the eldest daughter of Hassan." But she said it with no grace. It was uttered as a warning, almost a threat, rather than as a polite phrase.

Peter examined her homely face a moment with a faint smile, with one eyebrow slightly tilted, and murmured, "I am charmed, your highness."

Beyond her stood a boy of nineteen—a sullen, dark-haired, dark-eyed youth in whose mouth and nose Peter saw a royal resemblance.

With the same scorn and insolence of the homely blond girl, he said, "I am Prince Hassan—my father's eldest son—the successor to the throne."

Still with that amused smile, Peter responded, "I am Peter Moore, an American citizen."

"We have heard of your country," Princess Nairobe said.

"We have no wish to see it," Prince Hassan added.

"We feel that the people must be most stupid," Princess Nairobe said.

"Some of them," Jim Saunders said across the table, "even eat peas with their knives, A deplorable people!"

The fair stout princess regarded him with curiosity.

"Why," she asked bluntly, "don't the peas roll off?"

"Ah, your highness, the knives have grooves. Pea-rollers, as such people are called, usually become murderers."

Princess Nairobe gazed at him scornfully. "I have no wish to see such a country."

THEY HAD HARDLY finished this sprightly interchange—the golden gong was still booming—when Hassan the Fifteenth entered, and in himself he was a most amazing spectacle. He was taller than Peter had supposed, for he had seen this strange monarch in a sitting position. He must have been fully six feet four inches tall, and broad in proportion—a sensational figure with his great red beard, his flaming red hair, which grew in tangled, thick curls, and the gold-and-purple robe he wore. He might have been the high priest of some mystic and terrible religion. His eyes were the eyes of a Rasputin, only they were that fierce yellow-green, with inner dancing fires.

Here was a man of prodigious energy—and tremendous cruelty. In him, no doubt, the fierce and savage blood of the Barbarossas—the cruelest, most barbarous pirates ever to draw a sword—ran with all the fierceness of his notorious ancestors.

Those eyes were more than a little insane.

Peter Moore pictured him as his lovely half-sister had described him—posing for hours before a mirror, worshiping himself.

King Hassan the Fifteenth paused beside the great chair he was to occupy and stared fixedly at Susan; for a moment she met that greedy stare with her amethyst eyes, then she turned ghostly pale and glanced helplessly across the table at Peter. He tried to give her courage with his eyes, but he had at no time since entering this dreadful valley felt more hopeless than he did at this moment. For he sensed, as he had not sensed before, the barbaric savagery of this red-bearded giant.

The ruler of the Kingdom of the Lost stared at Susan for fully thirty seconds before he spoke, gloating over her slender, ripe loveliness.

In his deep, harsh voice, he said, "You shall always sit in this honored place on my right. You shall be the honored wife of my harem. You shall bear me sons who will rule my kingdom. I am apt to be so much putty in your little fingers. Let me see those charming fingers."

He seized her hand before she could snatch it away. He held it up and admired it as if it were a jewel. Among human hands, it was a jewel, that hand—so slender, so delicate, so beautifully shaped. Susan was vain of her lovely hands. But she was not vain of them now.

He said, when she tried to pull away, "Ah, you should not resist your bridegroom! You should not spurn the touch of Hassan the Fifteenth! You should be flattered!"

Susan cried faintly, "I detest you! I loathe you!"

He stared at her a little longer, without releasing her hand. His large red mouth became grim. His eyes went almost pure yellow with displeasure, resentment.

"In a little time, my dove, we will overcome that. Has my charming sister told you what happens to the woman or man who displeases me?"

"You're hurting me!" Susan cried.

He dropped her hand. It looked crumpled and bluish-white. He said heavily:

"I must remember not to hurt my little bride."

King Hassan seated himself, and gave the signal for the others to do the same. Even seated, he bulked almost a head taller than Peter. So far he had not glanced at Peter. He was still feasting his eyes on the loveliness of the American heiress. He sighed and said, "You were made for love, my little flower. I have seen beautiful women. But I have never seen a woman half so beautiful as you. You make me most happy."

Once he was seated, servants magically appeared with

golden bowls of soup. An Oriental stringed orchestra appeared as though magically. They settled down in a row against the far wall, a dozen men in purple, with guitars and fiddles of all shapes and sizes. They began to play softly.

IT WAS THE most fabulous, most incredible dinner to which Peter Moore had ever seated himself. In more ways than one, it was a remarkable meal. With each course went the appropriate wine—sherry with the soup, Chablis with the fish, sparkling Burgundy with the roast beef.

Peter could have ordered and secured no finer meal in the best restaurant in New York or Paris. The food was perfectly cooked, perfectly seasoned.

But he thought of that food, of the vintage wines, only in retrospect. His attention throughout the meal was secured wholly by the incredible red-beard whom he sat beside.

King Hassan jeered at Peter Moore; demanded, in his roaring voice, that he tell him tales of the "outworld."

"Let us hear some of the marvels of this great world from which you have come."

"Perhaps," Peter complied, "you'd like to hear about modern battleships—ships with guns so accurate that they can fire at and hit an object out of sight beyond the horizon. Or shall I tell you about the new warfare of the air?"

Hassan Barbarossa looked at him without kindness. "I do not believe this about your battleships. You are lying. But let us hear about the new warfare of the air."

"A modern bombing plane," Peter answered, "could fly over this valley, your majesty, and drop a bomb containing enough poison gas to kill off every member of your population."

"A lie!" Hassan shouted. "But tell us more."

"They would drop bombs containing disease germs in your water supply. If the gas bomb did not exterminate all of you, the germs would."

"More lies! What could such warships of the air do to cities like Hong Kong and New York?"

"A few such warships of the air," Peter answered, "could kill the entire population of the largest city in the world."

Hassan the Fifteenth began to laugh. He laughed long and heartily, in great gusts of sound.

"Entertaining! Most delightful! You could make me believe that black was white. How would I fare, with a fleet, against such destroyers of the air and the sea?"

"I leave it to your majesty to judge."

The egomaniac thumped his barrel chest and roared: "My men and my fleet will conquer the world! We will overrun the world! Its people will become our slaves! Why? Because no outworld nation can produce an army of soldiers so willing to die for their ruler! But there are no more rulers. Only I—I, Hassan Barbarossa—remain, the last, the only absolute monarch left on earth. Or so my emissaries tell me. Are they lying to me?"

"No, your majesty. You are the last absolute monarch left in the world."

"Why is this?"

"Because the day of monarchies has gone, your majesty. The people of the world have seized their rulers' power to rule themselves."

"That is called bolshevism!"

"In America, it is called democracy."

"In any land," his majesty roared, "it should be punishable by death. Kings are born to rule. The mass of the people are born to be slaves. I will show this outworld what a real king can do. One day, I shall rule this world."

IT WAS NOT as ridiculous as it sounded. There was something magnificent in this egoistic, red-bearded giant proclaiming his ambitious intentions. And, in him, Peter saw the stuff of the kings of medieval times—the kings who, by their very vanity, their self-esteem, ruined the business of kings.

And in Peter, Hassan the Fifteenth evidently saw a man who had little but contempt for him and his egoism. He became loudly talkative. He ate wolfishly, swilled down his food with wine and cared not whether he talked with a full mouth or otherwise.

He boasted of his ancestors, their power, their brutality. Once when the musicians were playing a weird, haunting melody, he shouted, "That is the song of the Barbarossas. My ancestors danced to that tune while they ate the broiled hearts of virgins!"

Once again, he burst out: "Your civilization is in ruins. Of all the nations of the world, only I have the perfect state—a king and a kingdom of slaves! I have never been into your world. I detest and scorn your world. It is full of weaklings. Some of my ancestors held otherwise. They wished to learn.

"My grandfather graduated from Oxford University. My great-grandfather attended Heidelberg and, later, your Harvard University. He became a great ship designer—an architect of the sea! Another of my ancestors went into the outworld and attended your universities and became a great doctor. But I need no doctors. I obey the first law of the universe—only the fit survive. Your world has grown soft and weak and confused. My kingdom has grown strong. There is no finer specimen of man in all the world than I. I am a greater man than any of my ancestors. They saw this world of yours and envied it. My father even tried to pattern our kingdom after the so-called marvels he had seen in your country and in England and elsewhere. But in him was a weak strain.

"He brought back stupid things—electricity! I tore out his electricity! My country has gone back to the older, better gods. The subject who does not worship me and my ancestors is invited to climb the blue tower.

"Perhaps you observed, when you came into the square from the tunnel, the little temple that is being built by my artisans on the great wall. It is a temple to myself and my ancestors. It is being made of the rarest, most perfect colored glass and crystal that money can buy. It is almost finished. When it is finished, it will be a jewel—a great diadem for my subjects to revere. It has already cost upward of one million dollars. Through my emissaries, for better than twenty years, I have ordered these sheets and plates of colored glass to be moulded and cut to my requirements. It is a fitting monument to the House of Barbarossa!"

He paused to admire Susan again. "You have eyes like jewels, my bride, and your lips are jewels, too—they are blood-red rubies. There is a glint of red in your hair. You shall bear me a red-headed son. My other wives have failed. If you do not bear me a red-headed son, this one"—he pointed his dripping knife at the sullen face of Prince Hassan—"will fill my shoes! But if your son shall be red-haired, this one will lose his name and your son will be Hassan—in time, Hassan the Sixteenth!"

HE RETURNED TO his favorite theme, then—his contempt for the "outworld."

"The meddling, scheming, treacherous woman whom you saw—at my command—whirl herself into death from the golden floor of the blue tower was the last of my emissaries in the outworld. What happened to her happens to them all. They grow ambitious. They acquire absurd ideas. They wish me to copy the methods and ideas of other lands.

"My father and my grandfather often sent a dozen emissaries into the world at a time. I do not believe in it. I sent my half-sister Lotus into the world merely to act as my purchaser and to command my raiding ship. But her hatred of the white race led her into trouble—led her to her death. Above all, she hated young women of the white race. Merely because her mother was a Chinese woman! The two bloods mixed badly in her. She was a fool. But her day is over. My next emissary will be a man with a level head."

Prince Hassan said quickly, "Send me! Send me!"

His father looked at him with suspicious yellow eyes.

"Bah! You are an even greater fool! You cannot look at a pretty girl without losing your silly head. The clever women of the outworld would make a dunce of you."

"Your majesty," Jim Saunders said recklessly, "since you have no more emissaries at present in the outworld, if this valley were bottled up now, you would be in a ticklish—"

"Silence!" roared Hassan the Fifteenth. "This valley will not be bottled up! It will never be bottled up! The man does not live who is clever enough to bottle up this valley!"

He sent a sudden, savage glance at Peter Moore. But the adventurer, thoughtfully nodding, as if with agreement, was gazing into his golden wine goblet.

The banquet in the Hall of Gold lasted for hours, and throughout it, Hassan the Fifteenth shouted and gorged himself and boasted—and now and then made love to Susan, who hardly touched her food—who had the look of a girl on the verge of fainting at every moment. To that high-spirited young woman, it must have been a terrific ordeal.

King Hassan ended that strange meal with an announcement. He had consulted his gods, he said, and would marry Susan tomorrow—for tomorrow, it chanced, was the Day of the. Greatest Whirling Ecstasy, when great numbers of the people whirled off the blue tower and into the ineffable rapture of the paradise beyond this life.

He said to Peter: "I have not yet decided your fate, my friend. It depends largely on your attitude. Do you wish to spare yourself unnecessary agony by telling me now where my diamonds are?"

And Peter, knowing that his life was safe as long as the diamonds were not found, answered, "No, your majesty."

Hassan sprang to his feet, as if he were about to strike Peter with his fist. But he only said, quietly:

"I will give you until dawn to change your mind."

He strode out of the Hall of Gold. The other members of the royal family began loudly to chatter. Throughout the banquet, all of them with the exception of Princess Nairobe and Prince Hassan had maintained an absolute silence, while their king shouted and boasted and noisily ate.

16

INTO HELL!

JIM SAUNDERS WENT down the table to where Princess Ailena sat. Susan said to Peter, above the uproar: "You'll have to help me out of this chair. I'm afraid my knees won't hold me. But I'm not really afraid any more."

"Why not?"

"I watched you while he was roaring at you. You aren't afraid of him. That gave me courage. If you aren't afraid of him, I'm not. I feel—"

She stopped, said nothing more until the four of them were returning to the bronze room. Then she said, "I think you have a scheme. I've always adored you. If you can get us out of this, I'll positively worship you!"

But the red-haired princess did not share Susan's optimism. She said, "My brother hates you, Mr. Moore, because he knows you are not afraid of him. He will not tolerate people who do not cower."

"I will try cowering," Peter said.

"I have heard ugly rumors. I think he intends to banish you. Until you will tell him where the diamonds are. And once you have told, he will kill you. If it were not for the diamonds, he would have killed you before this. He knows you and Susan are in love."

"Who told him that?"

"Captain Barberry."

"Why does he let the three of us roam about this place? Why doesn't he lock us up?"

"It is his way of showing contempt. He has this scorn for every one. What harm could you do?"

"We could kill him," Susan said vehemently. "I have a little automatic pistol."

The red-haired girl shook her head. "But what good would it do to kill him? His son is as cruel."

"We won't," Peter said firmly, "shoot our way out of this place. What kind of man is this Jengha?"

"A very proud man."

"Has he ever told you he'd like to get out of this piece?"

"Yes. He wants to get out. We all do."

"What's his real feeling toward Hassan?"

"Fear."

"Is he ambitious? Has he brains?"

Princess Ailena looked at Peter strangely. "If you are thinking of winning Jengha to your side, you are making a mistake. Jengha has no price."

Peter smiled. "But has he ambition—brains? Has he ever seemed dissatisfied with his job? Has he ever envied Hassan's power? Has he ever said he'd like to get out into the world and do something exciting? Or is he just another halfwit?"

"No. He is different. He is intelligent—and restless."

She waited for Peter to explain what he had in mind, but he dropped the subject. "Hassan intends to marry Susan tomorrow," he mentioned.

"I'll die first!" Susan cried.

Peter asked the red-haired girl to tell him something about the marriage ceremony.

"THE CEREMONY STARTS shortly after the noonday meal," Ailena replied. "Susan will go to her room and I will help dress her in her wedding gown. It is a pale-green gown, embroidered with emeralds. Then I and every one else in the palace with the exception of a few servants will leave. We will form a lone line extending from the palace to the opposite side of the square.

"Hassan will have left the palace sometime before in his wedding robe, which is purple. Susan will walk along the line of people, across the square to where Hassan will be waiting in a golden chariot that was brought here, I think as an ornament, by Hassan the First. It is kept in the stables which are against the cliff on the other side of the valley. It has figured in every marriage ceremony of a king since this valley was occupied by the Barbarossas.

"The horses are Arabs. Hassan the First was a great horseman, before he left Turkey and Arabia. He brought twenty white Arab horses here. It has become a tradition to keep that stable well stocked with the finest white Arab-horses. And it has been tradition for every Hassan since to be a good horseman.

"Susan will walk—alone—to that chariot. She will get in. Hassan drive the chariot completely around the square. It will come to a stop before the blue tower. And it will stop there while Hassan and Susan watch the sacrifices. Hassan will read the names from what he calls the holy list. As each name is called, the man or woman walks to the tower and starts to climb."

"And whirls off into space!" Susan cried. "How perfectly monstrous!"

"Hassan will call the names at about thirty-second intervals," Ailena went on.

"Who will they be?" Saunders interrupted.

"Men and women from the valley who may have, in the past year, made trouble among their people—in a word, any one who has shown any qualities of leadership. But I will be the first to go."

"By God—" the vice consul began wrathfully.

"Hold it," Peter said. "Let's have the rest of this."

"If you two men have, by then, been sentenced to die by the whirling death, you will follow me from the tower. If you refuse, you will be carried up and thrown off. But Hassan will probably decide on some other form of death for you—some form of torture to take place on the wall, so that the people can see you die. The commonest form is the tug of war. The victim has one end of a long rope tied to his ankles, another long rope tied to his wrists. Two teams of fifty men each take a rope and pull as hard as they can.

"There is no prize. The object of the game is to pull the victim apart, joint by joint."

"Just a jolly, wholesome game for the kiddies," Jim Saunders said.

"After the sacrifices," Ailena went on, "Hassan will drive the chariot across the valley to a small blue stone building. He will carry Susan out of the chariot and into this building. They will spend their honeymoon there—one night. The following morning, they will return to the palace."

SUSAN WAS BREATHING rapidly. She was pale. And her violet eyes were large with terror.

"I will!" she panted. "I'll kill myself first!"

"Don't kill yourself," Peter said, "until we've exhausted all the possibilities."

"But there aren't any possibilities! There isn't any hope!"

"A moment ago you thought there was. There still is, Susan." He gazed thoughtfully at Ailena. "How many keys are there to the control room in the tower?"

"Just the one—the jade key that Jengha carries. But it's useless to think of that key. Even if you secured it, you could not use it."

"Where will Jengha be?"

"Where he wishes."

"Not in the tower?"

"No. He has no duties that day."

"Where will you, Jim and I be during Susan's walk across the square to the chariot?"

"You will be in the line."

"Are you sure?"

"Yes. He will want you to see all of it, because he is so cruel. And it is a custom, too. Every one but a few of the lowest servants will be in that long line."

"Will we be at any particular place?"

"You will be wherever you wish, as long as you are in the line. He will insist on that."

"You, Jim and I can stand together?"

"If we wish."

Susan uttered a sentiment that she had used in most of her former predicaments. She wished she'd never been born. The stirring events of the day had utterly exhausted her.

Peter suggested that she try to sleep. And when the two

girls were gone, he and Jim Saunders entered their room and closed the door.

Peter went to the grilled window and looked out. There was a thin, high fog, and the moon was milkily shining through. He could see, for the first time, down the valley—the cliffs, like great shadows slanting downward from the fog—and the gray immensity of the valley. It seemed to stretch into infinity. To the left, he could just see the blue tower, in the glow of the torches set along the spiral stairway.

He could make out dimly a movement below him—beyond the great wall. It was as if a sea were impounded there, a sea that restlessly churned and tossed and moved. Another simile occurred to him: it was as if he were looking down on a great gray blanket on which vermin ceaselessly moved about. And this stir and movement was caused, he supposed, by the leprous idiots of the valley—the teeming thousands of clay eaters, the slaves with which Hassan the Fifteenth planned to conquer the world!

He turned from the window. Jim Saunders was sitting on the bed, looking at him curiously.

"Well, what's the dope, Pete?"

"There isn't any dope—yet. That control tower is the only solution, but I can't fit things into a picture."

"Anything would be better than what will happen to us if we don't strike fast and hard."

THEY WERE INTERRUPTED by a sharp rapping at the door.

Peter opened it. The red-haired princess stood there, pale and agitated, with tragic eyes.

She panted, "You are to be banished! He has sent me to

tell you to come to him at once. He is in a murderous rage. If you will not tell him where you hid those diamonds, you are to be sent at once into the valley!" To Jim Saunders, she said, "You are to wait here."

To the vice consul Peter said quietly, "I won't be in that valley long. While I'm gone, do just one thing: cultivate this Jengha—the keeper of the tower. He's our only hope. Talk to him. Find out his weaknesses. Try to make a friend of him."

Jim Saunders nodded dubiously. "Okay, I'll work on Jengha. But you're shooting at the stars with a popgun, Pete. We're cooked. There's no way out of this."

Peter said grimly, "We're already on the way."

He shut the door and went with Princess Ailena along the corridor.

"Hassan has been in a frightful rage ever since the banquet," she said. "He felt that you have nothing but scorn and contempt for him. He cannot be laughed at. He feels he is an object of worship, and when any one goes against his will, even in his slightest whims, he flies into a rage. He feels that you were laughing at his pretentions and his pompousness.

"He is more sensitive, more thin-skinned than you realize. I think you are the first man he has ever known who has crossed his will—dared to defy him. He would subject you to frightful tortures, to make you tell where the diamonds are, but he has killed so many men with torture that he hesitates. He is afraid you would die and he would never find the diamonds.

"I have never seen him in such a rage. Your sweetheart is begging him to spare your life, but she is wasting her time. I warn you to be more prudent. Say nothing more to arouse him, or we will all suffer."

Peter was alarmed, but not frightened. And he was determined not to tell that redbeard where he had concealed the diamonds.

King Hassan was in a large lofty room which, Peter guessed, was the throne room, but his majesty was not occupying his throne—a massive teakwood chair on a dais, both inlaid with mother-o'-pearl. He was pacing up and down the room, his purple robes bellying out behind him, his beard jutting straight out like the beard of a Pharaoh in a hieroglyph, his big red hands clamped to his waist.

Susan was cowering against a purple wall hanging as large as a mainsail of a big trading schooner. White and large-eyed, she watched Hassan Barbarossa as he strode back and forth.

When he saw Peter, he shouted,. "Where are my diamonds?" and stopped pacing. He rushed toward the American as though he intended to strike him. And when Peter did not answer, he roared: "I am sick of your insolence! Tell me where my diamonds are!"

And Peter said scornfully, "Tear your ship apart and find them!"

Hassan's face was angrily red.

"You are an insolent dog! You are a worm beneath my heel! I sentence you to banishment! Live with those lepers! Live with those idiots! Eat clay! Live in filth!"

Susan shrieked, "No!"

Hassan turned on her. "You love this man!"

"I do!" Her voice was thin and high and breaking with the panic of her heart. "Let him go! Free him! I will give

you my fortune if you will let him go free! I am one of
the richest women in the world. My wealth will buy you
diamonds—a dozen times as many diamonds as those!"

King Hassan violently shook his red beard. "I am not
interested in your wealth." He clapped his hands.

A half dozen men, among them Jengha, the keeper of
the tower, came trotting into the room.

Hassan said, "This man is consigned to the valley. Turn
him loose!"

Susan started across the room toward Peter. But before
she could reach him, Hassan had intercepted her. He seized
her elbow, spun her about until she faced him. And when
she struck at him, he grinned and said indulgently, "Picture
it! My little dove has claws!"

PETER COULD DO nothing. For the first time since he had
entered this incredible valley, he was being forcibly held. A
man on either side gripped his arm.

They took him from the throne room, through long
corridors and finally out into a walled compound. At the
far end of this was the great wall which extended across
the valley from black precipice to black precipice. Men
with rifles were grouped about a gate of heavy steel bars
in the great wall. Beyond, presumably, was the land of his
banishment.

Through the bars he could see faces—the first faces he
had seen of those unfortunates beyond the wall. For the men
from the valley whom he had seen thus far—the Langpo's
crew—were separated by years from the valley life.

His knees felt a little weak as he approached that gate,
with strong hands on either arm, holding him, as if forcing
him toward this loathsome fate.

At the gate, the group, with Peter at its center, stopped. The tall man, Jengha, produced a heavy brass key. And it was apparent that he was not only the keeper of the tower, but the keeper of the gate. His steel-gray eyes were uncompromising. In them was mysticism and strength.

In a deep voice, Jengha said, "Look through the bars. Look well, my friend. You still have the chance of telling his imperial majesty where the diamonds are."

Peter looked through the bars. Dimness of moonlight filtering through fog showed him blank-eyed, awful ghost faces. Faces disappeared to be replaced by others as awful. There was loud fool's laughter. Idiot eyes stared through the bars out of faces like death's heads.

Peter glanced back at Jengha. "You are a fair and just man, Jengha. What do you advise?"

"A slave cannot give counsel."

"If I told your master where the diamonds are, would I be a dead man in an hour?"

"In all fairness—" Jengha began.

"Whose knife would stick my throat?"

"Beyond this gate," was the answer, "is life worse than any death."

"Open the gate."

Jengha fitted the brass key into the lock. The other guards opened the gate a little way—just far enough to push Peter through. The heavy gate clanged shut behind him. And once the gate was closed, the mob beset him. Half-starved, half-naked wretches crowded about him.

They welcomed him to their living hell with idiotic shouts and gurgles and laughs.

17

LIVING DEATH

IN THEIR FRIENDLINESS, the lepers were horrible. Unclean, reeking, they packed about Peter. In the dim light, he saw faces vaguely—faces that sickened him and made him faint. Some faces without noses, some without mouths. These people pawed him—and this was meant to be the mauling of affection. He had the sensation of being packed in a soft mass of stinking flesh. Bony hands patted his face and stroked his hair.

He could not have fought them off. And he now realized that he was being passed from hand to hand. They wanted to touch him, to feel him. A woman, naked except for bits of rags, threw bony arms about his neck and attempted to enfold his head and kiss him.

He wriggled free of her. He felt nauseated. The stench of bad flesh, of unclean flesh, made him want to vomit. He had visited pestilential sections of China, where famine stalked, where starving Chinese ate the roots of weeds and the bark from trees, where disease epidemics raged. He had been sickened and revolted by the things he had seen, but he had never been so revolted as by the things he now saw.

He believed he would go mad if he stayed in this place a full hour. Yet he must stay until that vague plan of his was forwarded a little. He must be returned alive and intact to the palace.

The next man who tried to paw him he pushed away. He shouted at them to keep back. And as if by magic, an area about him was cleared. Accustomed to instant, doglike obedience, these tragic wretches recognized in his voice the tones of command, and they automatically gave way.

Thereafter, for a time he was not molested. Only the small, inviolate circle in which he stood moved. It moved strangely, to allow others to see him. But it was slowly penetrating these dull brains that the visitor was not here in the capacity of master. He wielded no whip and was otherwise unarmed.

They would presently realize that he had been cast in here to share their own lot, to compete with them for the scant supply of food. Their temper, in fact, was already changing. And he wondered if, as time went on, they would tear his clothes to shreds—would rob him of everything he possessed, leaving him stripped naked and reduced to their own shocking level.

He looked back at the great wall. Beyond it he could dimly see the lights twinkling in the palace—a forbidden fairyland. He could see the tower with its torchlights, and the delicate and beautiful glass structure which Hassan the Fifteenth was erecting to celebrate his glory and that of his ancestors.

He was thirsty, and he wondered where their drinking pools were. For it was obvious to him that they would drink from pools like animals. As far as he could see, there was no structure, no kind of house or other habitation. He presumed they lived in caves or slept in the open.

Once, the moon for a few moments flooded the valley when a great pale beam found its way through a rift in the rolling low clouds. He was standing then on an elevation, a mound, perhaps a burial mound. And what he clearly saw by that random beam of pale light was worse than any of his imaginings.

UP THE VALLEY, as far as he could see, was a great stirring, as if, the news spreading that a visitor from the outworld had been admitted into these awful precincts, the gray human animals were stirring from uneasy slumber, were awakening and scrambling to inspect the newcomer for themselves. He caught the impression of a human pack so large that it seemed as if all of the humanity in the world was packed into this small space.

New waves of sickening odor reached him, and this odor was almost as revolting as that of a corrupt corpse. And the movement of pale faces and arms far away was distressingly like the movement of maggots about a corpse abandoned and neglected.

No man could retain his sanity long in such surroundings. Peter thought of the men and, worse even—the young girls—who had been thrust into this foul and disgraceful enclosure, to be seized and destroyed mentally, spiritually and physically by these hideous living dead.

It was, indeed, the Kingdom of the Lost.

He thought of the Barbarossas who had perpetrated this sin upon the name of mankind, and he hated them as he had never hated men in all his life. Here, indeed, were human guinea pigs—victims of an experiment by ruthless, selfish men. Here, to an extreme the world had never witnessed since its beginnings were the results of an incredible, prolonged depravity.

No slaves in the long, sorry story of humanity had been reduced to such woeful straits as these. This valley was nothing, indeed, but a great breeding pen in which the horrible experiment of soulless rulers was being carried on through the centuries. Here were human bodies robbed through centuries of their souls, reduced to a level lower than that suffered by any animal. The lowest forms of vermin were better off than this tragic band. A hundred thousand bodies without souls, a hundred thousand humans robbed of every human privilege but that of existence and the right to breed, so that, in due course, a red-bearded monarch might muster an army with which to overwhelm the civilized world!

It was all so monstrous, so horrible that a sane mind could not grasp a fraction of its portent. Beyond these high, glittering black walls were civilizations the lowest of which in comparison was a towering triumph in human accomplishment. Beyond these black precipices were complex law enforcement agencies which patrolled the land, the seas, the very air, to assure to humans the rights which are their due.

Not in the darkest ages of the world had mankind sunk to a level so low as that which existed here.

Peter reflected that the United States is the most powerful, most advanced nation in the world because of the fact that it is a melting pot, where the races of the world meet and unite, where the fire of the Latin blends with the calm strength of the Scandinavian, where the adventurous, the best traits of the Scotch, the Irish, the Italian, the French,

"You dare to defy me!" the king stormed at Peter.

and all the others have been fused into a single trait of high courage and high zeal. Fresh blood. New blood. Flowing together to form a race of fearless pioneers.

Contrasted with that he saw the hideous result of in-breeding—the vacant eyes, the dull hair, the slack, drooling mouths, the blank faces of a race deprived of the freshening, invigorating influences of new blood. A hundred thousand men and women produced, so to speak, in the identical mould!

In all the history of the world, there had never been an abuse of privilege so monstrous as this!

Was it a wonder that men and women, thrust into this awful place, promptly lost their reason?

Why had these soulless creatures lived? Why had not some epidemic mercifully killed them all?

THESE REFLECTIONS AND others flashed through Peter Moore's mind in the measured seconds in which the beam of moonlight struck through that rift in the rolling white clouds and showed him graphically the extent of the Barbarossas' infamous influence over this mass of humanity under the iron heel of their power.

At that moment he could have killed Hassan Barbarossa with bare hands.

And at that moment the first stone was thrown. The idiot mob had sensed that he was not sent here as a master.

Then there was an interval of waiting. If he was a master, he would display in no uncertain terms his resentment at the thrown stone.

The stone flashed past under his chin, ticked the cloth on his shoulder. And it signalled Peter Moore into trying the plan on which all his hopes depended—a thread slender enough. The product of his inventive genius—the tiny radio receiver—was in the inside pocket of his coat—where it had been since he had played it for the amusement of Princess Ailena.

He did not remove it from his coat, but reached inside and quickly touched the dials. He was not, he realized, dealing with a collective human intelligence, but with an uncertain mob emotion.

Through his coat, a voice said the words, "Beethoven's 'Moonlight Sonata' will be the next offering of the Royal Symphonic Orchestra of Sydney, Australia." The announcer's voice blended into the first notes of that famous composition.

Peter adjusted the volume control to its loudest pitch. The music of a two hundred piece orchestra came swelling from the magical little instrument, and he prayed that the tubes of his own invention would not burn out, that the battery on which he had labored so many months would not suddenly go dead.

As the great tide of music swelled from the tiny instrument, as if poured from his heart, he raised his hands over his head. He had planned this moment carefully, and he executed the plan with dramatic purpose.

All about him, gray, idiot faces stared as if, indeed, they stared upon some miracle granted them by an unknown Heaven. Mouths gaped and drooled. Jaws dropped. Then there was a great whispering sound, as of countless thousands of throats uttering breaths of awe.

And suddenly, as far as the eye could reach in the dim light, the leprous idiots began throwing themselves on their faces—prostrating themselves before this deity, this tall blond god from whose heart poured in deep volumes the music of a moonstruck German composer.

No miracle, however clever, however amazing, could have struck awe in such measure into the hearts of any pagan people. The little metal box with its intricate arrangement of tubes and condensers and batteries and clever circuits—this pocket-size miracle had elevated a man on their own footing, a slave, to godhood. Peter Moore was suddenly a king in his own right—greater, more wonderful, more terrible in their eyes than the king they had been taught to worship. Yet it was a power of which he could use but a very little.

With it, he hoped to accomplish two small things—to plant an idea in the mind of one man, and to be delivered from this moonlit inferno.

HE MOVED DOWN from the mound on which he had permitted the miracle to occur. He shut off the "Moonlight

Sonata" only because he feared the tiny, delicate battery might be drained. And he had further uses for this ingenious little invention of his.

But that demonstration had been sufficient. Way was made for him as he advanced toward the great wall. He wanted to examine it, to ascertain if there was some way in which it might be scaled. But he had no intention of turning loose this idiot mob on the palace. To do so would frustrate his other plan. And with this mob on the other side of the wall, Susan, Ailena and Jim Saunders would not be safe. No one would be safe if the destructive power of this wretched million were ever turned loose.

His plan was of much smaller scope; much more subtle.

He walked the length of the wall, followed at a respectful distance by his worshipers. As he advanced, those in his path made way and prostrated themselves.

From precipice to precipice, the wall was about a mile in length. He counted forty sentries patrolling it. He found no stairs of any kind, and there was but the one gate—the one through which he had entered.

Having reached the far end, he started back. He stopped just below the fantastic structure of precious colored glass which the present Hassan Barbarossa was having erected to the glory of himself and his ancestors.

Peter stared up at this intricate, beautiful, fairylike structure for a long time. Then he stooped down and picked up a rock. With all his strength, he hurled it. There was a sound of glass falling in splinters.

A GREAT GASP went up from the human mass about him. He picked up another rock and threw it. There was another smashing sound.

Sentries were coming along the great wall on the run. His next rock he threw at a sentry.

Another gasp went up. So far, his rock-throwing had not been imitated. To have thrown a rock at the million-dollar glass monument or at the guards would have been in violation not of years but of centuries of abject worship and obedience to the red-bearded kings who lived on the other side of the wall—a worship and obedience which had been beaten into them for upwards of four centuries.

He had to overcome that powerful prejudice. He did so by shouting at them to do as he was doing. He threw more rocks. One struck a sentry in the hand as he was about to fire his rifle. Peter presumed that the sentries had been instructed to fire on him under no conditions. Once again, so he believed, his life was safe because of those de Sylva diamonds.

But the sentries began firing into the mob. And this firing and Peter's rock-throwing eventually caused the response he wanted. A man near him picked up a rock and, with a scream, threw it at the glass monument. Others followed this revolutionary example.

Instantly, it seemed, the air was full of rocks. Peter now stood back and watched. Thousands of eager hands were scooping up large and small stones and hurling them. The sentries ran about, firing at random into the mob, inflicting death and injuries, but never stopping that meteoric shower. Sentries fell. Others replaced them. These, too, were struck down.

And the glass monument to the glory of the Barbarossas was vanishing as a monument of snow vanishes in a downpour of rain. Rocks hailed upon it by the countless thousands, smashing the glass, bending and twisting the delicate metal frames on which the glass was being mounted. The million-dollar glory became, within a space of minutes, a twisted, mangled mass of metal and shattered glass.

When this vandalism was complete, Peter made his way toward the other end of the wall—the gate. Men on the other side of the thick bars were shouting his name. Servants of the palace were running about in the compound, dodging rocks.

Peter reached the gate. Through the thick bars he saw Jengha peering at him, his long gray face transfused with terror and wonder.

"You are pardoned!" shouted the keeper of the keys. "You are to be freed at once!"

"Not yet! Tell your master that if he does not guarantee the freedom of my friends—our instant delivery to the outworld—I will have this mob swarm these walls and destroy him and his palace!"

"He has told me to grant you any desire!"

"Then open the gate!"

Peter was not deceived. He knew that Hassan would grant any desire under heaven to have him delivered into the palace again—and then reverse his promise. Peter did not look behind him when the gate opened. He had seen, he hoped, the last of the valley of the leprous idiots. As long as he lived, he would wear on his very soul the scars of that monstrous place.

The gate clanged behind him. And as if that had been a signal, the rocks stopped falling. A moan went up, soft at first, then louder and louder until it echoed from precipice to precipice and filled the night—a moaning sigh of lost hope, of frustration, from the throats, the very hearts, of that great legion of the cursed.

18

PETER'S PLAN

THE ADVENTURER WAS swiftly spirited into the palace, and into the presence of his imperial majesty, King Hassan the Fifteenth. The red-bearded monarch had a wild look. He was pacing up and down in that room of the purple hangings, pale and gaunt of face, eyes tigerish yellow and insane with fury.

When he saw Peter, he whirled about and licked his pale lips. He was shaking with kingly rage—and with helpless human fury. Yet there was in his face a puzzlement and awe. "You—" he began, in a thin, cracking voice. "What did you do to my people? How did you arouse them in so short a time?"

"I have a dark magic, your majesty." Peter sent a glance at Jengha. The keeper of the keys was staring at him, his eyes still slight with that wonder and terror. And Peter was, for the moment, satisfied. He said nothing of Hassan's promise, and in the red-bearded king's next breath, his guess at the emptiness of that promise was verified.

"You dare to defy me! You dare to turn my people against me and against my works! You have the insolence—" He choked on his words. He beat his hands together. "You caused death and injury to more than a hundred of my guards! I will have you killed! I will have you drawn and quartered! I will have every inch of your insolent flesh tortured until—"

"But will that find your diamonds?" Peter quietly interrupted.

"I will think of a better way than hanging you by your thumbs! Go! Tomorrow—you die!"

Peter withdrew. His only fear was that, at this juncture, Hassan would order some form of torture to which Peter's knowledge of Yogism would not apply. Red-hot charcoal would have done it—perhaps. Threat of cobra poison would have done it, for Peter Moore had his weakness. Poisonous reptiles. He loathed and dreaded them.

As he left the purple room and the wrathful monarch, he realized that he had succeeded in bluffing Hassan the Fifteenth. The red-bearded king could not understand a man whose will he could not break. No doubt, in hundreds of years, that banishment among the dreadful humans who thronged the valley beyond the wall had, in a brief time, successfully wrung confessions and precious secrets from every victim of the Barbarossas. But Peter Moore had turned the mob spirit of that detestable human mass to his own advantage. By his destruction of the glass monument he had aroused the kingly ire. Yet he had come off first in the clash with Hassan's will and that monarch, hating him, was strangely in awe of his magical powers.

It had been a delicate and dangerous moment, but it was past. If he was to die tomorrow, he must work fast.

Peter made his way quickly to the bronze room. On his way he directed a servant to bring water for bathing. His skin was creeping from contact with the filthy flesh of the valley people. He felt soiled and polluted.

In the bronze room he found another man at his pacing. Jim Saunders, vice consul to Foochow, was striding up and down the room, wild of eye and pale of face, but these were not the symptoms of rage.

When he saw Peter, he stopped pacing, and stared "Good God," he said. "Didn't they put you on the other side of that wall?"

"They did."

"How in hell did you get out?"

Peter swiftly summed it up, and Jim Saunders stared at him with that same puzzled awe of King Hassan.

FOUR SERVANTS ENTERED. One carried wash cloths and brushes, another fresh clothes. Two staggered under the weight of a great bronze urn filled with water. They withdrew and Peter fell to scrubbing himself from head to foot. He asked Saunders if he had talked to Jengha, the keeper of the keys.

"I did! I've talked to him ever since you left. Ailena brought him up here. We both talked to him. And you can bank on only one thing—he won't betray our confidence. Not because of us, but because of Ailena. He worships that girl. She told him she loved me. He said he would like to help her escape—but he loves his life, too. It's a funny thing, the way people love their lives. So few lives are worth it!" He paused and narrowed his eyes. "What did Hassan say?"

"Among other things, that I'm going to die tomorrow. But I suspect it's only another threat. He's afraid to torture me, thinking I may die and never disclose the hiding place of those diamonds. He isn't being very clever. He should know that if he threatened to torture Susan, I'd come clean quickly enough. He's too furious to think, though. What else happened?"

"Nothing ever happens. Ah, yes. Here's a bit of news—a mere detail. But it may interest you. It proves that he's at least been thinking about something. Tomorrow is the red letter day in the Barbarossa calendar—The Day of the Greatest Whirling Ecstasy. As Ailena told us, Hassan is going to marry your girl and he's going to put on a big celebration. A lot of people he doesn't like are going to spin off into space, including Ailena. But I'm going to be a special treat."

Peter, getting into fresh clothes, cried, "What?"

"Have you ever heard of white leopards?"

"Albinos?"

"Perhaps. They have pink eyes—like white rabbits. These are half-starved white leopards, and they're kept downstairs in this palace. Tomorrow evening, to celebrate his wedding to Susan, I am going to be thrown to the pink-eyed leopards! That's the final dope. And now, unless I'm crazy, you'll join me! He'll throw us both to the leopards and in the meantime he probably expects you'll break down and tell where the diamonds are."

Peter was putting on his coat as a knock sounded at the door. The vice consul to Foochow opened it. Princess Ailena and Susan came in, both pale, both wearing looks of determination. Susan flew into Peter's arms, demanded to know if he'd been hurt. But even in her solicitude he realized that she had more hope, more confidence, than at any time since their arrival in this incredible valley.

"I knew you'd escape from that horrible place," she told him, kissing him. "It's the first time it's ever been done. Thousands of people have been turned in with those awful people—and you're the only one who's come out! Oh, darling, you're wonderful! If you can get out of there, you can get all of us out of here. Have you a plan?"

"I have. I want Jengha."

Princess Ailena returned to the door. "I'll bring him."

"One moment, Ailena. Whatever I say—if he looks to you—back me up."

"Yes."

JENGHA COULD NOT have been far away, for she returned with him very shortly. The tall, gray-eyed man came into the room with apparent reluctance. He advanced uncertainly, with his eyes on Peter's face as if fascinated.

He muttered, "No, no," in a frightened voice. "I know why you have sent for me. Your friend talked to me. It is impossible for you to escape. I cannot give you the key. If I did, you would be killed. And none of you would escape."

Peter looked at him grimly. "That is not my plan, Jengha. I wanted to talk to you. I wanted to know, first of all, if you wish to leave this valley."

The tall, gray-eyed man's mouth became stubborn. "Who has not dreamed of escaping from this valley? But it is not for me. I have a sacred trust. I am the keeper of the tower. Before me, my father held that trust, and his father before him. That trust has never been violated by one of my name. It will not be now."

"But have you no feeling of obligation toward Princess Ailena?"

"I have a greater feeling of obligation toward my master."

"Only because you are in terror of him."

"There is no plan you can suggest," Jengha answered, "that would succeed. We would all be killed. And I and my family would be disgraced."

"But, suppose it could be arranged—"

"There is no possible plan that could succeed," Jengha reiterated with firmness.

"Two hours ago you would have said there was no plan by which any man could escape from beyond that wall. That gate has opened to admit many men and women into the valley—and none has ever returned. You saw me return."

"I was amazed. How did you do it?"

Peter smiled. "That is my secret. If I had wished, I could have sent that mob swarming over the wall to destroy and kill."

"How did you do it?" Jengha repeated in a desperate voice.

"I could give you that secret. It would give you immediate power over that great mob. You would instantly become a general with an army of a hundred thousand at your back. You could send them over this wall. You could become king in Hassan's place! You could visit the outworld at your pleasure."

Jengha was staring at him, licking his gray lips.

"No, no, it's impossible! I would be killed!"

"You could not be killed! If you will listen to my plan—"

"No."

"But look here, pal," Jim Saunders interrupted, "you saw what he did. He used his magic out there. In less than ten seconds, he was the head man. It took him that time to turn a hundred thousand fighting fools against the Barbarossas. In ten seconds, he undid the work of centuries. You, too, can be that man!"

Jengha looked at the vice consul dubiously, then back at Peter.

"What was this trick?"

"It is a trick by which a man's heart makes wonderful music."

"A trick?"

"Your trick, if you will help us."

"A miracle!" Saunders cried.

Jengha panted: "Let me hear! Let me hear!"

Peter reached into his coat and touched the dials. There was an interval of silence. Then from the throat of that amazingly useful little invention of his surged a Spanish waltz. From a short-wave station in Madrid, across Europe, across Asia Minor and India and Cambodia, the waltz came through the vibrant ether. It was rich and golden melody.

PETER HAD BACKED away from Jengha. With a mystic expression on his face, with his hand under his heart—just under the concealed pocket radio—he watched Jengha.

The keeper of the keys had likewise backed away. He was licking his lips, staring with hypnotized eyes at the approximate region of Peter's thumping heart.

His pale lips worked, but no sounds came from them. He darted glances at Susan, at Ailena and at Jim Saunders. Peter reached into his coat and shut off the music.

And Jengha gasped, "How is it done? Truly, it is a miracle!"

"It is a miracle of modern science and invention," Peter

answered. He took the small black case from his pocket. Jengha stared at it fearfully. "Here, Jengha. Hold it in your hand!"

"No, no!"

"It won't hurt you. Ailena, show him."

The red-haired girl accepted the tiny instrument. She turned the knobs. And when the golden music surged from it, she laughed. Jengha seemed somewhat relieved, but he was still utterly amazed and awestruck.

Finally, he cried with eagerness, "Let me try!" He took the receiver and turned the control switch. And at the command of his fingers, the Spanish waltz leaped out again.

Jim Saunders tried to explain the mystery. "It is coming from Madrid, Spain. A powerful electrical station is sending waves through the air, and these waves carry the music of a large dance orchestra over thousands of miles of space to that little box. The little box changes back the electrical waves into sound."

But Jengha, of course, could not understand. He was as delighted as a child with its first toy train. Peter tuned in other stations and said, "It is safe to say that this will work at any hour of the day or night, because somewhere in the world, a station will be broadcasting either music or voices. And this little kit will pick up every station in existence."

Greedily, Jengha answered, "I would like to have that little box of magic."

Then his eagerness departed; there were too many objections. Just what, he wanted to know, was Peter's plan?

"Briefly, this: just before this lady"—he indicated Susan—"leaves tomorrow in the green gown, for the wedding ceremony, you will call at her room, and she will give you this magical box. She will then wait for you to go up and into the tower. That will arouse no suspicion, will it—your going into the tower?"

"No. But—"

"She will cross the square and get into the chariot. When Hassan drives it around the square, he will stop before the tower. Unless I am greatly mistaken, no one will be watching the tunnel. If I am wrong, correct me."

"So far, you are not wrong. But—"

"Very well. Here is the plan. You will throw the lever which opens the tunnel gates. You will then come down the tower. If what you have done is discovered, if any attempt is made at stopping you, you have only to turn on this magic box. But you will not be noticed, I assure you, Jengha. Because, while you are descending the tower, there will be great excitement."

"Of what nature, master?"

"This gentleman and I will have leaped into the chariot and overwhelmed Hassan. Princess Ailena will be with us. We will drive like mad down the square and into the tunnel. Before the gates can be dropped, we will have escaped."

"It is incredible!" Jengha gasped.

"But why won't it work?"

"It may work. It is astounding. But it may work. Yet what becomes of me?"

"You will have a job ahead of you. You will run to the compound and let yourself into the valley. You will let those million people hear the music from your heart. You will lead them in an attack. You will throw stones until a ramp has been made by which the wall can be climbed. With your million at your back, you will attack and destroy every living Barbarossa—and become the king yourself!"

"Ah, that is a mad plan, master!" But Jengha's eyes were no longer dull, and his face was not gray. It seemed to glow. Then his face grew long and his eyes went dull. He had thought of objections. He had, he said, a thousand objections.

Patiently, Peter answered them, met them, overcame them, one by one. And with each crop dispensed with, the keeper of the keys presented a fresh crop. Jengha's greatest doubt concerned his control over his idiot subjects once he had them on the other side of the wall. How was he to drive them back? How was he to establish his kingly authority? Peter answered that—the hardest question of them all. It was a long and elaborate answer, chiefly involving firearms, which must not fall into the mob's hands.

Once, Peter glanced at the window. It was an arch of gray light now. Dawn was here. A little later he saw the lighted valley.

AND, AT LENGTH, Jengha's last doubts were overridden. He would do it!

"I see no reason why we cannot carry through this plan as you have drawn it, master," he said. "I will be the king of this valley, and you, your sweetheart, and this other gentleman and Princess Ailena will escape to the outworld! But I must exact from you a promise. You will never breathe a word of this place to a living soul."

"You have that promise," Peter firmly answered.

"Very well, master. Then, just before the ceremony, I will call at the silver room—and this lady will give me the magic box."

"May I see that key?"

Jengha showed it to him—an intricately fashioned key of rare kingfisher jade, which he carried on a fine gold chain about his neck.

Then Jengha left the room with the swagger of a man already king. Susan was delighted with the resourcefulness of the plan. For the first time, she was the happy girl Peter had once known. She declared that the plan was perfectly wonderful. Even the lovely red-haired princess, always so dubious of any plan of escape, was enthusiastic. Yet she sounded a notice of caution.

"Susan and I will go now. We will stay in the silver room until it is time. And I advise you two men to stay here. There is only one possible complication—Hassan may decide to imprison you, or torture you, because of the diamonds, sometime before the ceremony. I will have food sent here."

Susan started for the door, then whirled about and ran to Peter. Her eyes were sparkling with excitement. And her lovely face was flushed. She impulsively threw her arms about his neck and kissed him.

"Darling," she said, "you're simply wonderful. Just think of it, Peter! By tonight, we'll be out of this place! In a few days, we'll be in Hong Kong. Civilization! We'll be married! Oh, I love you so much, Peter!"

He did not say that he loved her, too—he did not have the chance. With her beautiful sparkling eyes close to his face, she whispered, "But we won't go back to America, darling. We'll stay in China. America would be so dull?"

"Dull?" Peter echoed.

"Oh, life is so exciting in China! We've had such fun. We'll have greater fun!"

"More adventure!"

"Yes, darling!"

Peter's ardor cooled perceptibly. She wasn't joking. The little thrill-hunter meant it. In previous adventures, she had waited until they were clear of a dangerous predicament before wanting fresh excitement. With their freedom still to be fought for, with the odds tremendously against them, she already craved fresh, new adventure!

Loving Susan as he did, Peter was suddenly discouraged. She was incurable. She would never be cured of her capacity of plunging herself and others into trouble.

He kissed her gently and led her to the door. Peter asked Ailena if she could secure revolvers or automatic pistols for him and Jim Saunders. She said she could not do so without arousing dangerous suspicion. Susan offered him her .25 caliber Colt's automatic, but he told her to keep it.

WHEN THE GIRLS were gone, the two young men began a discussion of the details of Peter's plan. Unarmed, they must somehow secure a boat in which to escape from the black cave.

Food was brought to them. A message came, by a servant, from Princess Ailena, in which she said that Hassan was spending his morning trying to ascertain what kind of magic it was that Peter had used last night in the valley; that he was puzzled and troubled and irritable. The accounts he had received had varied. Some declared that a nimbus of holy light had shone about Peter's head. Others described his whole person bathed in a sacred glow. Many reports had it that he lifted his hands and that music flowed from the tips of his fingers. Others believed that he had drawn the divine music down to earth from the clouds.

As long as Hassan the Fifteenth was puzzled, worried, Peter was safe. Hassan would know that no torture could wring from Peter the secret of his magic. It was likely that the American adventurer would be safe until late afternoon at least. But Hassan had not changed his mind about putting the two Americans to death. They would be tossed into a bamboo enclosure especially erected for the occasion on the stone wall, and into this enclosure, one at a time, the white leopards would be loosed.

As the time for the ceremony approached, Peter became more and more nervous, as a fighter does, as the zero hour of his appearance in the prize ring comes nearer and nearer. He was not afraid. He knew that he had taken the only course open to him. His worry was the great number of possible ways in which his plan could go astray. It depended on so many unpredictable factors. Yet it had to be daring. It had to be spectacular and dramatic. On those very features its success depended.

Jim Saunders said, "You have done everything a man could. You have anticipated everything possible. The rest is in the lap of the gods. No one anticipates trouble, least of all that red-bearded rat. It is going to be a surprise party—and by the time the surprise wears off, we'll be long gone. And once out of this hellish place, we'll take our chances with the fog, the waves and the wind. You've hatched a wonderful scheme. You're a great guy, Pete. You're the greatest guy I ever knew."

They were interrupted by a knock at the door. It was a servant, to tell them that they were expected with the rest of the royal household in the square immediately.

19

THE SACRIFICE

THE COLLAPSE OF Peter's complex plan of escape from the Kingdom of the Lost was occasioned, as might have been expected, by Jengha. The keeper of the keys had been overwhelmed by the magic of the pocket radio. He had been captivated by Peter's plan for him to become the new king of the Valley of the Barbarossas. But as the hours dragged on, Jengha grew dubious. He was, after all, the product of centuries of breeding along a single narrow line of slavelike obedience. In generation after generation of Jenghas had been reposed the sacred trust of the blue tower—the control of the bronze tunnel gates. His dreams of power had been shortlived. Peter's arguments, though they had been true, logical and correct down to the finest detail, did not weigh as heavily in Jengha's brain as did his sense of slavelike duty to his ruler.

He did not return to Peter to argue it out. He did not have the courage. He did not wish to argue it out. He was afraid of the American and his black magic. Instead, Jengha waited until the time came for him to appear at the silver room, to secure the magical little black box from Susan. And by this time, it was too late for Peter to be of help.

Susan was alone in the silver room. Some minutes before, Princess Ailena had left to join Peter and Jim Saunders in the long line of people stretching from the palace to the other side of the square.

Waiting for the servant who would summon her, she went to the window and looked down. She could see Peter and Jim and Ailena, standing in a little group in the very center of the long line—standing not a hundred feet away from the base of the blue tower.

On the great wall, not far from the tower, was the bamboo enclosure which had been built as a sacrificial pen—for Peter and Jim. Susan gave it a glance of disdain.

She was thrilled as she had never before been thrilled in her life. The drama of the moment, and the promised drama of the ensuing half hour, set her heart to beating hard. Her eyes, in the mirror, had never been so beautiful, so large, so lustrous. She was glad she was so beautiful, for Peter's sake. She was glad that she would make him such a beautiful bride.

She said, into the great, deep mirror, "I'll make him a lovely bride." For Susan was fully aware how beautiful she was. She was proud of her loveliness, of her slim, exquisite body, of her small, beautiful hands and feet She was an aristocrat—one of the last of a race that will soon be extinct.

But Susan was as selfish as she was lovely. She loved Peter Moore as she had never believed she could ever love a man. She adored him. But she had no intention, after their marriage, of letting Peter spoil her life. There would be no children. There would be no settling down, no comfortable security—and respectability.

Why should they settle down? With the whole world

at their disposal—a world teeming with exciting and dangerous adventure for the asking. And her wealth—her wonderful millions—a magic carpet on which they would fly here and there and into the most fascinating and dangerous thrills.

More than anything in her life, she looked forward to this afternoon's wonderful excitement. All eyes would be upon her beauty. And at the end—the thrilling break for freedom! They would not fail. She trusted Peter. And Peter Moore never had failed her.

Looking down at him now from her window, his well-shaped head, his wide shoulders, his slender, erect carriage, she loved him more than ever before.

THERE WAS A hurried rapping of knuckles at the silver door. She took a deep breath. It would be, of course, the servant, for at that moment, far across the square, she saw the flash and glitter of the golden chariot, the snowy whiteness of its spirited horses. Seeing the purple figure in the chariot, she laughed. She threw open the door.

But it was not the servant. It was Jengha.

Susan laughed excitedly. She cried, "Ah! Just a moment!" And ran back into the room. She had almost forgotten that Jengha had failed to come for the little black box. Suppose she had left the room, forgetting, in her excitement, that important detail! It would have been like her, she reflected. "I am such a little rattlebrain."

But Je.ngha did not extend his hand to accept the little magical black box. Instead, with hands clutched nervously behind him, he shook his head.

"Madam, I cannot betray my king. I cannot go through with this."

Susan uttered a gasp. Her heart suddenly went cold, then it began to race with panic. Hysterically, she cried, "Jengha! You can't mean it! You can't back out now! You promised!"

"I am sorry, madam. But I have given it much thought. I cannot go through with it. The risk is too great. I was carried away by your lover's enthusiasm. But I am not the man for it. I would fail."

Thoughts confused, bewildered, desperate, came tumbling through the girl's brain. She was frantic. She was trapped. She did not know what to say or do. She begged him to reconsider. She begged him to have pity on her, on Princess Ailena, on the two men. But Jengha would not be argued with. The more she entreated, the more she argued and bullied, the more firm he became in his decision. No, he would not change his mind. He was sorry. It was his life against theirs. It was their wish against the honor and the glory of his family.

"Freedom for you and your friends, madam, means disgrace, dishonor, death for me."

Suddenly, into the agonized churning of her mind, penetrated an icy thought—a horrible thought. It was as if some one else were doing the thinking for her. Certainly, she herself could not have created such a chain of hideous, monstrous thinking. She had an instant in which to make her decision.

Jengha was turning to go. She made her decision. In a frightened little voice, she cried, "Jengha!"

He returned. "But it is useless!"

"Come into this room!"

Now he obeyed. She shut the door. She faced him. From the bosom of her pale-green robe she removed her little automatic pistol. She levelled it at him and whispered, "Give me that key!"

Frightened, he started back to the door. "No, madam! Oh, no!"

When his hand was on the knob, she aimed as steadily as she could at his head. Because of her shaking hand, the shot went wild. It tore a gash along his scalp. The next shot was better. It struck into his skull above the ear. As he tottered, she fired four more shots. Three of the silvery little bullets drove into his brain. The fourth struck the silver door, and, ricocheting, went screaming up to strike flakes of silver from the ceiling.

Susan returned the pistol to her bosom. The hot barrel burned her tender flesh, but she did not care. What mattered now what happened to her tender flesh?

She took the key from around his neck, placed the fine gold chain around her own, and dropped the key down between her breasts. Then she dragged the dead man away from the door, went out into the corridor, closed the door after her, and waited.

She was not afraid now. Her eyes were shining as they had never shone before. Her face was transfigured. It glowed as if with an inner light. For perhaps the first time in her life, Susan—spoiled, selfish, willful, greedy Susan—was proud of something beside her exquisite beauty.

PETER AND THE red-haired princess and the vice consul to Foochow watched Susan approach. Her chin was lifted. Her eyes were large and glowing. In the two years since Peter had first met her on the transpacific crossing, he had never seen her so lovely. Or so unafraid. There was courage in the way she carried her small, exquisite head, in the very way she set down her small dainty feet.

Watching her as she came, Peter was proud of Susan. She was playing her part, he reflected, with rare courage.

There was no sunlight. A little more than a thousand feet up the walls of the black precipices—just above the golden top of the blue tower—the fog lay like a blanket of uneasy ivory.

The light that came through was, however, brilliant and hard. In utter silence, Susan walked the length of the line. Her pale green robe floated about her, matching her slimness and grace. The emeralds with which the bodice was encrusted flashed and shimmered in lovely waves of sheerest green.

She was about to pass Peter. So far, she had turned her head neither to right nor left. But just as she was opposite him, she turned and smiled. It was a smile of such sweetness as he had never before seen at her lips, even at her tenderest moments when she was telling him how she loved him. He gave her back a smile for courage. He saw there was moisture in her large, amethystine eyes, and he presumed that this was only a revelation of the inner nervousness that she was otherwise concealing so nobly.

She passed on, and that smile lingered in his memory. It puzzled him. It troubled him.

He watched her approach the golden chariot. Hassan the Fifteenth was waiting, holding the eight white reins in his powerful red hands. He was watching her greedily, with a smile at his thick red lips.

Hassan did not help her into the chariot. According to the old ritual, the bride was supposed to come to the bridegroom, as if willingly, as if eager for him. That was the tradition. So Susan stepped into the golden car. Hassan cracked a long white whip, and the four magnificent white horses started off with a clatter.

It was like a pageant of the old and all but forgotten days of early empire. So might the victorious Cæsar have driven through the streets of Rome, or Hannibal through the warlike Carthage, or—an early Barbarossa, returning triumphant from piratical looting, through the cheering streets of Constantinople.

The golden chariot, gleaming in the diffused light from the clouds, went whirling to the end of the square. It passed the bronze door at the tunnel entrance. It swerved and came back, with a clattering thunder of hoofs, a ringing of thick iron tires, the purple robe and the green robe of its occupants floating out behind in a strange and remarkable banner.

By now, Peter knew that something was amiss. Jengha had not appeared. Long ago, Jengha should have slipped out of the palace and climbed the spiral stairs to the control room. For now was the time when the excitement should begin.

He whispered to Ailena, "Where is Jengha?"

And she replied, "Oh, something must have happened! We are lost! In only a moment, Hassan will command me to climb the tower. Then he will order the other sacrificial victims to be fetched. Then you and Jim will be taken to that cage—"

It was as if an iron band had suddenly been placed about Peter's heart. He felt an actual stab of pain. His throat was dust-dry. His knees felt weak. His plan, after all, had failed! Sickness, desperation went through him in waves.

Jim, beside him, panted, "We'll die fighting, kid! Believe me, it will cost them something. We'll go for that rat, anyway!"

THE CHARIOT HAD come to a stop just in front of them. Hassan had turned to face them. His eyes dwelled malevolently on his half-sister's white, beautiful face. His eyes rested possessively on Susan's shoulders.

And suddenly Susan twisted away from those great red paws. Both hands plunged into the bosom of her dress. She screamed: "Peter! Get him! Go! I've got the key!"

As if he were paralyzed, Peter watched. In a nightmare, he saw Susan point the little automatic at Hassan's head—saw the little spurt of flame. As Hassan staggered back, she leaped down from the chariot and ran toward the tower. In his sick confusion, Peter saw that she held high over her head Jengha's kingfisher jade key—the key to the control room of the tower!

It was not Peter but Jim Saunders who perceived, with the flashing speed of intuition, what Susan's plans were; realized that it was their only hope of getting out of this place alive—realized that Susan was offering her life as a supreme sacrifice so that the three of them could escape. Realized, too, that there could be no other way. And that Peter Moore would very likely spoil their plans when the truth struck him.

Therefore, the vice consul's first act was a surprise attack on Peter Moore. As Susan ran up the spiral stairway, he struck Peter a smashing blow with his fist in the side of the head. Peter collapsed in his arms.

Saunders seized his shoulders and dragged him toward the chariot in which Hassan the Fifteenth, not dead but dazed, was slumped. There was no time to get rid of the red-bearded king.

Ailena had followed him. She, too, had realized that Susan was giving to them their life and liberty by sacrificing her own.

SAUNDERS DRAGGED PETER into the golden car, told Ailena to hold tight to him, and picked up reins and whip. He cracked the whip.

And before the guards could come running, before the servants in the palace could reach the turret room, before any of the crowd in the square could act—Susan had reached the control tower.

By now, the golden chariot, with its strange crew—a half-fainting girl, two half-conscious men, with Jim Saunders at the reins, was rattling and clattering down the square toward the tunnel, the four white horses plunging at a full run.

The bronze gate was still closed. Jim Saunders sent a desperate glance behind him. He could not see Susan. But when he looked ahead, the bronze door was slowly lifting! She was in the control room—pulling that great lever!

The vice consul sent another glance arear. Members of the royal household were streaming after the chariot. Men and women were shouting, yelling, beckoning. Guards were frantically running to and fro along the great wall.

Suddenly, Susan reappeared—a tiny green figure. She was finishing her job. She was climbing to the golden roof!

Peter was recovering from that smashing blow on the head. And Hassan XV was recovering from the smashing shock of the glancing bullet. With growls and oaths, he was struggling up from the floor of the swaying golden car.

Peter shook his head, as a fighter, floored, does, in trying to clear the black mists from his brain. He shook his head and stared. He, too, saw that small figure climb to the golden floor.

He shook his head again. He shouted, "Stop! Stop!" But Jim Saunders did not stop. And Peter, with an awful groan, burst out: "She's going to kill herself!"

He saw the wind catch the folds of pale-green cloth— saw, or imagined he saw—the glitter of the emerald-encrusted bodice. Susan raised her hands slowly over her head. She slowly stretched her arms—in a gesture of farewell. Now she was pivoting on the golden floor. It was fantastic. Impossible! It could not be Susan. His Susan!

She spun about slowly twice. She seemed to crumple, as if the high courage that had sustained her thus far had suddenly run out of her. In her was not the strength to whirl into that state of rapture. She slipped off the edge. She began slowly to fall, tumbling over and over through the air.

Peter stared—and clenched his eyes. He could not watch that tiny, beloved figure be impaled on those horrible barbed spears.

A sigh reached him. It was a sigh of utter desolation— as if the world had given off a sigh of deep regret. Susan was dead! Susan had leaped from that tower and killed herself, so that he and Saunders and Ailena might gain their freedom!

It was incredible that she had done this thing—that Susan, living, breathing, warm Susan—his Susan—had leaped to her death. For death is the hardest of all facts for a lover to grasp. He loved her so much, he could not believe that she was dead. Other people died, but not the person you loved. It couldn't be true! He had saved her from so many dangers—had planned so carefully, with such thoroughness, to save her from this horrible place. He could not believe she was really dead. But she was. She had sacrificed her life to spare his.

20

ESCAPE

AT ABOUT THIS time, Hassan Barbarossa came strenuously to life. He made a snatch for the white reins. He gave them a violent jerk. He roared: "Stop this chariot! Stop it, I say!"

He gave the reins another, stronger jerk. The white horses swerved. Saunders struck the royal hand with the butt of the whip. He jerked the horses back on the original line of their madly galloping flight.

But would the horses enter the tunnel? Horses fear the unknown. They might, at the last moment, swerve in panic to right or left—might refuse to enter the tunnel. Such a hesitation would be disastrous. Doubtless, the chariot would upset. Its occupants would be scattered, perhaps knocked senseless. And the pursuit would be upon them.

But the horses did not swerve. Never hesitating, they plunged into the tunnel's mouth. The great bronze door flashed past overhead. Beyond, dimly, stretched the tunnel, with its other bronze doors, all lifted by the ingenious mechanism which Susan had set going a moment before she plunged to her death.

Peter was struggling with the red-bearded king. They were locked in each other's arms, striking, kicking.

It seemed to Jim Saunders that the bronze doors were starting to close. Doubtless, some one had hastened up the stairs to undo, if possible, what Susan had done—would attempt to trap the fugitives.

Between the fifth and sixth doors, Saunders saw the bronze slab Ailena had mentioned. He saw the ring in the wall—black with the corrosion of age and salt moisture. He would have liked to snatch the ring as he passed, but he was too busy with the charging horses. He realized now that they were running away—that they were utterly beyond human control.

The last of the gates flashed by overhead. It was beginning to close. All twelve, simultaneously, were closing!

PETER MOORE DISENGAGED himself from the powerful arms of Hassan and leaped out of the chariot. He fell and rolled over and over. He scrambled up and ran back down the tunnel.

Trying to fight the terrified horses, Saunders yelled, "Come back! Those gates are closing! You'll be trapped!"

King Hassan jumped out of the lurching golden car. He, too, sprawled, rolled over and over, and scrambled to his feet. He went plunging down the tunnel after Peter, and he was fantastic, even ridiculous, in his rich royal purple robes. He bellowed hoarsely. And from the folds of his robes he plucked, as if by magic, a long and shining dagger.

Jim Saunders now addressed himself solely to the four runaways. Just ahead, glimmering in the lights still burning on the Langpo, was the great basin. The horses were headed straight for it—apparently had no intention of swinging along the rock shelf to left or to right.

When he saw that the maddened horses would doubtless plunge into the water, the vice consul let go the reins, seized Ailena in his arms and jumped clear. They fell, slid and rolled. But neither was badly hurt. And as they got up, the horses and the chariot plunged into the water.

Unaware that Hassan was pursuing him, Peter raced down the tunnel. He passed the sixth gate. He reached the ring in the wall. He gave it a mighty jerk.

Instantly, between the fifth and sixth gates, which were slowly descending, the bronze slab swung down. With a crumbling, a thunderous sound of harsh friction, the hidden slab above came smashing down beyond it. It dropped with a tremendous thud—a slab of bronze fully a foot in thickness. For almost four centuries it had waited there for this moment—a grimly ironical moment indeed in the bloody history of the conquering Barbarossas!

For with this act, Peter had, in some degree, revenged the death of Susan O'Gilvie. He had bottled up the Kingdom of the Lost! But his revenge was not yet finished.

A moment after the great slab dropped down, Hassan arrived, knife in hand, upraised.

Peter threw himself at Hassan. And Hassan, in the dim, far light at the end of the tunnel, saw in the adventurer's face such demon ferocity that, in abrupt dismay, he dropped the knife. With a shout of terror, he turned about and fled.

Peter pursued. And it was an amazing pursuit. Slowly the bronze doors were swinging down. It was a question—a great question—whether he could reach the end of that fantastic passageway without being entombed.

He was not thinking rationally or he would not have wasted precious time in stopping to snatch up the dagger

Hassan had dropped. But he did snatch it up, and in so doing narrowed his chances of escape still further.

He saw Hassan scuttle under the twelfth and last door. It was dropping rapidly, or so it seemed. It was within sixteen inches of the floor when Peter reached it He dropped down, rolled under and, as he sprang up, grasped a handful of Hassan's royal purple robe.

He gave this handful of royal raiment such a tremendous yank that it set Hassan toppling off balance. The red-bearded king spun about. As he did so, Peter scrambled to his knees. In this kneeling position, with his left hand, he seized the king's beard. He pulled Hassan's head down close. Gripping the beard, he drove the dagger into Hassan's throat.

Then, springing up, he gave the dying king a great push. It was a final gesture of loathing, but it capped his revenge with a curious and somewhat horrible touch. Hassan rolled so that his head was under the closing bronze door.

And as Peter watched, the door slowly closed, crushing the head of Hassan as if it were an eggshell.

NOW—NOT TILL NOW—DID Peter blink the bloodmist from his eyes. He was still thinking only of avenging the death of Susan. He did not know—would never know—whether Jengha was living or dead at that moment. He knew only that Jengha had betrayed a trust, had broken a promise. And he thirsted for revenge on Jengha—on them all—the horrible valley full of them, the scornful, decadent members of the royal family—the countless hideous leprous idiots beyond the great wall.

He would bottle this valley forever—for eternity! Only dimly he saw the four Arabian horses struggling in the deep water of the basin; dragged down slowly, inevitably by the weight of the golden chariot.

Only dimly he saw Princess Ailena and Jim Saunders in each other's arms near the bow of the Langpo. He shouted at them to get aboard. He was hardly aware of the gray-faced men who swarmed about the ship.

These dull-witted creatures stared at him with awe and confusion. They had seen him kill their king. But whatever their mood might have become, it changed plastically under the ripping fury of Peter Moore's commands.

With his own hands, he swung the sledge hammer against the bronze stud in the black wall which operated the sea gate mechanism. Those mighty bronze doors were swinging ajar as he climbed aboard, shouting orders to cast off the lines, carrying the sledge hammer across his shoulder—his aspect terrifying, his voice savage.

Ailena and the vice consul stared at him as if he had lost his reason. And, in a sense, he had. The fury that filled him was murderous. It surged through him in a fierce and awful tide of hatred and destruction.

He roared and cursed at the ship's officers. He sent them scurrying into the pilot house. Driving them in ahead of him, he gave the signals with his own hand on the engine-room telegraph. And if these signals had not been obeyed, he would have gone below and executed them himself.

The Langpo backed out of the inner basin and into the great outer basin. Peter ordered the ship brought alongside the bronze stud in the black, shining wall. And with the sledge hammer, he struck it a terrific blow.

Then he returned to the bridge and, pacing back and forth, cursing, watched the massive bronze doors swing shut. He now maneuvered the ship until the bows were pointing at the bronze doors. He ordered the engines in reverse. When the Langpo had backed off a distance equal to a dozen times her length, he signaled for full speed ahead.

One of the officers protested. Peter swarmed upon him, battered him down with blows to the face. The Langpo gathered momentum. She was proceeding almost full speed ahead when her blunt bows crashed into the sea doors.

THE EFFECT WAS, in some degree, that of the irresistible force meeting the immovable body. The doors did not yield. But the bows did. They crumpled. It was surprising how slowly they crumpled. The heavy bow plates buckled and bent and curled with a tremendous snarling, ripping sound. There was clashing and rumblings and explosions. It was like the sounds of an erupting volcano. The ship pressed steadily and irresistibly against the gates, and they did not yield a fraction of an inch.

The momentum of the ship, with engines still spinning her screw at full speed ahead, poured itself out, thoroughly collapsing the bows.

Above the sounds of rending, splitting, bending, buckling metal now came the roar of inrushing water. The Langpo began rapidly to settle by the head.

Jim Saunders was getting a lifeboat ready to put overboard, throwing off the tarpaulin, untangling the falls.

The ship's hull had apparently been opened, by the strain, farther aft. She began rapidly to sink. Now the boilers began to explode, tearing out huge sections of the deck, aft, spraying the water all about with fragments of torn steel and splintered wood.

And in the midst of the tremendous, sustained uproar of a ship disintegrating, there was an amazing development. Peter was left alone on the bridge. As he paced from wing to wing, watching his handiwork, he saw the crew leaping overboard. Each man left on the surface, as he plunged, spreading stains of red. They were committing a form of hari-kari! Each man, as he leaped, plunged a knife into his heart!

It was the final fantastic touch to the most incredible, most terrifying experience Peter Moore had ever undergone. Doubtless, these dull-witted men had been instructed, in the course of their training, to do just this. In the event of capture, in the event of their defeat by any one from the outworld, they were simply to erase themselves from existence!

But even this shocking wholesale suicide of the Langpo's crew was a scene observed through swimming mists. His deeds he saw clearly. He looked with triumph at the great bronze doors. They were forever closed! Even if the frantic inhabitants of the valley should succeed, in time, in cutting through or around that slab of bronze in the tunnel, they would never cut their way through or around these sea doors! The Langpo, now on the bottom, jammed against the doors, would prevent their being opened.

The Kingdom of the Lost was bottled up forever.

How long, he wondered, was forever? How long could they exist without food supplies from the outworld? How long could they exist without salt? With their salt supply forever cut off, would not the leprous idiots in the valley go stark mad? Would they not insanely swarm over the forbidden wall and destroy the members of the royal household? Would not the prisoners, all the prisoners, in that valley suffer a swift moral and physical decay—dying in terror, in frantic agony?

Peter believed so. He had, in effect, issued the death sentence to more than a hundred thousand mortals. Yet he did not suffer the smallest pang of regret.

To him, the valley was not a valley of the living or the dying, but a tomb—a sarcophagus which contained the mortal remains of the only woman he had ever loved—or ever could love.

THE MAIN DECK was awash when he went down the ladder from the bridge. But the Langpo would sink no deeper. She was resting solidly on the bottom.

Jim Saunders had cast the lifeboat adrift. He was sitting at the oars, with Ailena, white-faced, sobbing, in the stern.

Peter looked at them for a moment. His face was gray, his eyes were haggard. He had become, in the past few minutes, a changed man—a man immune to the passions and the follies of the world, a man strangely and coldly detached, a man without love of life or fear of death. Thus, completely changed, he faced what life had left for him.

There was a strange and bitter smile at his lips.

Saunders said gently, "We'd better get going, Pete. We've got a long row ahead of us—out through those pinnacle rocks. But there won't be anything to worry about in the Jaws of Hell. You've locked them tight! You've settled that mystery forever. No more vanishing ships!"

Peter did not speak for a moment. He looked at the vice

consul, then he looked at the pale and frightened girl as if they were strangers to him.

He said quietly: "I came on this trip for two purposes. One was to save the girl I loved from an unknown danger. The other was to secure some diamonds belonging to a friend of mine. At least, I want to be able to say that I've accomplished half of my job."

Peter waded through ankle deep water to the funnel. He climbed the steel ladder to the top. He reached down inside.

Within, the funnel was thickly crusted with soot. In places it was an inch thick. He could not at first find the end of the fine wire he had attached to a rivet head, the rivet and the wire being so thickly encrusted with the greasy black dust. Soot in a busy funnel forms rapidly, like an evil fungus. Very shortly after Peter had suspended the box of diamonds in the funnel, he had known that the wire would be thickly crusted—invisible to the most prying eyes.

Only by tearing the ship apart, piece by piece, he believed, would those diamonds have been found.

He detached the wire and pulled up the little metal box. He rapped it against the funnel as he descended to free it of its thick casing of soot. Reaching the deck, he made his way slowly to the waiting boat.

THEY WERE PICKED up on the second day by a fishing junk out of Hainan. Two weeks later, on a little coastwise tramp, they reached Hong Kong. The two men and the girl had entered into a sacred agreement: So long as they lived, they would never mention the Valley of the Lost.

Peter delivered the fortune in precious stones to Dan

de Sylva, refused to make the slightest explanation, and requested, as payment, the whimsical little elephant-head ring, once the property of the now insane Sultan of Sakara.

He attended the quiet wedding of Jim Saunders and Princess Ailena, and spent their last evening in Hong Kong with them—gave them a wedding dinner, in fact, at the Colonial Hotel. The red-haired princess, still too dazed by what she had been through, still haunted by Susan's sacrifice, was only beginning to enjoy civilization. She would, in time, forget and become very happy—because hers was a happy nature.

Their ship sailed for San Francisco at midnight. Peter saw them off. He returned to shore in a sampan. He knew how risky it was to venture on the harbor of Hong Kong after dark in an unlicensed sampan.

But he was not concerned over his safety. He was not afraid of a knife between his shoulder blades. He knew that he would never be afraid of death again.

He watched the lights of that fabulous Oriental city as the sampan swung toward Blake's Jetty. Far up on the Peak, the lights mingled, blended with the stars.

Susan had loved Hong Kong. She had loved its lights, its fogs, its mysteries, its romance. For a moment, he had the mystic feeling that Susan was sitting beside him. He could detect the fragrance of her hair. He could, for an illusory, fleeting moment, hear the brightness of her gay young voice. Then the magical, intoxicating moment passed.

He sighed. Coolly he contemplated the city of lost dreams. And he wondered what fresh surprises life could possibly hold for a man who feared neither death nor the devil.

OVER THE DRAGON WALL

A dragon, green as an emerald, that ate men, was destined to shock Peter the Brazen into the most stupendous surprise of his life

1

"SHE LIVES!"

THE GLITTER OF the ugly little idol arrested the young American in mid-stride. He stopped, bent down and peered through the window of Ko Chang's jade shop.

Here, if he wasn't mistaken, was a treasure: a specimen of plum-blossom jade beautifully carved into the likeness of the Chinese god of wrath.

It should have been in one of the world's great jade collections. Wondering if the proprietor knew its worth, the tall young American went into the shop, a dimly-lighted place that smelled a century old.

Ko Chang, it quickly developed, was well aware of the worth of that bit of carved plum-blossom jade. It was not for sale. It was, he cheerfully admitted, nothing but a lure—and would the young masta seatee him and lookee-see other velly fine otticals?

The tall young American informed Ko Chang, in fluent and flowery Cantonese—for all this occurred in the busy port of Hong Kong—that he was the thrice-accursed offspring of a turnip, and that his ancestors had spent their lives filching coppers from the eyelids of the dead.

Ko Chang, who was old and fat and amiable, chuckled throughout this indictment, then fetched other items of merit. But the American was not interested in a Ming vase mended with gold, or a perfume bottle carved from a single white opal, or the rose quartz chop of an emperor.

He wanted the God of Wrath. Ko Chang, smiling benevolently, waddled to the rear of his shop for more treasures in miniature.

The American did not see a gray figure slip in from the street—a figure as gray as the fog from which it might have detached itself—and slide a small flat greenish object along the counter toward his elbow. In fact, the American was unaware that this creature of the fog had come and gone, so swift, so stealthy had he been.

But he presently became aware of the flat little object the mysterious unseen one had left behind. It was a perfectly round disc of about the size and thickness of a silver dollar. It was pale green in color and was probably one of the many cheap Japanese imitations of jade.

One side of the stone disc was smooth. On the other had been hastily engraved two Chinese symbols. It looked at a quick glance like a good luck charm, and the symbols might have meant long life or happiness or any of a number

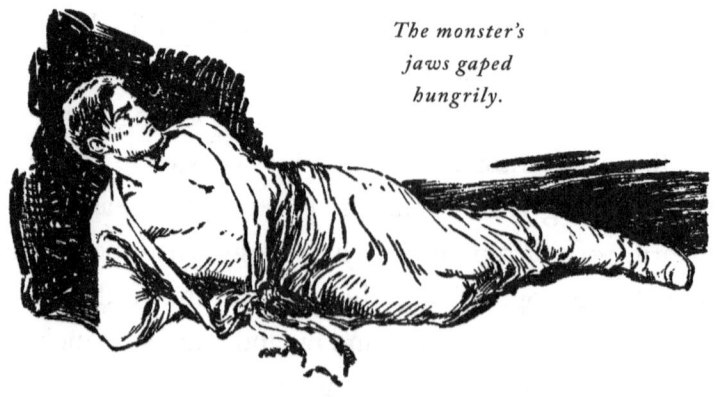

The monster's jaws gaped hungrily.

of such banal sentiments. But these characters spelled nothing of the kind. They conveyed sharply to the young man's startled brain the concise message: *She Lives!*

The young man snatched up the imitation jade disc and brought his fist smashing down on the counter. Ko Chang came waddling, a beaming smile at his full lips, a gleam of silver in his hand.

The American sprang up. His face, gray and haggard a moment ago, was flushed with anger and his eyes were sapphires of dancing wrath.

"What thing?" he snapped.

The shop keeper stared at the pale green disc and, with a puzzled air, shook his head. "My no savvy."

"Why did you putee it my?" the young man shouted.

"But I did not putee it you, masta!"

Ko Chang stepped back a little, for the American had

the look in his blue eyes of a man who might become dangerously violent. Savagely, he threw the disc of imitation jade to the stone floor, but there was evidently little satisfaction for him in seeing it break into a dozen fragments, for his eyes did not change, nor did his face lose its threatening dark look. He strode out of the jade shop, leaving Ko Chang staring after his broad back with beady, bulging eyes.

HE STRODE THROUGH the dusk of Hong Kong, blind to the beauties of the south China evening, softened by the thinning mist—the purpling sky, the lights sparkling like fabulous jewels flung down from the eminence of the Peak.

He strode to and into the nearest bar. It was cocktail hour in Hong Kong. Frosty shakers were singing their tinkling songs. Voices were raised in laughter and convivial conversation.

The American found a place at the bar and ordered a Scotch and soda. A voice behind him boomed: "Pete Moore! You big palooka—just the man I'm looking for!"

Peter Moore turned. A tall, bronzed man of about his age was reaching for his hand. He said without enthusiasm, "Hello, Fordyce."

He had never liked Jim Fordyce, a rich man's son who had been sent to China to occupy an unimportant post in his father's banking house. He had once seen Fordyce strike a rickshaw coolie with his stick, and Moore had little use for that breed of American.

"I heard you were in town," Fordyce was saying.

"What will you drink?"

"A daiquiri."

Moore gave the order to the barman and Fordyce said,

"My sister and my fiancée just came in on the Empress of Britain. They've both heard all about you. Dying to know you. You never met Doris, did you?"

"Doris?"

"My little sister. You'll love Doris. She's just your type. Loves adventure—any kind of excitement. Oh, she'll eat you alive. We'll have dinner, then go down to Recourse and dance. What, what?"

"I'm sorry," the other began.

"Now, now, now! Don't go and get pious on me, Pete. You're not doing a damned thing, or you wouldn't be here drinking alone. Nasty habit, drinking alone. I never drink alone except the first two hours after I get up. Doris is a grand little egg, even if she is my own sister. And she isn't a prude. The chances are, she'll be in your lap an hour after she knows you. She's the demonstrative type. Is it a date?"

"I'm sorry."

The somewhat blurred gray eyes of the other American became a little sharper as they centered on Moore's face. Fordyce swiftly acquired the ugly look of the spoiled only son when thwarted. He became nasty.

"What's happened to you? Have you been sick? You look like hell!"

Moore, with his gaunt eyes and tragic, embittered mouth, looked haggard, old. He said nothing. Fordyce, still staring hard at his face, cried: "Say! What's become of that little American cutey you were running around with—the one with that big pile of money? O'Gilvie, that's it! Susan O'Gilvie! I'm glad to see you've given her the air. With all her money, she was nothing but a little bum."

Peter Moore's right fist snapped in an arc to the Fordyce

mouth. He had sensed it would happen. It had to happen. He had supposed that people had talked about him and Susan O'Gilvie, for with her wealth and her capacity for dangerous mischief, it was inevitable that she be discussed. He could not yet bear to hear her name mentioned, and Jim Fordyce's insult had released a little of the desperate fury corked up in him.

There was an instant of confusion in which he saw Jim Fordyce stretched out on the floor, blinking up at him, with blood trickling from his mouth. Men seemed to be milling about. Then a tall Mongolian with a scar—the Hong Kong version of a bouncer—came pushing through the crowd. When he laid rough hands on Peter Moore, the young man slugged him, too. And in the greater confusion made his way to the street.

He was sorry he had acted so hastily.

He wasn't in the habit of going about punching people. Yet Fordyce had had it coming.

HE PROCEEDED TO his hotel, the Colonial. He knew he should not be living on such a lavish scale. His funds were almost gone. Soon he would have to begin casting about for some means of livelihood. Yet, in the passing months since Susan had killed herself, he had lost all passion for life and all respect for death. For life without Susan, her loveliness, her lively companionship, had proved barren and bitter.

As he entered the lobby, a gray-haired man arose from a chair and came toward him, faintly smiling—a short, brisk man with a round, ruddy countenance and twinkling eyes. He appeared to be about fifty-five, and Moore might have been amused could he have known that this chubby, merry-looking, middle-aged person was little less than a handmaiden of destiny.

He said, in a cheerful voice, "You're Peter Moore, aren't you?"

Moore   stopped. "Yes." The round beaming face was vaguely familiar.

"Do you remember meeting me in Shanghai a couple of years ago?

Peter Moore

I'm Judd Burton. There was a little unpleasantness with a number of Japanese soldiers. Specifically, they shoved me and the lady who was with me off a sidewalk and into the mud. Then a Jap sergeant insulted us—and you took a hand. Remember?"

Peter Moore nodded. He had forgotten all of that incident but the insolence of the Japanese sergeant and the indignation of a middle-aged American gentleman and an elderly woman who were standing in mud to their ankles.

"You showed us some nice jujutsu, and you said your name was Peter Moore, but it didn't mean anything at the time. Since then, it seems to me I've heard your name everywhere I've turned."

Peter Moore dryly remarked: "I'm supposed to be a pretty shady character."

Mr. Burton looked amused and he made a grave statement. "My business is collecting wild animals."

Moore smiled. "And you want me for your collection?"

"The truth is, I have a very difficult job for someone, and I believe you are the only man in the Far East capable of doing it. Shall we have a drink and discuss it?"

Peter Moore assented. They went into the bar. In a secluded corner, over a table adorned with two highballs, Judd Burton went into detail.

"I'll admit, I've had you checked up," he said. "I heard plenty about your courage, your daredevil feats, and—I hope you will accept my deepest condolences for the death of Miss O'Gilvie."

The young man sharply interrupted: "What did you hear about her?"

"Very little, Mr. Moore. I heard that she was, at the time of her death, the richest young woman in America, if not in the world. And that she had gone into adventuring in a big way in the Far East, and that you had sometimes, quite magically, succeeded in getting her out of a number of very dangerous scrapes.

"And I heard that she had somehow lost her life in a strange place in the north of Indo-China."

"A valley of death," Moore amended moodily. "With only one avenue of escape—a tunnel, full of bronze gates, at the dead end. She climbed a tower in the top of which were the gate controls." The young man's eyes were bleak with that dreadful memory.

"She opened the gates and then she jumped from that tower so the rest of us could get away."

"How horrible! Who lives in this valley?"

"A race of inbred human monsters—thousands of them." Moore hesitated. His eyes were rather wild. "I gave my word I'd never breathe a word about that place, but I can't help it. I'm losing my mind. I've got to talk about it."

HIS VOICE HAD risen to the point where other men in the bar were turning to stare. He became aware of this and stopped, glaring down at his clenched fists on the table. He snatched up the highball glass and swiftly drained it.

"You can be sure," the older man said, "I'll respect your confidence. Get it off your chest. Waiter—two more."

Peter Moore talked. He described the voyage of the mysterious ship which had taken him and Susan, both virtually prisoners, to that hateful valley; he told Mr. Burton of the soulless beings who inhabited this valley— these horrible slaves who had been ruled for centuries by descendants of the original Hassan Barbarossa, the Mediterranean pirate who had established a hidden kingdom there. And he related the dramatic story of his escape from that monstrous place.

"I bottled it up," he said in a low, venomous voice. "I jammed the sea gates by sinking their ship across the entrance. None of them will ever escape! The thousands of them will die like rats. Without food, without salt, they can't live!"

Once again, Moore's voice had risen with the emotion of that shocking narrative. Once again, he got himself under control.

His eyes were as fixed, as lusterless as those of a dead man.

Exhausted by the emotion of that experience re-lived, he said huskily, with irony, "Mr. Burton, you're enjoying the privilege of looking at a man who has murdered a half million people!"

Judd Burton, staring at him with fascination, vigorously shook his gray head. "No, Peter," he said gently. "I can't look at it that way. You deserve nothing but sympathy. I think," he went on more briskly, "I have something to take your mind off that ghastly experience. What are your plans?"

The young man shrugged.

"Then mine may interest you. I want to secure some sensational animal freak for the C.C.A. Something that will—"

"The C.C.A.?"

"Consolidated Circuses of America. Actually, this isn't up my street. I supply circuses and zoological gardens with animals and reptiles of all descriptions—but normal, run-of-the-mill specimens—tigers, elephants, snakes. This is an exceptional situation, calling for exceptional skill. You may know that the circus business in America has fallen upon very lean years, due to the depression, the movies, the radio and other changes in the national life. Circuses have to fight to keep alive—to attract the crowds. They even shoot men from cannons. Nothing is sensational enough. And I'm here to find something exceptionally sensational for the Consolidated sideshow department.

"It must be something the press agents can play up to the limit—something that will attract people in mobs."

"Quite a large order," Peter commented.

"I've found it!" The animal collector paused to sip his drink and light a cigar. He exhaled rich blue smoke and whispered: "It's a dragon!"

PETER MOORE'S CLEAR blue eyes regarded him over the top of his highhall glass, but the young man made no comment.

"A real Chinese dragon!" Mr. Burton declared. "As green as an emerald! And it's not a croc and it's not a 'gator. You don't believe it!"

"Perhaps I never happened to drink the right kind of liquor."

"It's a temple dragon," the animal collector explained. "And I've checked up on it. It's alive. It can't be wholly a fake. Too many people have reported it to me—and the reports jibe! I've convinced myself that it exists."

"Where?" Moore asked quietly.

"It's a hill temple in a big town—a city to the west of Indo-China, on the fringe of eastern Tibet, actually in the Himalayan foothills. Ever hear of Sandrakar?"

"Yes."

"Ever been there?"

"No."

"It's the Moon tribe, a branch of the Moosars, mixed with Tibetan."

"I know that tribe. Some of them are tree pygmies."

"These men aren't pygmies. They're big men—pale yellow men. And devilishly clever and as barbaric as a Chinese execution. What I've heard about this beast, this so-called dragon, convinces me that it's unusual—a true freak, what scientists call a sport. Maybe it's a throwback to the dinosaur age. Maybe it's painted green. I don't care. Too many natives have brought me reports on it."

"Any white men?" Moore interrupted.

"No white men." Mr. Burton's polished blue eyes became a little narrow. It gave him an effect of shrewdness. "It's dangerous territory for white men. If it weren't, I wouldn't be trying to enlist your aid. The description, briefly, is this:

the monster is emerald green, or grass green, perhaps twenty feet long, perhaps a little under that, and twice a year it becomes white hot."

"And it's alive?" the other murmured.

"Absolutely alive! Mind you, Moore, I don't say this description is accurate. It is a sacred animal—the central figure of a comparatively new but powerful religion—an abortive kind of Buddhism."

"Then no man could get it out alive," Moore said flatly.

Mr. Burton nodded understandingly. "I've heard about some of your adventures with strange oriental religions. Yet you took chances as great as this—and came out alive."

"Not with a twenty-foot white-hot dragon."

The older man laughed nervously. "It's worth trying, son. It's probably as dangerous as any expedition you ever embarked on. It should appeal to you. Certainly, it will snap you out of your doldrums."

"And it probably isn't a dragon," Moore argued.

"I DON'T CARE a damn what it is. I want it. I'm convinced it's a freak, a sport. Here, briefly, is my proposition. I will place ten thousand dollars, in American money, in escrow in the Bank of Hong Kong, payable to you on delivery alive in Hong Kong of this creature, whatever it is. In addition, I will advance you, on your word that you will undertake the expedition, a sum of five thousand Mex for expenses. If it proves to be a croc or a 'gator, painted green, then I lose. But I don't expect to lose. The Moosar country—the lower country—is a 'gator and crocodile infested region. Those people aren't going to nominate a croc or a 'gator for a new god."

Mr. Burton, flushed from the exertions of persuasion,

drank the rest of his highball and ordered two more. His eyes were shining now with the eagerness of a high pressure salesman.

"And you won't go at it single-handed," he went on. "I've arranged for the best help you could possibly have. In the village of Khava, about thirty miles from Sandrakar, a man named Charlie Ling is now camped with a caravan of fifteen elephants and upwards of forty mahouts, gun bearers, beaters, and roustabouts. Charlie Ling procures most of my Burmese and Siamese specimens for me. He is courageous, dependable, and absolutely loyal."

"What's his nationality?"

"Eurasian. Chinese and English."

The light of interest in the young American's eyes faded. Judd Burton saw it fade. He leaned forward with an earnest air.

"I know how you feel about Eurasians. They're ordinarily cowardly and treacherous and lazy. Not Charlie Ling. He's an exceptional fellow. I've had him for fifteen years. He's been through countless jams with me. You can count on Charlie Ling. He has saved my life. He has saved me from crooks and footpads and thieves. He is a man you can trust without stint or limit. He will obey your orders implicitly. I will give you letters to him, of course."

Mr. Burton paused again, with his shrewd eyes on the adventurer's lean, hard, tanned face. Evidently the animal collector was not reassured by what he saw there, for he cried, "Now—now—now! Before you make a negative answer—and I'm afraid I can see it in your eyes—let me make a fatherly suggestion. I know how you must feel over the loss of your fiancée. Wouldn't you really be happier, easier in your mind, if you were in action—matching your wits once again with difficulties and dangers?"

"I've lost my respect for danger."

Mr. Burton's flexible features were swiftly mobilized into an expression of deep concern. "I don't want you to walk deliberately into suicide!" he said sharply.

"I have no intention of committing suicide."

The animal collector seemed relieved. He grinned and said, "That's better, Peter! You'll get some good healthy excitement, going over the wall for that dragon!"

And Peter said, as if to himself, "Over the dragon wall!"

"Yes, I know that expression," Mr. Burton said hastily. "It's Chinese for death—the act of dying. But there's another meaning—the ascent to any earthly plane of happiness."

"Will I find that," Peter asked gravely, "on the other side of that wall?"

Mr. Burton chuckled. "You'll certainly find excitement, which is one form of happiness. Will you go after my dragon—matching your wits, once again, with dangers—difficulties?"

Peter hesitated a moment longer. Then, "Yes," he said crisply.

It was because of the obvious risks involved that Peter actually decided to undertake this strange mission—to attempt to steal and deliver in Hong Kong a twenty-foot dragon, green as an emerald, that ate men and twice a year became white hot!

2

—

SUSAN'S ESCAPE

FOR SUSAN O'GILVIE—GAY, beautiful, mischievous
Susan—for whom he had been mourning these past six
months—was not dead. And the manner of her escape
from the Kingdom of the Lost was even more amazing
than the fact of her existence.

To Peter Moore, her death had been a matter of utmost
certainty. He had seen her race up the spiral stairway of
the tower—that fantastic pillar of stone called the tower of
whirling ecstasy—had seen her emerge, in her green cere-
monial robes, on the little floor at the top of the tower. He
had seen her whirl about and topple from the edge, and
he had assumed that she had plunged to her death on the
barbed iron spears set into the ground far below. Actually,
he had not seen her fall. He had shut his eyes, and he had
heard a gasp from the thousands who were watching. He
had thought that this great sigh, emitted by that multitude
had been one of horror and regret at her doom. But he had
not seen the first of the Barbarossa soldiers, swarming up
the stairway, reach the top of the tower; had not seen one
of these men race out, reach out at peril of his own life to
grasp a fold of the green gown the instant Susan O'Gilvie
fell. Thus, he did not know that the vast sigh, the gasping

of thousands of throats, was one of relief at her miraculous salvation.

He had presumed she was dead before he and the two others with whom he had escaped from that valley of horrors had reached the narrow tunnel which led to liberty. He only knew that she had killed herself, sacrificed herself, so that he and those others might escape.

That interval had been, in fact, one of sick confusion to Peter Moore. He had escaped through the tunnel, and he had sealed the one escape from the valley forever by ramming the great bronze sea gates with the Barbarossas' ship—sinking the ship against those gates so that they could never again be opened. To him, it had not been murder—the penning up forever of those half million human monsters. It had been the sealing of the tomb of the only woman he had ever loved.

Susan O'Gilvie, in his heart, would never die. But in his mind, in his embittered thoughts, she was dead. In his mind's eye, a thousand times, he had seen that slim, beloved figure falling through the air to sudden, shocking death. Her escape from the death he had pictured so morosely so many times, and her escape from the dread valley constituted a chapter of miracles.

Thousands saw that soldier seize the fold of her green gown, snatch her back from the brink of oblivion. Among them was a Burmese, a prisoner on the other side of the great wall which divided the valley, with its unscalable, cliff-like sides, into two unequal parts—the smaller part where the rulers lived, and the larger part, where the innumerable slaves of the Barbarossas existed like animals.

This Burmese was called Lak Lon. He was an old, old

man, a white-bearded, rheumy-eyed old man from the Province of Tashwar, in northern Burma. Five years previously he had been captured from a Malayan felucca by the raiding ship of the Barbarossas. He had been on an errand for his master, the sultan

Susan

Pra Ki Saludin, of Tashwar. He had been brought into the Kingdom of the Lost aboard the Barbarossas' raider—a true raider of the deep—and consigned to the living death of the human animals who lived on the "other side" of the great wall.

In spite of his age, his white beard, his palsy, Lak Lon was shrewd and clever. And since the moment of his imprisonment, he had been perfecting a plan of escape from this hideous place. This plan, it chanced, was ripe—quite ripe—on the day when Peter Moore and the two whom he had helped escape made good their getaway through the tunnel and forever sealed up the only exit from the valley.

Old Lak Lon had watched the slender girl in green run up the spiral steps and into the control room of the tower. He knew about that machinery, too. Because of the excitement about him, he knew that the girl in green was racing to the control room, and he knew presently that she had succeeded. He heard the shouts and cries of alarmed sentries on the great wall. He heard the uproar of the unseen people on the other side of the wall as Peter Moore and his two friends made good their escape—the first time in the history of the valley that anyone had escaped.

Shrewdly, he reasoned that this girl had sacrificed herself to race up the stairs to the control room, to throw the great levers opening the series of bronze gates in the tunnel, so that someone else might escape.

HE SAW THIS girl's attempt at suicide. And he saw presently that an even greater excitement was agitating the ruling class on the other side of the wall. Shortly the rumor reached the enslaved wretches, of which old Lak Lon was one—the terrifying rumor that those who had escaped through the tunnel had corked up this valley forever!

Having spent most of his life in the most turbulent state in the world, which is India, Lak Lon was accustomed to mob excitement, the frenzy of politico-religious mobs. Yet in all his life, he had never seen any mob behave quite so madly as this.

The half-idiots about him—the leprous, inhuman beasts, men and women and children, of which this great howling mass was composed—had passed that rumor from mouth to mouth, and all had lost what little reason was left to them.

The sealing up of that tunnel by those who had escaped meant that the valley was doomed—for through that tunnel trickled the valley's food supply, and almost as important as the food, the supply of salt without which this mob would soon be reduced to a state even lower than that to which it had attained.

Life could have meant but little to any of these poor wretches, yet their rabid protests against death proved how ferocious is the will to exist under even the most miserable circumstances.

They shrieked and howled. They ran about aimlessly, babbling. They flung themselves on the ground. Many of them engaged in fights to the death. The cries, howls, shrieks from their throats became a profane and dreadful roaring which shook the sultry air and reverberated in awful waves from precipice to precipice.

Then, leaderless, with a singleness of purpose that would have chilled the blood of the most fearless onlooker, they rushed at the great wall. The sentries had disappeared. The first wave of humanity broke, like the senseless wave of an ocean, against the wall. Others surged in after it, upon it. Others swarmed upon the fallen. Successive waves that followed reached the top of the wall and broke over it—this mass of screaming human monsters.

The little food, the little salt, remaining in the valley was in the possession of the Barbarossas.

Lak Lon was knocked down and trampled on when the mob first surged toward the great wall. He picked himself up and watched with the calm detachment of shrewd, wily old age. His plan was already taking form in his mind. He would escape, but not alone.

Except for the crippled, the blind, the dying, he was the last man left behind the wall. The gate, on the palace side, had been opened. He walked serenely through and into the forbidden territory. A few guns were blazing, but these few firearms in the possession of the rulers could have no more checked that flood of insane humanity than if it had been a tidal wave.

Lak Lon looked calmly, shrewdly over that mad scene.

The palace and its grounds were almost invisible under the swarming slaves. They were going in at doors and at windows. They were crawling up the façade. They reminded Lak Lon of so many starving lice.

HE WAS LOOKING for the girl in green. His plans for her were very simple. If he returned to his sultan, after these five years of absence, no explanations, no excuses would be acceptable, and Lak Lon would lose cast, for Sultan Pra Ki Saludin was a monarch of very little imagination.

But if Lak Lon were to return to Tashwar with a beautiful white girl as a gift for Pra Ki Saludin, the sultan would require no explanation. For Pra Ki Saludin was a great admirer, a lover of beautiful women. He had many in his harem. And there was always room for one more. If Lak Lon could somehow deliver this beautiful girl in green to his master, Sultan Pra Ki Saludin would reward him fittingly, and life would be very pleasant for Lak Lon to the end of his days.

There, in a nutshell, was Lak Lon's plan. It remained only for him to find the girl in the green robes and to spirit her out of this dreadful valley.

Lak Lon found her, as he had hoped he might, at the base of the tower, where her rescuers had abandoned her when the rumor spread that the tunnel was forever closed.

She was unconscious—lying in a little crumpled heap where they had dropped her. Lak Lon studied the pale, beautiful face long and thoughtfully. And was delighted, for she was even more beautiful than he had hoped. He permitted himself a moment of great self-satisfaction. Yet he was quickly aware of his need for haste. For the time being, the mob, in its hysteria, thought only of food—food and salt. But the time would soon be here when a beautiful young girl would be in the greatest danger.

Kneeling down, he slapped her face briskly, and when she opened her eyes and stared up dazedly into his face, Lak Lon cried, in clear English: "Up! Up! We must escape!"

He helped her to her feet and Susan O'Gilvie stared with large, dazed eyes at the maddened scene about her. Yet it hardly registered on her senses. It was all, in truth, a meaningless confusion. A curtain had snapped across her brain. Her memory was gone. And the shock of her experience had numbed all the departments of her brain.

Only vaguely was she aware of any of this insane uproar and mob hysteria. Lak Lon, with his rheumy eyes, his tangled beard, his rags, his urgency to hurry, hurry—he, too, was the filament of a dream.

He had to help her most of the way. She did not remember passing through the gate and entering the dreary land on the other side of the great wall.

Her brain was clearing a little, but when she tried to think of what had happened beyond a few minutes ago, her brain refused to help her. She remembered being on top of a high tower with several strange, yelling men about her, men who looked alike, with strange, death-like faces. It was as if her life had begun at that point. She did not know who she was or what she was doing in this amazing place. She asked the hurrying old man beside her who he was, and he answered impatiently, "Lak Lon—hurry, hurry!"

And when she asked him what this place was and what she was doing in it, he only glanced at her sharply and made no reply.

"But who am I?" she cried.

His answer to that was a shrug, and: "We are what fate makes us. Hurry!"

She gave it up for the time being. The pace he was setting used all her breath, all her energy. The strangeness of the great valley frightened her, and her inability to remember the past made her want to cry.

IT SEEMED TO her that they walked and walked for an immeasurable time. But at length they came to that part of the valley, half way between the wall and the farther end, which Lak Lon had studied all these years so cannily, observing a little niche here, a projecting rock there, in the fresh crevice, result of a slide, up which Lak Lon was certain a man could climb to freedom.

For five years, day in and day out, the old Burmese had studied that crevice, had made mental measurements, had firmly decided that escape by that avenue was more than a possibility.

Old age on his part, weakness and confusion and uncertainty on the part of the girl, made it a long and heartbreaking performance. It was dusk when they began that tremendous undertaking. Rocks gave way and started small avalanches below them. Niches on which Lak Lon had counted proved to be nothing but discolorations. If there had been anyone to hinder them, if there had been the usual sentries, they could never have undertaken even the first fourth of that perilous climb. But there were no sentries. There were, however, other prisoners who now saw what Lak Lon had so painstakingly studied out over these past five years.

Long before dark, at least a hundred of those leprous

wretches were following that painfully blazed trail. When dark came, it was necessary to wait.

While they rested, Susan, after she had caught her breath, told the old Burmese that she had lost her memory, and she asked him questions.

"Who am I?"

"If you do not know," he answered, "how can I know?"

"But what was I doing in this place?"

"I have no answers to such questions. I lived with those on the wrong side of the wall. You lived on the other side. You lived with kings and queens, yet you are not one of them. You speak only English. I think you came from a land across the sea, a place where white barbarians live in houses a mile tall and ride about in vehicles made of the purest gold. Only Buddha knows these answers."

"What was I doing on that tower?"

"You were about to throw yourself into space."

"Why?" Susan gasped.

"I know nothing of the way of the Barbarossas."

Perched there in the darkness, high on the side of the cliff, with a chill wind in her face, with a soft continuous roaring sound coming from far below, Susan was suddenly terrified. She had a sense of awful loneliness. She was a soul lost between worlds. She pressed her palms to her throbbing temples and tried to think. But she could not remember who she had been or how she had come to this place, or from where.

When Lak Lon told her that the Kingdom of the Lost was in northeastern Indo-China, it meant nothing to her.

He told her the story of the Kingdom of the Lost, of the cruel and selfish Barbarossas, but he was evasive when she asked him where he was taking her. "To a safe refuge," was all he could say. And at his evasiveness, her feeling of helplessness grew. He boasted of his cleverness in planning and plotting this escape. And he told her how fortunate she was that he had selected her to save. "You would have been a little white rabbit in a den of wolves."

A mountain peak beyond the far side of the mountain began to glow palely. A tip of the moon appeared. "We climb again," the old man said.

When the moon set, another long wait was necessary. Many hours later, dawn came and they commenced again, and the human chain below them lengthened and became a long, thin, winding snake.

Near the top, the crevice narrowed, and at the very top it was precipitous and hardly wide enough to admit the passage of a human body. It was necessary to squirm and writhe and claw one's way through this part.

LAK LON WAS the first to squirm, claw and wriggle through. Then he reached down, snatched at the girl's hands and dragged her up to safety. But Lak Lon wasn't finished. He hated that valley and its denizens with the peculiar cold and malignant hate of which only an Oriental is capable. He had blazed the trail, but he was determined that that mob of leprous idiots would not profit by his patience and cleverness.

There were any number of boulders lying about on the great green plateau on which the two refugees found themselves. Lak Lon undertook to roll the largest of them over the crack up through which he and the girl had squirmed, but he was not quite fast enough. Three men—a Mongolian prisoner of several years, and two of the death-like valley men—came squirming up and went their ways before Lak Lon could roll the boulder into place. It did not cover enough of the crack to suit him, so he rolled others.

Some of the stones were too small, and fell through, and they accomplished, in another way, what he had set out to do. They plunged through the opening, and they started a slide. And as they bounded down through the crevice, they started other slides. The long line of men, following Lak Lon's and Susan O'Gilvie's trail, was checked. Many of them were brushed off into space and sudden death by the accumulating slides, and when these rocks and the slides they precipitated had finished their work, the path had been wiped out of existence.

Susan watched some of this, and was terrified by it. As if she had just been born into this world of cruelty and horror, she remained in a state of helpless loneliness. She was afraid of this crochety old man with his curt answers to her questions, his elusiveness as to her fate. She knew that he had some scheme for her, that his interest in her was not unselfish. Yet there was no one else to whom she could appeal. If she could only remember who she was!

Lak Lon and Susan started off in a southwesterly direction. They saw no more of the tall Mongolian and the two valley men. It was, perhaps, this Mongolian who, upon reaching Hong Kong, saw and recognized Peter Moore and stealthily placed at his elbow in Ko Chang's jade shop the mystic message which had so upset the young man, for Peter Moore had hosts of unknown friends among the natives.

Of that trek across the great green plateau and later, across the almost impenetrable jungles which followed it, Susan O'Gilvie would never recall more than random details. She remembered it chiefly as a passage through the most desolate and friendless and tortured country she had ever seen.

THERE WERE DEEP canyons to cross, and areas strewn with giant boulders—a country so tortured, so danger-ous that it was, to Lak Lon, easy to understand why, in all these centuries, no one from the outside world had ever discovered that great crack in the earth's crust known as the Valley of the Lost.

But he said nothing of any of this to Susan. His was a race that held women in little respect. Yet Susan had no real cause for complaint. He treated her considerately. He saw to it that she had enough to eat and drink. And on two occasions, he went out of his way to save her life—once when they were climbing along a precipice, and she slipped and fell to a ledge below, and once when they were cross-ing a swift, little mountain stream, and she slipped from a mossy rock and fell into the icy water.

Yet her distrust of him did not diminish. As time passed, her brain grew clearer, yet her old memory, it seemed, was gone forever.

On one score there can be no question: if Lak Lon had not been a jungle man, and had he not been intimately familiar with jungle ways, jungle animals, and jungle meth-ods of securing safe, edible food, they would never have emerged on the other side of those trackless tropical thick-ets.

With nothing but a small knife, he hollowed out a log and fashioned it into a crude canoe, and with no other implements he fashioned a paddle. And with the same tool, he hacked their way through a lacework of lianas which would have otherwise been impenetrable. In fact, without Lak Lon's jungle knowledge, and without Lak Lon's knife, that journey could never have been attempted.

Armed only with the useful knife and his jungle sense, the wrinkled old Burmese took the richest girl in America through that first jungle, then through other jungles in the swamp lands of northern Siam, and over mountains. He was careful about villages. Never once did he permit Susan to enter a village. He himself went in alone, leaving her hidden safely. He would beg food and clothing and ointments to soothe their insect bites. He was doubtless pursuing a course, almost as straight as that of a homing pigeon, with nothing but the sun, the stars and his unerring instinct to guide him, toward his province and his sultan.

Weakened by exertion, frightened by the animals and reptiles she saw daily in the slimy swamps and the sightless jungles, Susan saw all this in nightmarish distortion. Nameless—a truly lost soul—she was utterly forlorn. The meaning of existence, if there was a meaning, was lost. Without a past, her present had no meaning, her future was a terrifying question mark. She was at the mercy of whatever fate this silent, crabbed old man might have in store for her. And in their infrequent meetings with natives when she might have appealed for help, she, unfortunately, could not speak the language.

As far as Lak Lon was concerned, her helplessness was fortunate, and it was the kind of helplessness that would appeal greatly to the Sultan of Tashwar.

In spite of her thinness, because of their terrific exertions, and in spite of insect bites, Lak Lon knew that this girl with violet eyes was the most beautiful woman on whom his sultan would ever have gazed. If his courage and his energies ever flagged, this certainty was what drove Lak Lon on.

Perhaps it made the old man a little reckless, but perhaps his fate was written in the stars—as he truly believed—long before he was born.

They had reached higher altitudes, with the jungle well behind them, when Lak Lon's tragedy occurred. They were in Moosar country, crossing a corner of Tibet, where the nights are bitter cold and the men of the great Moon tribe have sharper intelligence than their kinsmen of the swamps far below.

3

TRAPPED

TOWARD DUSK, UNWARNED, the two pilgrims were surrounded by tall, pale-yellow men who wore goatskins and leopard hides, and who materialized about them as though produced magically by the very underbrush.

They were on the outskirts of the great trading town of Sandrakar, and Lak Lon had planned to steal in and beg a little food, leaving the girl hidden, as usual, a safe distance from the town.

It was the end of the pilgrimage, as it was the end of that wily old schemer from Tashwar.

The prisoners were hustled into the city—a city of many streets, of houses of baked and whitewashed clay—and into the presence of a fat yellow man who sat on a throne of teakwood with a great peacock fan in his hand.

This was Ram Chan, the ruler of Sandrakar, half-priest, half-king, a middle-aged, graying man with a thin, high, shrill effeminate voice.

The trial—if it could be called a trial—was the soul of briefness. The captors explained, in a strange, nasal tongue, and the captives, not knowing the tongue and without benefit of interpreters, perforce said nothing at all.

Before Susan O'Gilvie's shocked eyes, the wrinkled,

bearded old man who had escorted her with such patient care over so many trackless miles was stuck in the throat with an ugly little knife, as a pig is stuck, and died at her feet, gurgling his fealty to the Sultan of Tashwar.

The girl was saved for a more ceremonious fate. She was taken from this smoke-darkened throne room and through the streets of Sandrakar, now dusky violet with approaching night, and to a hill—a sharp and sudden little hill, in the very center of the city. It was indeed the very heart of Sandrakar, for the streets radiated out from the base of the hill like wagon spokes from a hub.

A small dark edifice crowned the hill and toward this the procession of which the American girl was a member slowly made its way. The building at the top Susan would have identified, if her memory of all past events had not been curtained. In full possession of her faculties, she would have recognized it as a temple of some sort—a temple the architect of which had been influenced by pagodas.

A door in dark masonry opened as the procession reached the hilltop. A bald-headed old man in black robes stood in the doorway, while shouts went back and forth. Then the door closed, and an adjoining door opened—a door in a wall. And Susan O'Gilvie was thrust through this into a high-walled enclosure. The door closed with a clang and she looked apprehensively about her.

Through a panel of vertical iron bars as thick as a man's wrist, she saw the procession taking its departure. She saw the last of them go down the hill, but she did not see a native boy of about fifteen, with large excited eyes in his pale yellow face, who crept back and peered through the bars.

For at that moment the American girl discovered that she was not alone in the walled and barred enclosure. And had seen the movement of something—some animal, some creature—in the shadow cast by the pagoda.

Charlie Ling

She stood rigidly, watching, scarcely breathing. From out the darkness emerged a huge creature with a slowly lashing, scaly tail. The dim light gleamed on the green hide of its great back. At the end of a long neck a reptilian head moved slowly with a strange, hypnotic motion, and three pale green eyes glowed evilly at the girl. Great jaws slowly opened and closed, as if savoring the approaching feast.

Things of its sort she had seen enough of in the jungles to realize, without calling upon that poor dark memory of hers, that it menaced her life. Yet it was neither alligator nor crocodile. A huge, malignant creature of another world, it advanced upon her, its claws clicking on the flagging, its horrible head moving from side to side.

DAZED AND HELPLESS, the girl stood and watched the green monster approach. It came slowly, with a fascinating deliberation, its great long jaw hanging slightly open, its gleaming green eyes fixed on her.

The native boy at the bars, forbidden under penalty of

death to watch this sacred beast devour its kill, watched all this with a leaping heart and shaking limbs. He had defied the edict which measured out death to anyone, young or old, who lingered to watch this sacred performance. His curiosity had overcome his fear even of death. Never, in all his life, had the boy seen a being so radiantly beautiful as this girl who had been doomed to be eaten by the green dragon. He had lingered because of a sudden and dazzling infatuation for this beautiful girl. It was more than childish curiosity that held him at the thick bars.

Panting softly through his teeth, staring at this lovely being from the outer world, the boy watched the girl and the dragon. He saw the green monster approach her and stop.

The boy did not see a door in the temple wall open and a skinny hand beckon to the paralyzed girl. All the boy had eyes for was the fragile loveliness of this girl waiting for the green beast to attack, to destroy, to rend the flesh from her bones.

The dragon came close and stopped, its tail slowly lashing from side to side. The boy saw the girl reach up with a steady hand and begin stroking the beast slowly, gently, above its three eyes.

Screaming, the boy ran from the bars, and still screaming, ran down the hill and into the city.

PETER MOORE HAD made his way without difficulty through the jungles of north Indo-China and so into the foothills of the Himalayas and a higher atmosphere. In the friendly and peaceful village of Khava, actually a trading post, he found Charlie Ling, the Eurasian, occupying the caravansary with Judd Burton's fifteen elephants, and forty mahouts, gun bearers and assorted servants.

Khava was on the other—the safe—side of the Tibetan border. Peter entered it late in the afternoon, exhausted by almost a month of travel on rented elephants, which he dismissed when he found Charlie Ling's caravansary.

Lean and pale and delicate in appearance, Charlie Ling welcomed him with a certain cool reserve. But when Peter mentioned his name, the Eurasian's liquid dark eyes brightened with interest. He said he had heard of Peter's exploits.

"You are really a legend," he said, in his intelligent voice. "I have envied you from afar. This is a great honor, I assure you."

And when Peter had presented to him the credentials from Judd Burton, the young Eurasian's remaining reserve melted.

"I am delighted," he said. "I prefer nothing better than to turn over this caravan to you, lock, stock and barrel. You are from now on the boss, and I gladly take your orders. Securing that so-called dragon is going to be at least a two-man job. Myself—I look upon it as a pretty hopeless undertaking."

He took Peter about the encampment, showing him the equipment and the elephants.

Until late that night, the two young men sat over a table in the tent assigned to Peter Moore, poring over maps and other data which Charlie Ling had painstakingly accumulated. Boiling all this information down, Peter was in possession of a few brief and not at all promising facts:

Sandrakar was approximately forty miles from Khava.

The road was uphill all the way.

The population of Sandrakar was about 90,000, and its people were notoriously cruel, clever, proud and barbaric. **SANDRAKAR WAS RULED** by a king named Ram Chan, who hated all whites, in fact all outlanders, and would put them to death upon capture, either by knife or by feeding them to the sacred dragon.

The dragon temple was presided over by a priest, who lived in the temple alone. Actually, this priest was a prisoner, and under the thumb of the powerful and ruthless Ram Chan. There was a story, or legend, that the priest had brought the dragon to Sandrakar twenty years ago, had set up a strange, dragon-worshipping religion, his intention being to dominate the people and wrest Ram Chan's power away from him. But in this he had failed. Ram Chan had somehow outwitted him.

Charlie Ling said he had heard more recent rumors of a puzzling nature that the priest was dead and that a priestess now presided over the dragon temple. But he had been unable to verify this rumor.

The Eurasian had not seen the dragon, and did not know whether it was a freak of the saurian family, or a true member of the fabled breed. He emphasized what Judd Burton had told Peter: the dragon was no "croc" and no "'gator." It was actually a living creature, not a clever mechanism. The populace worshipped it. It lived in a high-walled and barred enclosure beside the temple erected in its honor on the top of the central hill in Sandrakar.

Peter spent another day in the caravansary in Khava, finding out what he could about Sandrakar, its people, its customs, its king, and its dragon temple. But he realized that little help was to be gained from second-hand information. He must make his inquiries for himself.

He announced on the following morning to Charlie Ling that he would leave for Sandrakar as soon as he could disguise himself properly.

The Eurasian asked him if he had a plan for carrying off the dragon single-handed.

"I'll probably make my plans as I go along," Peter answered. "I want to look the ground over. Some kind of stratagem will be necessary. I want to see Sandrakar and that dragon with my own eyes before I decide what steps to take."

Charlie Ling hesitated and said, "Alone?"

"Unless you want to go with me."

"Of course I want to go with you, master! It is no task for a man to undertake single-handed."

Disguising themselves in the costumes of the country, the two young men set out for Sandrakar afoot. They slept overnight beside the road, and the next evening arrived at Sandrakar. Throngs of people filled the ill-lighted streets—goat-herders, hunters, priests, beggars, elephant men and camel drivers.

The language they spoke was familiar to Peter. He cound understand it, but he could not speak it.

The two young men made their way through the crowds toward the small but prominent hill in the center of the city. As they progressed, the American studied the city as a general would have studied a battlefield. No detail escaped his vigilance.

But there were other sharp eyes in Sandrakar that night, and it was to the mountain-sharpness of a street urchin's eyes that the presence of the white man, in his careful disguise, was discovered.

It was no fault of Peter Moore's that his eyes were as blue as sapphires, and that when he was excited, or under the pressure of danger, they took on a brilliant sparkle, not at all like the subdued glow of oriental eyes, no matter how strenuous the excitement.

Moosar eyes are little and brown and generally close-set. Wide-set sapphire eyes in Sandrakar are a curiosity—a sensation!

In the stream of light from a bazaar, the street urchin saw the unusual eyes. He uttered a shriek of *"Jen bibo!"*—The eyes!

Others glanced, out of simple curiosity, at the tell-tale sapphire eyes of the outlander, and others took up that disconcerting cry, "The eyes!"

PETER AND CHARLIE Ling with one impulse broke through the suddenly forming circle and started for the nearest open space—the little hill on which stood the temple of the green dragon. They had reached this dubious haven, with shrieks and yells growing closer and louder all about them, when a detachment of Ram Chan's guards, armed with Mannlicher rifles, saw the two runners and shouted at them to halt.

Half an hour later, the adventurers were escorted into the presence of fat, gross Ram Chan, who squatted on a teakwood throne gently waving a great peacock fan to and fro under his triple chins.

And at the foot of this bizarre throne, Peter was to receive the greatest and most mortifying surprise so far.

The garments were stripped from the impostors to their

waists. The fat and shrewd Ram Chan stared from one half-naked man to the other, and asked questions in his high, thin, effeminate voice.

He listened to the stories of the guards and witnesses, and promptly sentenced the prisoners to death at the jaws of the dragon.

Then Charlie Ling began babbling. Words, in the native tongue, spilled from his terrified lips. He was begging for mercy. Not only begging, but bargaining.

He was bargaining that his life be spared, and that the American be fed to the dragon.

Peter Moore had faced the awful grin of death before, and in company with other men, but it was his first experience in such a situation, when a companion in battle and danger showed the white feather. It was in complete violation of Peter Moore's code. In a similar position, he would, if possible, have risked his own life to any extent, if by so doing he could have helped Charlie Ling. And at first, he could not believe his hearing—that Charlie Ling was using all his oratory to persuade Ram Chan to sacrifice the American and let him go free.

Peter listened in bewilderment and growing anger. This was the man—this Eurasian—of whom Judd Burton had stated:

"He is courageous, dependable and absolutely loyal. You can trust him without stint or limit—"

And the truth suddenly dawned on our American adventurer: Charlie Ling was—must be—an impostor. Just what this impostor's scheme had been, Peter would probably never know.

The bargaining was becoming lively. Ram Chan was

beginning to weaken. His only stipulation was that one of the captives must remain his prisoner. Yet Charlie Ling had made no attempt at persuading Ram Chan to let the two of them go free.

"Three elephants, your majesty!" the Eurasian shouted.

And it was settled on that basis. The American was to lose his life, the Eurasian's was to be spared on condition that he deliver to Ram Chan three able-bodied elephants.

Peter had stood speechless and motionless throughout that brisk dickering. Now his fury let go. He leaped at "Charlie Ling," intending to destroy him with his bare hands. But he did not reach the treacherous Eurasian. As he leaped, with fists upraised, a rifle butt in the hands of a guard came cracking against the side of his skull.

The American staggered back, vainly fighting off the blackness that swarmed in upon him. He staggered against a wall, with blood streaming from the broken skin down the side of his chin. He was taking great, deep breaths and heaving them out, trying to beat off that awful influx of darkness, fiercely willing himself to stay on his feet, to reach the perfidious Eurasian, to fight, not to fall.

RAM CHAN, WITH his triple chins resting on a fat fist, watched him with twinkling little brown eyes. When the white man collapsed to hands and knees, shaking his head, trying to clear his senses, the plump oriental monarch bent forward, watching his grotesque efforts as, hundreds of years ago, a Roman emperor might have watched the futile struggles of a man in a lion pit.

Still fighting off unconsciousness, still on rigid hands and knees, Peter succumbed to the blackness. And Ram Chan made a little gesture with his unoccupied hand.

The victim of the Eurasian's treachery and cowardice recovered partly from that blow on the head as he was being dragged through the streets toward the temple on the little hill. A man had him by either leg. He was being dragged unceremoniously along a rough road of dried mud. People were yelling. Stones were thrown at him.

He was numbly aware of both insults and injuries. The world had become a sick and aching confusion to Peter Moore. Lights flickered and died. A great thumping was taking place inside his battered head. Dimly, he recalled a glimpse of that rifle butt as it sliced through the air. He had never felt so ill. And some remote rational corner of his brain assured him that his skull must be cracked.

He did not realize he was being dragged up the hill. Drunkenly, he saw, as he lay on the hilltop, a grim dark structure. Then a door opened, and a partition was let into the blackness—an oblong area with an arched top from which yellow light poured.

A figure in black robes was holding a dancing yellow light high over its head. Voices spoke. There were shrill shouts, then the door closed. And Peter now heard a clanking. Again he was picked up, and this time, when he was unceremoniously thrown to the ground, all babbling ceased.

He lay on the ground where he had been thrown, unable to lift his head or to move hand or leg. He was partly on his side, with one leg doubled under him.

There was another clanging, and then silence fell. As if he were lapsing again into unconsciousness, all sounds perceptibly withdrew. Far away, a faint roaring might have been that of the city—or the protest of cells in his throbbing brain.

His eyes presently made out a dense twilight—a soft diffusion of light far away which etched the outlines of a nearby building. And he heard a curious clicking sound on the flagging of the enclosure into which he had been tossed. Pale green eyes glowed at him. The clicking sound came closer. The great body of some huge monster loomed near him.

His burning eyes delivered to his brain the ironical information that he was, after all this effort, at last in the sacred precincts of the green dragon of Sandrakar. Over the dragon wall!

He was unable to move any muscle below his neck. His eyes strained in the direction of the clicking sounds. The creature took form.

A great saurian monster, it loomed above him in the darkness, its head moving slowly from side to side. Three green eyes gleamed at him. The monster's jaws gaped hungrily, closed with a blood-chilling snap.

Little rivulets of ice seemed to be trickling down Peter's spine. He fought against terrible fear, against his physical weakness, against a supernatural dread. A dragon—a Chinese dragon of myth become terrifying actuality—was advancing upon him, advancing to tear him to bits and feast upon his carcass! He must escape—back—back over the dragon will!

He tried to move, and could not. The evil head of the dragon was slowly coming closer. He stared into its glowing green eyes with an awful fascination. In a moment—in just a moment—those powerful jaws would open wider, wider—and close down relentlessly on his body.

He made a final desperate effort to get up. A crackling, splitting sensation occurred in his head. Someone was grasping his shoulders, dragging him toward a rectangle of golden light in the wall. He felt the flagging bumping along under his heels; he heard desperate panting sounds behind him.

The dragon of Sandrakar seemed to recede, as if it were backing away. Its lower jaw was pendulous. It seemed to be laughing at him. Then a heavy door slammed.

He must have lost consciousness again, for he did not recall having been dragged or carried through the dark corridor, with its flickering oil tapers in niches, into which he had been taken from the enclosure.

4

PLAN FOR ESCAPE

HIS NEXT AWARENESS was of a large and lofty room. He opened his eyes upon a new scene. More oil tapers flamed and guttered in niches in darkened stone walls, losing their rays in the blackness of a lofty arched ceiling and splintering into paler rays against sheets of glass behind which, in recesses in the walls, hung strange, bright satin and silk garments.

He was lying on his back, and a face was bending over him, and dark pools of eyes were searching into his.

He knew now that all of this was the stuff of dreams, or the hazy outlines of the half-world to which the recent dead go. For the slimly beautiful face hovering over him, with its great deep eyes, not blue but an amazing dark violet, with its breathlessly parted lips, was that of Susan!

He tried to say it, but his throat was too choked. But his heart shouted it—his whole being shouted it. And if this was death, he cared for no more life. And he knew, even as his senses cleared a little, that it could be nothing but death, for had he not seen Susan fall from that high tower in the Kingdom of the Lost? And even if she could have been miraculously spared from death, there was utterly no possibility that she could have escaped from that dreadful place with its high, unscalable, soaring walls.

Yes, she was dead, and one of the miraculous and merciful things about death was that you bore no scars from your previous existence. Susan must have been horribly mutilated in that fall from the tower upon the barbed iron spikes below, but she was now intact, unmarred—as beautiful as he remembered her. Yet why had he carried into death the scars of his last living hour?

It occurred to him that it was a little unfair for a man who had slipped from life into death to have such aches and pains and such weakness as afflicted him. He should have cast off, as a useless garment, all the ills and hurts to which mortal flesh is heir; he should have been gloriously reborn, in this new life after death, in possession of all his earthly strength and clear-mindedness. Hadn't Susan?

But this would, presumably, pass away. And he was content for the moment merely to know that he had found her again. He had never known happiness quite like it—to be reunited, after all these heartbroken, bitter months, with his gay, beautiful, thrilling Susan!

All this time, while he gazed up, trying to smile, into that lovely hovering face, Susan was regarding him with an air at once dazed and puzzled.

And it struck him forcibly, with a sinking heart, that she did not recognize him.

To her, he was a stranger! She did not know him! He, her lover—the man she had professed to love more than any living human being—the man she had been planning to marry—this man was, to her, a stranger!

Peter Moore's opinion of the life after death underwent

a quick revision. If lovers who met again after death were to be strangers to each other, then death was cruel indeed.

But there was one compensation. The awful throbbing in his head was subsiding a little, and he found suddenly that he had a voice—a faint and feeble voice to be sure, yet it could manufacture speech.

"Susan!" he whispered.

And the girl stared at him uncomprehendingly.

He tried again. "Susan! Don't you remember me?"

She shook her head a little. Lights danced in her beautiful eyes.

"No. Who are you?"

It pained him to have to give the answer to that. "Think hard. I am Peter."

And he saw, in her vague and puzzled eyes, that his name meant nothing to her.

"Think!" he gasped. "Try to think, darling! We were alive—in that valley. You jumped from the tower. I thought you were dead and I escaped. Thank God, we're dead."

Again she shook her head. "I don't remember. But something is wrong. We aren't dead. We are alive."

He stared up at her. "I died outside this temple."

"No, no. You didn't die. I dragged you inside. Whoever you are—you didn't die. And I didn't die."

A REALIZATION THAT there might be a grain of truth in this caused Peter to try to sit up. He succeeded partly. Then his head took up its banging and he let himself fall back.

"You leaped from that tower," he said harshly.

"But I didn't leap. An old Burmese who took me out of that valley told me. I started to fall. A soldier grabbed a fold of my gown and saved me. Then this old Burmese and I climbed out of that valley and we came here. He was killed."

It sounded plausible. It actually sounded convincing.

Peter, staring up at her, wondered. And then Susan said, "I do not know who I am. For a time I was utterly dazed. But my head has grown clearer and clearer. I can remember everything that happened since the old Burmese helped me escape from the valley, but I can remember nothing before that. I can remember people—men and women—running about and shouting. And I can remember our climb out of that valley. But I do not remember anything that happened before."

"Not even your name?"

"Not even my name."

He told her it was Susan O'Gilvie. And she pronounced the syllables as if she were quite a stranger to them, then said, "And yours is Peter?"

"Yes, Susan."

She did not know him. She sat on a stool beside the couch on which she had placed him, and looked at him with eyes that were dark and bottomlessly deep, and that dazed, puzzled look remained. It was as if, far in the back of her mind, his name echoed hollowly, without meaning, and his image meant nothing likewise. She stared and stared at him. And he wondered if Susan would ever regain what she had lost.

He accepted without further question the fact that he was alive. Having found Susan, after these bleak and empty months, he was too glad to care whether he was alive or dead. And he was almost too sick to care.

The room went darker and darker, slipping off presently

into a whirling black nothingness in which red sparks floated and spun. Then he felt cold water on his face. She was bathing his temples.

Sitting on the stool, she was watching him, never taking those beautiful violet eyes, with their strange vagueness, away from him. Streaks of gray light were coming in at openings. He had slept for hours. He was, he realized, much better. His head still ached, still throbbed when he tried to move. But the awful sickness of last night was gone.

Not yet awake, he thought of his miraculous escape from the green dragon. His brain was clear enough, now, to realize what the creature actually was. To any untutored eye, the creature might readily be mistaken for a true dragon of myth. It was neither crocodile nor alligator. But it was, the injured man was now certain, a species of lizard—a freak, no doubt, or what Judd Burton had called a sport. Perhaps it was a gigantic specimen of a common enough breed of the lizard family. Peter had heard of similar lizards in South America, and in the Galapagos Islands, off South America. He had never before seen anything like it in the Orient.

The third eye of the creature still puzzled him, but he was beginning to suspect what that third eye might be.

COMING AWAKE, HE grinned. And the girl smiled at him. But it was a child's smile, tender and wondering and awed. And the young man wondered if her experience had changed Susan so—or whether this was a change due to her loss of memory. He had never seen Susan so subdued, so meek, so gentle. She had been so gay, so exuberant, so mischievous.

She said quietly, "I have spent the whole night, sitting here, looking at you, trying to remember." She gave a funny little shrug. "I can't. I'm afraid I'll just have to begin life all over again."

The light shifting into the temple was a brighter gray now, tinged with yellow and pink.

"Susan, tell me how you happen to be here?"

She told him, simply, of Lak Lon's death, and of her amazing adventure with the dragon.

"It came toward me, and I don't know why I wasn't afraid of it. I wasn't. I felt sorry for it. The poor thing looked so unhappy, so lonely. It was supposed to eat me alive. But it didn't. It let me scratch its head. And one of the native boys, who defied the law and stayed to watch, saw this—and he ran screaming down into the village to say— What could he have said?"

"That a goddess had come to town," Peter guessed.

"They killed the old man, the priest, who was here before me. I've had plenty of time to think and wonder. I don't think that dragon was ever vicious. I think he's always been as gentle as a lamb, although perhaps he's just old. I think that old priest built up the tradition—the law—that no one was to stay behind and watch the dragon eat his victims. He must have been a tricky old rascal."

"Is that third eye of the dragon an emerald?"

"Yes. It has been set in his thick hide in his forehead."

Peter had never before seen an emerald of such size. It must have been, he recalled, fully three-quarters of an inch in diameter. It must be worth a rajah's ransom, and it occurred to him that this emerald doubtless explained the spurious "Charlie Ling."

Why not? There were no lengths to which one of these rascally half-breeds would not go. Doubtless the impostor—if Peter's theory was the correct answer—had killed or somehow done away with the real Charlie Ling, and had merely awaited Peter's coming to Khava. How he had obtained advance news of Peter's coming was neither mysterious nor miraculous. There were grapevines on which rumors flowered from one end of Asia to the other.

It was probable that the false Charlie Ling had wanted Peter's help in stealing the dragon, or in obtaining access to it. But when they had been captured and taken before Ram Chan, he had preferred to lose Peter rather than his own life.

Peter said, "Am I the first victim since you've been priestess?"

"Yes."

"Yes, Peter," he said.

"Yes—Peter," she complied, and blushed.

"What did he do with the others?"

"I think he killed them and threw them into the old well in the compound in back. There are bones in the bottom of it, and there is clothing of all sorts and sizes piled in another room."

"How long have you been here?"

"I don't know. Months, I think."

"Can you come and go at your will?"

"No. I am actually nothing but a prisoner. There is a guard outside, day and night."

"How much of a guard?"

"One man. But he won't let me out. And he or someone brings me food every morning—rice and fruit and things."

"What does this lizard eat?"

She smiled again. "He is a vegetarian. I'll show you the garden. Can you walk?"

Peter found he could sit up. Experimentally, he stood up. His head throbbed, and he felt dizzy. But he could stand up. He could walk.

HE WENT OUT into the garden with Susan—a tangle of undergrowth surrounded by a wall at least fifteen feet high. He looked into the deep well she had mentioned—saw the human bones at the bottom.

But he was much less interested in his surroundings, and in the plight in which he and Susan were placed, than in Susan herself—this strange, shy, changed Susan.

Her eyes were shy. She would glance at him, then hastily glance away—and blush. It was altogether as startling as if he had found a girl—a perfectly strange girl—in Susan's skin. In appearance, she hadn't changed. Possibly she was lovelier, but she looked no older for her shocking experience.

He could not reconcile himself to this change which seemed to affect her whole personality. He could not understand how she could so completely lose her memory of all past events beyond her leap from that tower, and at the same time retain, as she had, her speech, her vocabulary.

Where she had once been willful and headstrong, she was now submissive and meek. Where she had once been arrogant—an arrogance due, no doubt, to her great wealth—she was now humble. And in place of her champagne-like gaiety, her craving for adventurous thrills, she was now gentle and sweet.

He told her something about herself—how they had met, almost three years before, on a transpacific liner bound from San Francisco to the Far East. How they had shared adventures. And how they had come to be prisoners in the Kingdom of the Lost.

She listened to him, large-eyed, with frequent gasps and little exclamations. And he presently realized that he might as well have been telling a child a fairy tale. She was fascinated, but it was not part of her.

Since he had met Susan, on that exciting transpacific crossing, she had told him a great deal about her child-hood and girlhood—the strange existence of the richest orphan in America.

"When you say that I am the richest girl in America, or in the world, it means nothing to me except this; Why, if I am so rich, did I expose myself to such dangers when I might have enjoyed a full life quietly and safely?"

"I asked you that question once. Your answer was that you'd rather have five cents' worth of adventure and excite-ment than a million dollars' worth of safety and security."

Susan shook her head with a wondering look. "I can't understand it. I hate excitement and adventure and danger. I'd like nothing better than to live in some quiet, sunny place where there was a huge flower garden."

In the face of her new shyness, her demureness, he could not bring himself to tell her that they had been engaged to be married. And as the morning wore on and he talked and she demurely listened, he became aware of the strang-est development so far. This strange, beautiful girl was falling in love with him. He dismissed her shyness at first as strangeness, but as time passed and he saw in her the symptoms which had heralded her love for him in the first place, he was stunned.

YET THERE WAS a difference. The old Susan had not let him stay in the dark about it for very long. She had told him excitedly, joyously that she had finally found the one man she could really adore—and he was it! And she had been astonished but not hurt at his resistance. She loved resistance! She loved conflict! She would win him if it took the rest of her life and the last dollar of her huge fortune. And at last she had battered down his objections to marrying the richest girl in America, if not in the whole world.

This new Susan, on the other hand, might have been a fresh convent graduate. Her demureness, her shyness, her blushes were those of innocent girlhood. It was as if Susan were determined to fall in love with him all over again in this embarrassing way.

Peter might have construed it to mean that their love was unquestionably of a lasting sort; he might have been delighted at her naïve approach to their old relationship. But he could not rid himself of strange notions.

He tried to batter his way through that closed door into her memory. He tried going about it gently, persuasively. He tried more violent approaches. He went so far as to seize her by the shoulders and shake her and shout: "Susan! Snap out of it! Look at me! For God's sake, look at me!"

And when she looked at him, with eyes dazed by the shaking, but with that meek, shy smile, he shook her again, then cried impatiently: "Go over there and bang your head against that wall!" And she would have done it, if he hadn't laughed and told her not to be a ninny.

Susan came back and looked up at him adoringly. He wanted to kiss her. He wanted to snatch her in his arms and kiss her with the ardor he had once used. But he would not take advantage of this appallingly young, starry-eyed girl.

Briskly, he said, "Susan, we have got to get out of here."

"Yes, Peter," she said, and in such a voice that he looked at her with hearty hope, but it was not the old Susan.

"How can we escape?"

"I don't know."

"Haven't you thought about it?"

"What would be the use?"

"We're going to get you out of here," he said fiercely. "We're going to get you back to civilization. We're going to look for the girl you used to be."

"Yes, Peter."

She showed him more of the temple. There were winding stairs into a little room at the top of the tower, and there were slits in the tower, like old gun ports, from which he could look out over the roofs of Sandrakar.

Peter settled down to a long study of the situation. He walked from slot to slot, looking down the narrow, congested streets, looking along the roofs. There were a dozen roads spoking out from the little hill on which the dragon temple stood, but none of them was an avenue of escape.

He looked out wistfully over the surrounding country. Off to the west were the foothills of great mountains. Far, far away he could see them, floating like clouds in the thin blue air of the country. The greatest mountains in the world, these—all but impenetrable. Through here was one of the roads to that other forbidden city—Lhasa.

TO THE SOUTH, the hills tumbled away into a green and promising haze. Down that was Burma. A little to the right, if one took a straight course, was India. But in neither of these directions was Peter interested. Their flight, if they could somehow escape from this city of barbarians, would be toward the northeast, along the route he had followed— straight across the jungles of northern Siam, and then through Cambodia, through Angkor and to the civilized seaport of Saigon, the capital of French Indo-China.

The route was the one by which he had entered Khava. It wasn't safe. None of these routes were safe, but he was more familiar with the one from Khava to Saigon.

All afternoon he studied, tried this plan and that against the keen edge of his experience, only to discard them all. And late that afternoon, he believed he had found the solution.

The streets which led due north from the temple were the shortest of them all. The houses were in a solid row, and this row of houses ended against the flank of a brown hill. He saw a ladder leaning against the nearest wall.

The rest was easy. He would surprise and overpower the guard on duty at the temple doors. He and Susan would run to the ladder, climb to the roof and make their way as speedily as possible across the rooftops to the flank of that hill.

Once away from Sandrakar, in the open country, they would take their luck as they found it.

He outlined this proposition to Susan. She listened with glowing eyes.

Peter spent the remainder of the afternoon considering disguises. Rummaging about in one of the rooms, he made an interesting discovery. It was a dark room, or he wouldn't have made the discovery.

It was a glass jar with a screw top, and the jar bore a Japanese label. Peter, familiar with written and spoken Japanese, read the label: *Paint That Glows in the Night and Other Places of Extreme Darkness.* And in the murk of the room, the jar glowed as if it were whitely afire.

Peter unscrewed the cap and sniffed at the contents—a greasy gray paste which glowed and shimmered and smelled evilly of phosphorus. Whatever it may have been intended for by its manufacturers, he realized that its purpose here was, twice every year, to make the green lizard appear to be white-hot.

Smeared with this stuff from snout to tail, the dragon of Sandrakar would no doubt become—after dark—an awesome spectacle.

He put the jar aside and continued his rummaging. He found clothing which had once been worn by men who had, he supposed, been sacrifices to the dragon. He suspected that none of these victims had been harmed by the great lizard, but had been murdered by Susan's predecessor. None of the clothing showed tears or holes that might have been caused by an attack by the dragon, and he found blood on none of them. He presumed that the old priest had clubbed the men to death in their sleep, removed their garments and thrown their bodies down the well in the compound.

Among these garments, he found several suits which had been worn by white men, presumably English adventurers or traders who had come to Sandrakar by way of India.

HE ASKED SUSAN what had become of the old priest. She told him. When she was in the walled and barred enclosure with the big green lizard, a door into the enclosure from the temple—the same door through which she had dragged Peter—had opened, and an old man had beckoned to her. She had gone inside the temple and he had closed the door. She supposed he would have killed her if that native boy had not seen her miraculously subdue the dragon with a touch of her fingers.

"I don't think it occurred to Ram Chan," she said, "that there was nothing miraculous or magical about it, but that the lizard was really harmless. He or the rest of the village took it for granted that the dragon had spared me because I had some special kind of oriental merit. And they must have thought that the old priest had lost his power, or been bewitched, or both.

"Anyway, they came and banged on the big north door until he opened it. Ram Chan ordered him to come out. When he started down the steps, two soldiers with swords stepped up and cut him down. They dragged him through the streets. And Ram Chan gave me to understand that I was the new priestess of the dragon temple. I don't understand anything of this language, but he managed to make it quite clear."

Peter, studying her with a frown, was more puzzled than ever. She talked so intelligently, so rationally—just as she had used to talk in her rare solemn moments.

She had started to pick up a blue jacket from the pile of clothing. He shouted "Susan!" Startled, she dropped the jacket and stared up at him. But the transformation hadn't occurred. Her eyes remained vague and puzzled.

She smiled understandingly and said, "It's no use, Peter. It's a locked door. Maybe it will never be unlocked." Then her smile vanished and she softly cried: "Am I so dreadfully changed? What was I like before?"

"There was more trouble in the tip of your little finger," he told her, "than there is in a herd of wild elephants on the rampage. You could think up mischief faster than any living human. You got yourself and me into so much trouble that the American consul-general in Hong Kong finally kicked us out of China."

Susan stared at him with wide glowing eyes of amazement. Then she shook her head.

"You liked me better that way?"

"I did—emphatically. Because you were you. There was never anyone like you, Susan. You were a little devil. You were the original thrill-hunter."

"And you loved me," she whispered. "And you can't love me as I am now."

She was so pathetic, so hurt, that he wanted to take her into his arms. Tears came into her eyes. She turned away from him suddenly.

He did not know if this was the right way to go about it. But he would try any expedient. He knew that, for a person with her strange mental kink, there was no help from surgery. But how did one go about breaking down a door that had closed not only upon memory but upon personality?

He was sorry for this Susan, and he would, in time, love her. The beauty of her face and the slim rounded perfection of her body would make it difficult for any healthy young man not to fall in love with her. Yet the thing that had gone out of her—the fire of the spirit—had been one of Susan's strongest attractions for him. He had heartily

disapproved of her capacity for getting herself into dangerous scrapes, but her very adventurousness and fearlessness
had made him love her as he never had and never would
love another woman.

And he wondered if some sudden excitement would
break down that stubborn door. As sweet, as charming as
this new Susan was, he wanted the old one.

He selected drab and colorless native costumes as the
disguises they would wear on their break for freedom.
Susan would dress, he announced, as a beggar boy, and he
would dress as a priest.

He made this decision on finding a rough brown cloak
of camel's wool, with hood attached. With the hood over
his face, no one would see his telltale eyes.

When their costumes were assembled and ready, Peter
continued his tour. In another room, he found a jar of
stain which would do to change Susan's whiteness to pale
brownness. It was necessary to stain only her face, neck,
hands and ankles, as the beggar boy costume covered her
everywhere else.

In the room in which he had first opened his eyes, Peter
found other items of great interest. Susan declared that
she had never hit upon any satisfactory explanation for the
bright satin and silk garments in the wall recesses. They
hung in these recesses behind protective sheets of glass—
robes of various sizes and of brightest colors—jade green,
sea-blue, blood-red and sheer snow-white. Some of these
robes were jeweled, others were severely plain and simple,
but all were of the finest and richest kind of satin, doubtless hand-loomed.

And at the back of one of these recesses, Peter came

upon an object that puzzled him more than anything so far. It was a kind of harness, made of white leather straps, strongly sewn, and these straps were liberally studded with emeralds. The carving was crude, the color was slightly off, but they were authentic emeralds.

5

"CHARLIE LING" AGAIN

PETER REMOVED IT from the peg on which it hung, and stretched out the harness on the stone floor. It puzzled him for a long time. If it had been made for a horse, or pony, the animal must have been of strange conformation indeed. And there were no reins, only a leash-like strap about fifteen feet in length ending in a thick elephant-hair loop. It dawned on him suddenly, "It's for that dragon!"

If he could have, in any way, delivered the green monster to Judd Burton, he would have liked to deliver this amazing harness to him also. Then it struck him somewhat forcibly that he could not break his word to Judd Burton. Peter had once declared, perhaps recklessly, that the word "impossible" had better been left uncoined. He knew that he could not rest until he had exhausted every possibility of securing this green monster for the animal collector.

First of all, however, he must deliver Susan to safety. That done, he would return with a better organized plan of getting the dragon. Somehow he must secure and deliver this big lizard to Judd Burton!

The sun was setting now. Slanting rays of purple-red light were stealing through windows and niches high in the temple walls. And Peter and Susan got busy with their preparations for escape. He dyed her face, her ears, neck, hands, wrists, ankles and feet with the stain. Then, while he got into his monk's raiment, she went into another room, disrobed and put on the khaki shorts and blouse left behind by some ill-fated, slender youth. These were for travel through the jungle—the most practical outfit she could wear. Over blouse and shorts she put on the long shabby, woolen robes of a beggar. She tucked up her dark curling hair, and hid it completely under a goatskin cap.

When she returned, Peter had become a bent-shouldered monk, with a cape well down over his eyes. Beside him, on the stone floor, was a long, thin club. It was the only weapon of any description he had been able to find in the temple.

He climbed again into the dome of the temple, for a final survey of their route of proposed escape. There had been people on those roofs throughout the day, but with the setting of the sun, a wind came flowing down from the high, snow-capped mountains of Tibet, and this wind poured down upon Sandrakar with the biting cold of a mountain stream, driving the last of the women and children from the roofs. It should be clear going.

As he was preparing to descend, he saw, in the pure ruby light of almost horizontal sunrays which shot over the city and against a wall of trees on the outskirts, the silhouettes of three lumpy shapes—black objects that moved slowly against the trees along the road from Khava to Sandrakar.

He identified them presently as elephants, and would have dismissed them from mind at once except for that lingering, bitter memory of "Charlie Ling's" treachery. Three elephants! The Eurasian had bargained with Ram

Chan, had named three elephants as the price of life and liberty.

The ruby rays of the sun flicked off as the sun dropped behind the Himalayas. The three plodding elephants vanished into fee blue haze of the valley evening. Darkness would come swiftly.

Peter descended from the dome. He said: "The roofs are clear now. Even the streets are almost empty, with everyone at the evening meal. Ready?"

She was looking up at him with meek, adoring eyes.

"Yes, Peter."

"Scared?"

Her prompt headshake was that of a small girl. "No, Peter," she said stoutly, "not with you to protect me. You've saved me from too many scrapes."

HE STARTED TO pick up the club. Now he straightened up and stared at her. It was almost as if the old Susan, in one of her demurely mocking moments, had spoken. But she was only referring to some of the adventures he had described.

Earlier in the afternoon, he had liberally oiled the hinges of the great north door, and had drenched with oil the ponderous iron bolt which held it closed against the world.

As far as was possible, he was in readiness for the attempt. Susan had told him the guard was changed twice daily, at noon and at midnight. There would be no confusion on that score.

He picked up the club and went to the door with Susan close at his heels. His heart was hammering. Once they opened that door, there was no returning. And if this venture failed, all hope was lost. They would certainly be apprehended. Their lives would certainly pay for it.

With the utmost care, Peter slid back the ponderous iron bolt in its great wrought-iron sockets. It made no sound. Cautiously, he pulled open the great door, and this maneuver, too, was without the slightest attendant noise.

And with the door open, the club ready in his hands, Peter found himself face to face with a sentry armed with a rifle! There had been no opportunity to peer out, to make certain that the guard was facing the other way.

Peter was sure that this tall man in goatskin was the more surprised of the two. If he had not been so completely taken by surprise, he would have had that rifle up and ready to fire. It was not ready. Its butt was resting on the flagging.

For the fraction of a second, the beady little dark eyes stared at the two in the opening door. Then the rifle came up. But as it came Peter rushed, raising the club as he went. He brought it cracking down on the sentry's skull. And so far that was the only sound—a dull thump of hard wood meeting hard bone with a goatskin cap between. As the guardian of the temple gate sagged, Peter reached for the rifle, snatched it up before it could fall with the inevitable hard clatter.

He had planned on securing the guard's rifle, but he had not planned on a modern Mannlicher, with a shell in the chamber and a full magazine!

Luck played such a large part in an affair of this kind! Peter congratulated himself. Now if their luck, so auspiciously begun, would only hold!

He abandoned the club and took Susan's hand in his free hand. With swift stealth, they descended the temple steps and then the northern side of the hill. Night had come. The wind from the high mountains was sharp and fresh and scented with ice. Tibetan star-herds marched brightly in the sky.

The ladder still leaned against the whitewashed baked mud wall. And Peter hoped now that his lengthy surveys of the scene had been accurate. As far as he had been able to tell, the roofs were joined in an endless flat to the very end—to where the hills on the north began.

They swarmed up the ladder. It made creaking noises, but the song of the wind drowned these, as did the hearty voices of the occupants of the house. Cooking smells were in the air, mostly the rich pungence of broiling mutton fat.

On the rooftop, Susan clung to his arm, shivering.

"All right?" he whispered.

"Yes, Peter!"

He had two high hopes. One, that they make good this escape, with all its excellent promise. The other, that the suspense, the threat of danger would break down that door in Susan's brain, that she would lose this frightened-little-girl personality and regain her other, her real self.

They cautiously crossed that roof, and others. They met no one. It had been a simple, good plan, and they were executing it nicely.

Just ahead of them now, looming in the star-glow, lay the flank of the little hill beyond which was, Peter devoutly hoped, freedom.

And with only three more roofs to cross, the stratagem came to sudden and unexpected doom.

FROM THE LAST house in the long row flames suddenly burst forth. And it was as if this fire had been, with deliberate cunning, set off for the sole purpose of foiling their plans. That it was incendiary, Peter did not for a moment doubt. The flames burst alight and instantly began to roar into the sky, with a great belching of black smoke. And these clouds of smoke were heavily fragrant with the fumes of kerosene!

It did not seem possible that anyone could have had such diabolical cunning as to devise this means of frustrating their escape. Yet there could be no doubt that someone had deliberately set that house afire, with every intention of creating a fierce and terrible blaze.

Certainly, all hope of escape in that direction was now ruined. People were bursting from doorways. Others were swarming on the roofs behind them. A small mob was choking the streets. And the fired house had now become a giant torch, throwing light across the hills as if they comprised the setting of a great stage.

It was possible that, in the moment's excitement, they might make a break for it—and succeed. But the risk was too great.

He said swiftly, "We'll go back to the temple, cut around back, and slip out the south way. There's another chance, but it's too risky."

"Will we dare go through the city—any way?"

"Why not? This fire is going to be good. It's going to be a humdinger. This whole end of the town will be blazing before long. Caked mud on rattan! It's going to burn like a last year's bird nest. We won't be noticed—if we hurry while the hysteria is on."

Peter hid the Mannlicher in a fold of his robe. They descended to the street by a ladder and made their way through running, surging crowds. In the uproar, they escaped detection, and when they were within a block or two of the temple hill, the crowds thinned, and the last part of the way was through a deserted street.

But there was excitement at the temple. Men were shouting, and the blue-red spurts of rifle fire flashed against the velvet night. A bullet sang close to Peter's head, and he instinctively ducked. For some time, he believed that all this excitement was due to the discovery that he and Susan had escaped. Then he saw that two groups of men were carrying on this fight. And as he watched, the smaller group backed down and scattered. A volley of shots was fired at the fugitives. And in a random ray of light, Peter saw that those who had done the firing were guards, or soldiers. And he wondered who the others were.

The company of Ram Chan's men were now racing toward the south end of the temple, firing as they ran.

A suspicion of what was behind all this furor was dawning on Peter.

He said, "We got to get into that temple a moment—until these soldiers have scattered. It's risky, I know."

Susan, clinging to him, was shaking with terror. He seized her arm to steady her, and half-carried her the rest of the way to the hill and up the hill. The guards were shouting in back. The two fugitives ran up the temple steps down which they had so recently—and with such high hopes—escaped. The temple door was still open, as they had left it, but the guard was gone. The yelling soldiers came closer.

ONCE INSIDE, PETER closed and bolted the door. He looked hastily into the other rooms, making sure they were not occupied. The shouts of the soldiers were drawing away now. Ram Chan's men were still pursuing their quarry, and their quarry, it appeared, had decided on westward flight.

Peter peeked out the door and saw all this. It seemed to him that the fire was not blazing so fiercely. Now was the time to put his alternative plan into effect. And there could be no delay. They would push on out through any of the streets running southward. Once out of Sandrakar, they would discreetly encircle it to the Khava Road. And if that scheme proved unwise, they would keep going straight south, to Burma, or, farther west, to India. Unknown and dangerous territory all the way to the border, but there was, once again, no choice.

And as he started to pull the heavy door open, a deep and heavy groaning arrested him. It seemed to come from the dragon's enclosure. Peter hesitated a moment, then ran to the bolted door which gave upon the walled and barred enclosure.

Three men were lying there. Evidently they had climbed the dragon wall, had been shot as they leaped, or had been struck down by bullets fired between the thick iron bars.

Two of the men were dead. Peter recognized them. The third was laboriously, noisily breathing, uttering agonized groans.

Lying flat on its belly near the outer wall, the great lizard watched Peter, not moving.

Charlie Ling was the unconscious one. He had, Peter guessed, delivered the three elephants to Ram Chan, and had then had some of his own men fire the house as a decoy—to distract attention from his main plan. This plan had been to enter the great lizard's cage. He had come here, Peter was now certain, not to steal the dragon, but to rob from its forehead that priceless green emerald.

Behind him, Susan, shivering wailed: "Peter! Hurry!

There isn't a moment to lose! The fire is dying out, and some of the people are coming back! What—what's this?"

"This one isn't dead, but I think he's dying. He's the man who sold me over the dragon wall for three elephants! Let's go!"

"But you can't leave him here for Ram Chan to find!"

"It's Charlie Ling or us!"

"But Ram Chan would torture him!"

"It means losing our chance to escape!"

"Peter, I'd never forgive myself—or you—if we ran away from this wounded man. We can't leave a wounded white man to these barbarians!"

"He isn't white! He's Eurasian—the kind who would cut your throat for the price of a pipe of opium!"

But he gave in. Susan was right. Even as he despised the man, Peter couldn't leave him here for the tortures which Ram Chan would certainly inflict on him.

Telling Susan to close and bolt the door, Peter picked up the unconscious man and carried him into the large room. Susan had meanwhile gone to the north door to make observations.

She returned with the depressing news that the fire was out. The mob was scattering.

"I'm sorry, Peter. We might have escaped. But I couldn't leave this wounded man to Ram Chan."

The Eurasian was breathing noisily, in short, awful gasps. Peter had torn open the heavy *lemba,* or loose woolen jacket, and found the wound, a bullet hole just below the heart. Blood was pulsing from it, and running down the chest of the spurious Charlie Ling. Considering its location, Peter did not see how a man shot just below the heart with an expanding bullet could possibly live.

His diagnosis was verified with grim irony at that moment when the wounded man, with a final convulsive heaving of his chest, stopped breathing entirely. A last gasp rattled in his throat, and he mysteriously seemed to diminish in size. Charlie Ling had not, ironically, recovered consciousness since he had been shot.

And even as that last dying breath was wrenched from him, a hammering of rifle butts set up a small thunder at the north door.

Susan was clutching Peter's hand. She whispered: "It's my fault! It's all my fault! We're trapped! There's utterly no chance of escape!"

Then she gave a little laugh. "I don't want to live. I don't want you to be killed, but I don't want to live! You hate me as I am. And I can't ever be what I was before."

She laughed again, this time more hysterically. "Isn't it ironical and funny, Peter? Ever since you met me, on the transpacific crossing, I've been a perfect bane to you—always getting you into the most terrific trouble. I've gone and done it again—the last time! If I hadn't insisted on our trying to save this dead man, we'd have escaped! Before they break down that door and grab us, tell me—oh, Peter, tell me you might have loved me as I am—just a little!"

Peter grasped her hands and said grimly: "Susan, pull yourself together. There's still a chance. We may be killed trying, but we won't be shot like rats."

Above the uproar of shouts and the banging of rifle butts against the door, he heard the thin, high shrilling of Ram Chan's voice.

And Peter went about the hasty execution of the bold and daring plan he had considered and discarded earlier, the first step of which was to lure, or coax, or somehow compel the great green lizard to enter the temple.

6

A BOLD IDEA!

WORD HAD SPREAD through Sandrakar that the blue-eyed man who had been supposedly devoured by the dragon was alive and safe within the temple walls. The sentry who had succumbed to that swift blow of the white man's club had recovered and spread this news. Other sharp-eyed citizens had, it appeared, seen the white man and the priestess run up the steps and into the temple only a moment ago.

It was said that they had started that mysterious fire. Other rumors flew and reached Ram Chan, who deserted his throne and hastened to the temple, where a great mob of citizenry and soldiers had assembled. Soldiers were banging at the massive doors.

The fat monarch of Sandrakar took charge of the situation. He now gave the order that soldiers try the only other door—the one that led into the temple from the little compound where the dragon was kept.

Fear of the green monster held the scouting party back for a time. But Ram Chan, having given them the key to the dragon gate, bullied them on. And the scouting party returned shortly with the amazing information that the dragon was gone! He was, it appeared, inside the temple with the two white barbarians!

This rumor went from mouth to mouth in a rising roar of wonder and incredulity. Hysteria and supernatural fear took hold of the mob. Soldiers and citizenry alike backed away from the great north door and stared at the temple with awe and speculation.

Ram Chan, who feared no dragons, was the only man who dared approach that silent door. And as he approached, it opened. And as it opened, a roar of terror went up from those closely packed thousands.

For within the doorway was an awesome apparition. It glowed as spirits in the half-world are said to glow, with a strange and horrible pale fire. And as the mob stared and Ram Chan, no longer self-confident, fell back a step, the apparition took form, with waves of white fire shimmering about it.

A tall man with golden hair—a tall man, naked to the waist—was striding with slow, majestic steps toward them. His face, his arms, his hands, his chest glowed and shivered with unholy fire. In his upheld hand was the end of a long leather strap. At the other end of this strap, or leash, was the green dragon of Sandrakar!

The great lizard seemed to have grown to twice its usual size, an illusion that was no doubt due to the fiery glow which surrounded him like an obscene halo. Meekly, obediently, the lizard followed the white man, slowly, but willingly, step by step.

But the marvel did not end with that Sitting coolly astride the glowing green monster was the priestess of this temple—a creature of dazzling splendor, in a robe as white

as the snows which glistened on the distant moonstruck
Himalayan peaks. Her chin was high. Her air was scornful.

The sudden uproar of the mob was instantly silenced.
Only Ram Chan, it appeared, was not taken in by this
amazing spectacle. Alone, halfway up the temple steps, he
stared and began yelling commands at his soldiers.

Their failure to obey, set him into a frenzy. In his shrill,
rasping voice he ordered them to fire. But for once in his
life, Ram Chan was not obeyed. Supernatural fear held his
soldiers in a clammy, paralyzing grip.

And with a final shriek of rage, the fat monarch took
matters exclusively into his own hands. He whipped from
its sheath at his plump middle a long and wicked knife that
glittered. He leaped, not at the glowing demi-god who led
the dragon, but at the perfidious goddess on its back.

Peter had not been prepared for this. He had assumed
that even if Ram Chan were in the multitude, he, too,
would have been too deeply impressed to move. He had
not counted on Ram Chan's amazing shrewdness.

HE DID NOT have time to whirl about and defend Susan
from that utterly unexpected attack. But even as Peter,
faltering in that slow, deliberate stride, looked back, the
dragon itself had acted. Faster than Peter had ever seen
any living creature move, the lizard raised its forelegs, and
made a great lunge, as smaller members of his species,
almost since time began, have lunged at fat and juicy flies.

The thick neck of Ram Chan was seized in those powerful jaws. There was a sickening snapping sound. And this
was the sound of Ram Chan's neck breaking.

For a moment, Peter was frozen by the fear that the giant
lizard would now spoil everything by devouring his kill.

But the lizard did nothing of the kind. It dropped Ram Chan and, as if fully appreciating the deliberate drama of this astounding spectacle, it resumed its slow, grotesque march behind Peter.

Fortunately for the successful carrying out of this stratagem, Susan had not screamed. One hand had flown to her mouth when Ram Chan had leaped. And when the great lizard had lunged at the fat king, she had almost been unseated. Then she had recovered her balance. She did not even glance at the dead monarch as he rolled down the steps. Her chin remained tilted, her eyes uplifted, as if her thoughts never descended lower than the stars.

And except for a short, incredulous gasp, that great mob, with its glistening, spellbound eyes, remained still. It gave way, it moved, with a faint shuffling of bare and sandaled feet, as the man, the dragon and the girl advanced.

Sweating plentifully under the phosphorescent grease, Peter congratulated himself. He had been utterly unprepared for that attack by Ram Chan. He had thought that his plan was ruined. He had thought that Susan would be killed before he could act. And when the lizard had attacked Ram Chan, had snapped the man's neck in those great jaws, Peter was certain that that, too, was the end.

He knew that all members of the lizard family were possessed of very limited intelligence, that their brains, in proportion to their bulk, were smaller than those of any other living creature. Yet it was as if the lizard were cleverly using brains—as if the lizard understood perfectly what all this was about. And it now occurred to Peter that the explanation was much simpler—that the beast, in the months Susan had been virtually a prisoner in the temple, had developed a great affection and a truly dog-like devotion for her. It had leaped so suddenly at Ram Chan, simply because the life of this loved creature on its back was being threatened.

But Peter had no thoughts for further speculation. The mob was parting to let him and the dragon through. And he knew that this strange parade must continue for two miles, perhaps three. The clicking claws of the lizard made the only sound now in a breathless hush. But had this green monster the endurance, or the willingness, to crawl such a distance?

Once it balked, once it refused to take further part in this strange pageant, Peter and Susan would be in a tight corner indeed. He realized that these people were held entirely by the smooth continuity of the performance. It was as if they were under hypnotic influence. But if the big lizard talked, that spell would certainly be broken.

DOWN THE STREET ahead of them the mob surged and swirled. And that street seemed to go on and on forever. No walk that Peter had ever undertaken had seemed quite so long as this one. And another of his worries was Susan's endurance. She was under a terrific strain. She must sit there, eyes front and lifted, hardly daring to move a muscle. She must be, in the eyes of these people, a goddess untouched by earthly stares.

Peter had been in many uncomfortable corners, but he could not recall a dangerous situation that was so prolonged. Any moment, one of these staring, silent people might throw a stone; any moment, one of them might burst into jeering. And it would not take a minute for this mob, suddenly inflamed, to close in and assassinate this striding, fair-haired godlike man, and this haughty princess in her snow-white robes.

But no stones were thrown, no shots were fired, no jeers were uttered. Never, in its history, had this remote, barbaric city been so silent. Silent crowds packed the streets and the side-streets. Mobs were lined up on the roofs all along the way.

At the outskirts of the city, where the street they followed joined the road to Khava, Peter anticipated trouble. This awed, perhaps worshipful, mob must not follow. And it was evident that the mob was firmly determined to do nothing else. Perhaps fifty thousand people were in the procession which was strung out now behind the man, the girl and the dragon.

At a brightly lighted bazaar which marked the last northeastern outpost of Sandrakar, Peter turned about and held up his arms. He did not stop. With the golden light from the bazaar flooding him, he lifted his arms and shouted into the silence two words of the language which he knew.

"Naga lan!"

They meant: Go back! And for the first time since the lizard had snapped the fat neck of Ram Chan, an audible muttering went through the spellbound mob. It resembled the rippling of a wind through dry leaves. It became, in the distance, a sullen roar.

And it was successful. The mob stopped. Perhaps no one cared to follow this awesome procession of a man, a woman and a dragon into the blackness of the Tibetan night. Perhaps none of them cared to defy the command of a golden-haired god who glowed with unholy fire.

At all events, no one followed. And at the same pace, the god who glowed and the dragon that writhed and shone with the same hellish fire and the goddess who had eyes only for the stars—this amazing trio started down the road for Khava.

When they were safely into the darkness, Susan dismounted. She ran ahead and took Peter's arm. She was shaking uncontrollably, and smothering sobs. It had been a horrible ordeal.

"Now what are we going to do?"

"Keep going," Peter answered. Unless he was badly mistaken, he said, they would find an elephant caravan encamped a few miles farther along the road. It would be the caravansary of the spurious Charlie Ling, who would have left all his men and elephants there, ready for a quick getaway with the great emerald in the lizard's forehead, or the lizard itself, if he could somehow contrive to secure that.

"If I've guessed wrong about the caravansary, we'll walk to Khava," Peter said.

A MASTER OF adventurous intrigue, Peter had guessed correctly. Some five miles along the Khava road from Sandrakar they came upon the caravansary. It was busy with preparations for departure. Word had come—delivered by some of Charlie Ling's men who had escaped Ram Chan's soldiers—that Charlie Ling was dead. The camp was being broken up. Elephants were being loaded.

Into this brisk scene, Peter, Susan, and the dragon came and precipitated confusion. Elephants stampeded and mahouts climbed trees.

Peter undertook to restore order. And this voice of stern

authority eventually commanded the situation. Elephant men came down hesitantly from their perches, went about the arduous job of rounding up the elephants.

Susan wanted to know what Peter intended to do with the "best friend we have on earth."

"Deliver him to Hong Kong. He isn't too much of a load for a big elephant. And at Saigon we'll put him on a steamer."

But the mahouts objected. No elephant would tolerate that green monster as a cargo. Peter suggested blindfolding the largest elephant until the lizard was aboard. And this scheme was eventually successful.

Shortly before dawn, the caravan started for Khava— and the great seaport of south Indo-China. It would be, Peter knew, a journey beset with every sort of peril. Most of the route ran through untraveled, hostile country. But there was no other course now.

Peter started out with a heavy heart He had devoutly hoped that that tense ride on the lizard through Sandrakar would restore Susan's memory, her old personality. It had done nothing but terrify her.

And as the caravan went down through the foothills and into the swamps and jungles of northern Siam, he cast about in his mind for some method by which he could make the transformation in her.

The journey was half over when he suddenly had the inspiration. Several factors contributed to it. One was his head mahout, who was a tall, powerful man, a Punjabi, who spoke excellent English—a man, it proved, who had graduated from a British college in Bombay. The next stimulus was Peter's happening to see, in one of the few friendly villages through which they passed, a mask hanging before a temple of thatched nipa-palm—a grotesque mask carved of some translucent blue stone resembling sapphire.

Peter halted the caravan and, unknown to Susan, sent back Shan Hatma, the head mahout, to exchange a good rifle for the blue mask. And Shan Hatma returned without the rifle, but with a bulge at his breast and a certain light in his handsome brown eyes.

Shan Hatma had told Peter how the spurious Charlie Ling had come to be in charge of the caravan. He offered, at least, a reasonable explanation. This caravan had been bought and assembled in Burma by Judd Burton. The famous animal collector had placed Shan Hatma in charge, had instructed him to proceed to Khava, where Charlie Ling would join them. Shan Hatma had never known or seen the real Charlie Ling, nor had any of the other men in the caravan. The impostor had reached Khava with ample credentials from Judd Burton, and Shan Hatma had taken his authenticity for granted. How the impostor had secured these credentials from the real Charlie Ling, or what the latter's fate had been, no one, in all probability, would ever know.

The head mahout fell readily in with Peter's proposed scheme for shocking Susan into normality. But there were many details to arrange, other materials to secure. One of these was blue glass. Another temple along the line of march provided Peter with what he wanted. This was a temple in what had one time been prosperous farming country. Many years ago, the village had been abandoned. The jungle had reclaimed it.

AS THE ELEPHANTS plodded through the single village

street, with its underbrush now as high as a tall man, Peter heard the familiar tinkling of wind bells. These were tiny strips of glass, perhaps three inches long by an inch in width. They were strung close together along the eaves, and when a breeze agitated them, the little pieces of glass would give out a shivering sweet song. Some of them were colored—green, blue, red. And from this source Peter secured the blue glass he needed for his experiment.

The scheme he had in mind was, in a way, cruel and rather dangerous. It was to confront Susan suddenly and unexpectedly with the man whom, in the old days, she had feared and dreaded more than any man she had ever known. He was a wealthy and powerful Chinese named Mr. Lu, to whom fabulous things were ascribed. He was said to be hundreds of years old. He was said to have been all but killed in youth, in a fall from a high cliff. And a great surgeon of the time was said to have replaced his ruined brain with a magic brain of purest kingfisher jade. Dwelling in the remote mountain fastness of his castle in the impenetrable Shan Mountains, he exercised his malevolent power over thousands of people.

What truth there may have been in any of the stories told about this human monster—the "man with the jade brain"—Peter had never been able to learn with any real satisfaction. He knew only that Mr. Lu was powerful, exceedingly clever and very dangerous. And he had verified one incredible rumor—that Mr. Lu was a man without a face; that instead of a face Mr. Lu had gone through most of his life with a repulsive, horrible oval of gray scar tissue.

In a temple not far from where he had received his latest inspiration—the Temple of the Coiled Serpent—Peter had, in hand-to-hand conflict, killed or mortally wounded this powerful Chinese who had no face. And Susan had seen this fight to the death.

Yet it was certain that, behind that closed door of memory she still loathed and dreaded Mr. Lu, and that he had stood, in her imagination, for the most terrifying human being on earth.

It was Peter's plan to confront Susan unexpectedly with the apparition of this man whom she had feared and hated so. Since his reunion with Susan, he had told her very little about Mr. Lu. He knew she would be terrified. He knew that it was a cruel trick. But there was no choice.

And so Shan Hatma had been taken into the conspiracy, and so, in time, had all the other mahouts and servants of the caravan, and this was dangerous, for the scheme might be spoiled by the very superstitious and supernatural fears which controlled these brown men.

And one night, after the evening meal, the scheme was tried. On it, Peter staked his last hope of resurrecting the Susan he had known.

They were seated and lying in a circle about the camp fire in a clearing in the western Cambodian jungle—a dozen of them, including Peter, Susan, and the mahouts. Each man was, in turn, telling the story of his greatest adventure, his closest squeak with death. And these were strange and stirring stories. Susan sat beside Peter, staring into the fire. She did not understand the language of these story tellers, but their voices stirred her to dreamy contemplation of the red coals and the leaping flames.

SUDDENLY, BEYOND THE fire, appeared the apparition—a tall figure in blue wearing what appeared to be a sapphire mask. He seemed to emerge magically from the blue mists of the jungle night. And as he stepped forth, with arms folded majestically on breast, blue lights about him began to glow like will-o'-the-wisps. These lights shed upon the apparition a blue and unearthly glow.

In bewilderment and growing alarm, Susan stared at the tall, ominous figure in blue. Suddenly, she seized Peter's arm. She cried, "Look!" and pointed.

Peter looked in that direction. He said, in a puzzled tone, "What is it?"

"That man in blue!" she cried.

"But there's nothing there," he protested.

"There is! Look! That tall man with—with the blue thing—the mask over his face!" She was trembling.

The mahouts who had been telling stories stopped. As one man, the mahouts turned to peer where Susan was pointing. They shook their heads. No, *memsahib*, nothing was there nothing but the blue mists of the jungle.

The man in the sapphire mask was slowly approaching. The light playing upon him seemed to grow more dazzlingly blue. It glinted on the polished angles of the sapphire mask. In its eyeholes, eyes glittered malignantly.

Thus had Mr. Lu looked to Susan when she had climbed the long steps leading into the Temple of the Coiled Serpent, when, believing Peter dead, she had ventured an attack upon the life of Mr. Lu. Thus had Mr. Lu looked when, despite her clever disguise as a Chinese maiden, he had known who she was, had spoken her name! Doubtless it had been the most terrifying moment of her life.

The apparition in blue had stopped on the other side of the fire, beyond the ring of mahouts.

Susan uttered a little scream of terror.

"Peter!" she cried. "I—I can't be imagining it! He's coming closer!"

And he repeated, soothingly, "But there's no one there, Susan, or we would see him. You must have a touch of the sun."

"No, no! He's there!" she sobbed. "Wearing a sapphire mask—blue robes! He's looking at me!"

"Perhaps we'd better give you a bigger dose of quinine," Peter said.

She did not hear him. She was starting to her feet. She would have fled if Peter had not seized her hand and pulled her back. She was shivering. Her teeth were chattering. She stared at the apparition in blue.

And for the first time, the tall and sinister figure spoke— uttered in a harsh and awful voice, the words: "Miss O'Gilvie, I—want—you!"

She screamed again. "Peter!"

"What is it?"

"You heard him!"

"I heard nothing."

"Miss O'Gilvie," that dreadful voice spoke again, "I— want—you—to—come!"

"No!" she screamed. Her hand had flown to her convulsing mouth. She was gnawing her knuckles in terror.

And then the man in blue removed the sapphire mask. And the leaping flames of the fire played upon what had been beneath—not a human face, but what appeared to be an area—a horrible area—of gray scar tissue, with holes where the eyes were, holes where the nostrils were, and an awful slit for a mouth.

SUSAN SNATCHED HER hand away from Peter. She was screaming on a high, sustained note. But she didn't run. She stared for a moment at that hideous thing—as she had once stared in horror at the oval of scar tissue which had served Mr. Lu for a face—and then she collapsed. And Shan Hatma withdrew into the jungle.

She did not quite faint. She was breathing hard in little gasps, and Peter, in an agony of suspense, waited.

Susan seemed to shake herself. Then she sat up and stared in bewilderment at the faces about the fire, then at Peter. Her eyes, it seemed to the agonized young man, were actually changing, as if an invisible veil were being withdrawn. Never had he seen those eyes so brightly violet in color.

She stared at him, as if in dazed wonderment, and gasped, "Why, Peter! I have the funniest—" She stopped. She shook her head a little. "That tower. I was on top of that tower!" She put her hand over her eyes, then snatched it away and looked at him again. The vague look was gone. She began to smile, and this was not the shy smile of the Susan he had come to know in these past few weeks, but the gay, thrilling smile of the real Susan.

She cried: "You old humbug! You old devil! Why, darling!" She threw her arms about his neck. She kissed him. She began to laugh. Peter tried to laugh, but couldn't.

"You almost scared the living daylights out of me!" she cried. "It was Shan Hatma! What a perfectly marvelous piece of acting!"

She was gazing into his eyes, still laughing a little, with her hands on his shoulders.

"Darling! How utterly weird it all is! Now I remember

the whole thing—and it's simply incredible that I didn't know you when I saw you!" She clutched him. "Why, it just doesn't seem possible that I couldn't remember you—and—and everything we'd ever done together. And it's so unbelievable that I didn't *know* you—and then fell in love with you all over again. Oh, I think it's perfectly priceless, darling!"

She shook him a little. "Oh, Peter, Peter, how swell it is to be with you again!"

He caught her into his arms, held her fiercely and kissed her. And when he let her go again, she cried: "Darling! You didn't have any use for me!" She was laughing again. She tilted up her head and, still laughing, kissed him. "You positively loathed me!"

"No," Peter denied.

"You did! I don't blame you! What a sissy I was! What a little simp I was! Peter, tell me you like me better this way! Tell me you adore me!"

"I do."

"Peter—darling—wouldn't it have been simply awful if I'd never remembered? Wouldn't it have been too utterly frightful if I'd just gone on and on like that? It was so clever of you to think of Mr. Lu. But you are clever. You're so damned clever I positively couldn't live without you. Tell me you adore me, Peter!"

Peter had wondered if—provided her old memory was restored—she would retain her more recently acquired memory. It was very apparent that she had. And with the recovery of old memory, it was quite obvious that with it was restored her old personality.

The rest of that long journey to the coast of the China

Sea was, to Peter, a march of triumph. For Susan, despite that lapse of memory and personality, had lost none of her gayety, her vivacity, her high spirits.

She insisted that they would be married by the very first person they met who was qualified to do so. And they would never, never be separated again. It was a Methodist missionary in Angkor who read the marriage service.

TO PETER IT was the most exciting moment of his life. Compared to it, all their other adventures together paled.

As the voice of the missionary bound them together, Peter looked down at Susan's lovely face. Her lips were parted and her violet eyes were bright. She sent him an adoring glance.

He grinned at her. He was very happy.

And when it was over and he kissed her, Susan said, "I just can't believe it, Peter! I'm so happy! I simply can't believe that after all we've been through, we're finally married. The way I pursued you, and you'd have none of me—"

"And then I'd change my mind and pursue you, and then you didn't want me!"

"And then the time I thought you were dead, and then you— Oh, darling, isn't it grand that it's all over!"

They left Angkor that evening on a river steamer for Saigon. Shan Hatma was left in charge of the caravan.

Peter would, he said, get in touch with Judd Burton, and Mr. Burton, who owned the elephants, would give Shan Hatma instructions by cable or mail.

In Angkor Peter had built a large and comfortable crate of teakwood for the dragon of Sandrakar. In Saigon, this crate was transferred to a steamer bound for Hong Kong.

And in due course, the fabled dragon was delivered to the delighted Judd Burton in Hong Kong, and Peter was duly paid the $10,000 which they had agreed upon.

Peter and Susan remained in Hong Kong for a few days. Susan did not want to leave the dragon. The strange creature had truly been a faithful friend.

She was fond of it.

She had, she said, so much money—why couldn't she buy it back from Mr. Burton?

Peter tried to argue her out of it. In part, he succeeded. But she insisted on going to see the lizard before they sailed for America.

Mr. Burton himself took her to the great pen where the lizard was being kept until he should begin his sea voyage to the United States.